THE SOLITUDE SAGA

STALKER'S LUCK

CHEEKY
MINION

THE SOLITUDE SAGA

Stalker's Luck
Stalker's Bounty
Stalker's Exile

OTHER BOOKS BY CHRIS STRANGE

Don't Be a Hero: A Superhero Novel
Mayday: A Kaiju Thriller
The Man Who Crossed Worlds (Miles Franco #1)
The Man Who Walked in Darkness (Miles Franco #2)
The Man Who Lost Everything (Miles Franco #3)

www.chris-strange.com

CHEEKY
MINION

Cover art by Jarrod Owen
www.jarrodowen.com

Originally published by Cheeky Minion 2015
First Edition
Copyright © 2015 Chris Strange
All rights reserved.

ISBN: 1502321386
ISBN-13: 978-1502321381

1

In the cold light of the system's distant sun, the *Solitude* dropped into orbit around a gas giant of pale blue. The Feds met the ship like they always did: with orders barked and weapons locked.

Behind the *Solitude*'s helm, Dominique Souza loaded her sidearm and eased into dock with the Feds' orbital outpost. The maglock clunked against the hull with a shudder that ran through the ship and down Dom's spine. The comm unit squawked instructions from the Fed communicator. Dom obeyed, shutting down the *Solitude*'s engines, releasing the airlock controls to the Feds, and powering up lights throughout the ship's cramped interior.

"Prepare to be boarded," the Fed's voice crackled through the speaker.

"Yes, sir." She switched the comm unit off. "Motherfucker."

She unbuckled herself from the pilot's seat and stooped to make her way down the corridor, pulling on her duster coat as she went. Her boots clanged on the walkway grating. The *Solitude* whined as the engines spooled down. Dom patted the bulkhead. "Tell me about it, girl. Me too."

She stopped at the closed airlock, spread her legs, and clasped her hands together behind her back. An ancient computer buzzed on the other side of the airlock. The Feds were taking their sweet time. But something else tickled her hearing. A faint sound of screeching and synthetic beeps. Was the ship damaged? Had she docked her too roughly?

She turned on the spot, following the sound. Her eyes fell on a closed metal hatch. She sighed.

With a glance at the still-closed airlock, she took two quick strides to the hatch and hammered on it with her fist.

"Turn that noise down," she yelled. "We've got company."

There was no answer. Son of a bitch. She spun the handle and wrenched open the hatch. A cacophony of what she could only guess was supposed to be "music" assaulted her.

Inside, Eddie Gould lay on his bunk in a one-piece sleepsuit, one leg crossed over the other, bouncing in time with the synth music. His eyes were closed.

"For the love of Man, get dressed," Dom said. "And turn that off."

Eddie's head rolled to the side and one eye drifted half-open. "This is the new Sin Tower album. This is good stuff. The Feds might like it."

"They won't."

"How do you know?"

"Get up."

Eddie sniffed and closed his eyes again.

"Turn that off or I'm leaving you on Temperance when we depart," she said.

"You wouldn't."

"It's my ship. I do what I want with it."

Eddie's eyes opened. He yawned and swung his legs over the side of the bunk. With a touch of the wall panel, the music went silent. "How long until the Feds arrive?"

She glanced back at the airlock. "About five seconds."

"Okay." Eddie stood, stretched, and groaned. "Do we have any coffee left?"

"I don't know. Hurry up and get dressed."

He ignored her and climbed out of the hatch. A warning siren sounded and the airlock began to hiss open. Eddie wandered off down the corridor, towards the ship's common room.

"Where are you going?" Dom said.

"Coffee," he said simply. Then he disappeared through another hatch and out of sight.

She took a step after him. *I'll kill that son of a—*

She didn't manage to finish the thought before a voice boomed out of the rapidly widening airlock. "Show your hands!"

She threw her head back in exasperation and raised her hands. "Come on, gentlemen. You do this every time. What do you think I'm going to do?"

Boots stomped on the walkway. Three Fed marines in grey fatigues swept past her, submachine guns tucked against their shoulders as they rushed through the ship. One headed in the direction of the kitchen. A moment later, she heard him calling through his vox. "Hands! Put them up! Put down the cup."

"It's only coffee, Jack," Eddie's voice drifted back. "Take it easy."

There was a smash of metal clattering against the floor. "Hands!"

"You've gotta be kidding me. This your first week on the job, Jack? If you're pissing your pants about a bit of coffee, I don't think you're going to make it to Friday."

Movement in the airlock drew Dom's attention forward again. A white-haired Fed officer with a boyish face strode along the gangway and cast his gaze up and down Dom. His face was pocked with old acne scars. A heavy pistol was holstered to his belt. The slashes on his breast marked him as a lieutenant. No high-ranking officer would get stuck manning this outpost at the arse-end of Eleda space. They left that to the kids. The petulant ones that no one wanted back on Babel.

"Big, aren't you?" the lieutenant said as he stopped in front of her.

It was going to be one of those days. "I suppose so, sir."

There wasn't any supposing about it. Dom was tall enough and broad enough to break the lieutenant's back over her knee. And she was tempted to. But she just lowered her hands and tightened them into fists behind her back.

Out of the corner of her eye, she spotted one of the marines wrenching open the hatch to her quarters. A moment later there was a crash of food bowls and cinevid files being swept to the floor. Dom cringed internally.

The lieutenant brought up his tab and scrolled through.

"The *Solitude*. Registered at Carousel station to Dominique Souza." His eyes flicked up to her. "That'll be you."

"Yes, sir."

"And your companion is…" He scrolled further. "…Eddie Gould. Your husband?"

"No, sir."

"Hm." He lowered the tab and called to his men. "Anything?"

"Clear," came three replies.

"Care to show me to your common room, Miss Souza?" the lieutenant said. He glanced in the direction Eddie's voice had been coming from. "This way, I presume?"

Dom led the lieutenant down the corridor and through the hatch. Eddie sat with his legs up on the table, arms folded across his chest. A metal coffee cup lay on its side in the corner of the small common room, brown liquid dripping through the grating. One of the marines stood over him, fingers twitching on his submachine gun. Between the four of them there was barely enough room to move.

"Gather the others and wait by the airlock," the lieutenant said to the marine. With a final glare at Eddie, the marine shouldered past Dom and called to his friends. Eddie waggled his fingers at the marine's back as he went.

The lieutenant took the last remaining seat at the table, leaving Dom to stand. She didn't object. The Feds liked to remind everyone that they were in charge. They were all bluster, until they weren't anymore. She'd spent her youth killing Feds, destroying their facilities, stealing their supplies. She'd probably killed three or four dozen if you included the ones who got blown to chunks by the bombs she'd planted. But that was the problem with the Feds. No matter how many you killed, there were always more.

The lieutenant stared at the soles of Eddie's shoes resting on the table. "Do you mind?"

"Mind what?" Eddie said.

"Putting your feet down."

He shrugged and lowered his feet to the ground. "No problem, Jack."

"It's Lieutenant Pine."

"Yeah? How about that? That'll be three hundred vin, by the way."

"What will?"

Eddie nodded at the spilled mug. "The coffee. That's good stuff. Real, not synthed. Imported from Tarut. Expensive."

The lieutenant's mouth formed a thin line. Dom threw a look at Eddie. He was going to get her ship impounded if he kept this up.

"Well, I'm sure when you've successfully completed this job you'll be able to replace your coffee without any trouble," Pine said. He brought up his tab again. "Although I see Miss Souza is still paying off her considerable debt to the Federation." He smiled up at them. "Perhaps you'll have to be more careful with your expensive coffee in the future."

Eddie smiled back with all of his teeth.

"Can we get on with this, gentlemen?" Dom said before anyone decided to start shooting. "It's my understanding that Temperance only has about two weeks left before the last oxygen generators shut down and it becomes uninhabitable. It's in all of our best interests to ensure the job is done before then."

"Quite right, Miss Souza," Pine said. He tapped the screen of his tab and laid it on the table. "This is your quarry. Roy Williams. Former leader of the White Hand syndicate, convicted on three dozen counts of murder, assault, torture, and extortion. Sentenced to life plus fifty at the Bolt supermax facility in the Outer Reach. Four months ago, Mr Williams enlisted the aid of a guard to smuggle twenty-six kilograms of IL-KEM high explosives into the Bolt. He used them to stage a breakout. That guard and twenty-two others were killed in the explosions. Five prisoners—including Williams—escaped on a hijacked Federation prisoner transport shuttle. Federation ships attempted to pursue, but Williams evaded them."

"Yes, sir," Dom said. "We're well aware. We've followed the reports. But they don't say why he fled to Temperance after they abandoned the shuttle on Segan."

Eddie peered at the tab. "There's no picture."

"What?" Dom leaned over the table. She glanced at Pine. "You don't have a picture of him?"

Pine shook his head. "We have been unable to obtain any recent civilian photographs of Williams. All municipal records were transferred to the Federation following his arrest. But during the breakout, it appears Williams had a fellow prisoner hack the local databases and wipe most of the records."

Dom understood now why the Feds had been so cagey ever since they'd taken the contract on Williams. The Feds were protective of their technology, but the truth was they didn't really understand how it worked. It was all old tech, like the oxygen generators and the solar collectors and the grav drives that powered their largest ships and kept the artificial gravity operating in stations across the system. Technology from before the collapse of the Gypsy Gates, from before the Lonely Years, before the Gravity War, from the time when the Solar Federation was spread through thousands of systems across the galaxy.

The collapse of the Gypsy Gates had cut the Eleda system off from the rest of humanity. Now all they had left were the remnants of that age. The Fed databases, the stations, ships like the *Solitude*. They'd lasted three hundred years. But time had been hard on them. One by one, the remnants were breaking down. And the system was dying.

Not that the Feds wanted to admit that, of course. The party line was that the Gypsy Gates would one day reopen. That one day the Eleda system would be welcomed back into the arms of the Solar Federation, that these few million souls on the galactic frontier would once again be united with their billions of brothers and sisters of humanity.

What a crock of shit.

Eddie scrolled through Williams' records on Pine's tab. "There's not even any identifying information. Height, weight, tattoos, age, nothing. Are we even sure he's a man?"

Pine scowled. "I'm informed that he is in his fifties with a strong build." He glanced at Dom. "About your size."

"That's it?" Eddie said. "How many people are on Temperance?"

"Eighty thousand."

"That's just residents," Eddie said. "How many tourists

you got down there partying it up, dropping a few hundred thousand vin on roulette tables and hookers? Another thirty thousand?"

"More or less," Pine said.

Eddie pushed back his chair and picked up the spilled mug. "I'm getting some more coffee."

"What *can* you tell us?" Dom asked.

Pine shifted in his chair like he was trying to decide whether to stand up and make himself taller. "Not much. We lost all records of his known associates. Most of the ones we know of are dead. Williams is a dangerous man."

"No shit," Eddie said as he poured himself another mug. "That's why we're here."

"We recently received a message from a man on Temperance who claims to have information on Williams. Reverend Benjamin Bollard. The address is in the file."

Great. A preacher. Just what she needed.

"We haven't been able to question him," Pine said. "The Accord has seen to that."

Dom didn't have to ask what accord. Since the Lyon Accord was signed, the Feds had control of inter-colony space, but had no jurisdiction on any station or colony except for Babel, the capital colony.

"The higher-ups have seen fit to give you the sole contract on Williams," Pine said. "So I'll be monitoring your progress."

"We prefer to work independently, sir," Dom said. She immediately realised it was a mistake. The lieutenant's pinched lips pulled back in a sneer.

"I'll expect to be kept up to date, stalker," he said

slowly, rising from his chair. "And I expect you to do your jobs quietly and efficiently. I do not want business disrupted on Temperance. But I will not allow Williams to die on that rusted hunk of metal and sin without facing the Federation's justice. Do you understand me?"

Dom looked down on him, looked at his acne-scarred skin and the veins snaking through the whites of his eyes. She could smell the sweat rising off him. How many like him she'd killed. How many Federation uniforms she'd left drenched in blood. But they had her. She was on their leash. She was their dog now. So she barked.

"Yes, sir. I understand you, sir."

Eddie strolled up behind the lieutenant, sipping his coffee. "Reward. Remind me. How much?"

Pine kept his eyes on Dom. "Eleven point one million."

"Plus?" Eddie prompted.

Pine turned to Eddie and smirked. "Plus the six point five million time sensitive bonus."

Eddie whistled and smiled at Dom. "Sounds sweet, don't it? What did I tell you? Last chance bounties are where the money's at."

"Come to think of it," Pine said to Eddie, "I don't recall your purpose. Miss Souza is the registered stalker for this contract. What is your job, Mr Gould?"

"I'm a writer."

"A writer."

"Uh-huh."

Pine glanced back at Dom, as if he thought he was being made fun of. "And what does a stalker team need with a writer?"

"I'm what you call the moral compass in this motley crew," Eddie said. "Also, I'm a pretty quick draw. No reason a stalker can't be a writer as well."

"I suppose not," Pine said. "I don't recall ever hearing your name before. Would I know anything you've written?"

Eddie shrugged. "Maybe. *Massacre at Fractured Jaw*? *The Slow Death of Louie the Liar*?"

"Ah." Pine nodded as if everything had become clear. "I thought you meant you were some kind of reporter. But I see. You write for the dimes. Little stories to entertain the working classes, correct?"

Eddie smiled and took another sip of coffee.

Pine gave his sneer a bit more practice, then nodded. "Very well. You have your contract. I look forward to hearing from you. You will return to the outpost when you have Williams in custody. The Federation thanks you for your service. Good hunting."

He turned and strode back down the corridor and out the airlock. A moment later, the bootsteps of his marines clanged away. The airlock siren sounded once more. The door slid closed with a hiss.

Dom took a deep breath and forced the tension from her shoulders. She rubbed her forehead. Her head was throbbing. Fucking Feds.

"He never paid me for that coffee," Eddie said. "Who does that? Who spills someone's coffee then doesn't pay for it? It's rude, is what it is."

"Leave it alone. That's not Tarut coffee. We picked up the whole sack for five hundred when we resupplied at

Karm station."

"Well, he didn't know that." He tipped his mug in the direction of the airlock. "How old do you reckon he was? Did you see the way he looked at you? I think he was sweet on you, Freckles."

"I told you not to call me that."

"It suits you."

"I don't even have freckles."

Eddie shrugged.

The ship groaned as the maglock disengaged. Out the port hole she could see the outpost's gangway umbilical retracting back into the small Fed station. Beyond, the swirling blues of the gas giant Eleda VI filled space. A half dozen major stations orbited Eleda VI. They were all scheduled to die sooner or later. But Temperance would be next. If they didn't capture Roy Williams before the station went cold, Dom's bounty would go with it. And she'd be that much further away from paying off her indentured servitude to the Federation. That much further from being free of the Feds' leash.

"Don't you need to—you know—pilot this ancient crate?" Eddie asked, dragging her out of her thoughts.

She grunted and strode back to the ship's helm. She could hear Eddie shuffling along behind her.

"How long until we touch down?" he asked.

"Sixty-two minutes."

Dom climbed into the pilot's seat and wiped the finger-prints off the cracked control screen. The screen was one of the few remaining pieces of Pre-Fall tech in the helm. All the rest had long been replaced by the chunky, temperamental systems Eleda engineers had been building to replace the old tech as it slowly failed.

She touched a button and—with a little urging—brought the solid fuel engine coughing back to life. When she glanced back, Eddie was squinting sceptically at the rumbling coming from above them.

"It's getting worse."

"She's fine. She's a good ship."

"Whatever you say, Freckles. I'm going back to bed. Wake me when we're there."

Dom nodded and gave the manual throttle a gentle twist. Her stomach lurched for an instant before the gravity compensators caught up. There was a splash behind her. Eddie sighed.

"I'm never going to finish a coffee again, am I?" His footsteps quietened as he strolled back towards his quarters.

"Hey," Dom called over her shoulder. "Don't turn that bloody noise back—"

A flood of synth music roared out of Eddie's quarters. Dom set her teeth and started the *Solitude* on a course for Temperance station.

2

When Dom banged on his door to announce that they'd set down, Eddie crawled out of bed, tucked away the tab he'd been scribbling on, and strapped on his gun.

He yawned as he tugged open his door and shuffled out through the open airlock. He never could sleep properly on the *Solitude*, especially not when they were taking the dark roads through the system. A two day stretch in one of them was enough to put his cheek muscles in spasm, the way the ship creaked and groaned and screamed through the compressed void of space.

Sleep would be on the menu tonight, a good sleep in a good hotel with real goddamn coffee in the morning. He started to whistle to himself at the thought.

He wandered down the enclosed boarding tunnel, casting glances out the windows at the ships docked next door. Temperance had always been a tourist station, a getaway for the soon-to-be-poor and the desperate-to-be-rich who came to test their luck. And the tourist docks were once more crammed with passenger ships, even in the station's last days. Because of them. Different stations died in different ways. Some struggled, desperately attempting to jury-rig repairs to the life support systems, just to give themselves a few more days of life. On some stations they prayed. On others, the residents gathered with their loved ones and ate their last meals laced with cyanide. But Temperance was different.

On Temperance, they partied like it was the end of the world. And everyone wanted a bit of the fun.

Eddie emerged from the spaceport onto a shrewdly placed viewing platform and took his first look at the station's interior. The sky above was covered with transparent panels, revealing the slow rotation of Eleda VI and the storms raging across its surface hundreds of kilometres away. Those panels would be hardened against all the usual threats to a station's survival: meteors, debris, and of course, small arms fire. The ancients had learned that particular lesson early on, when the Second Colonial Expansion gave way to the Fracturing.

The station-wide lights were all off, casting the city into twilight. A grav train rocketed along an elevated rail that carried it swerving among billboards and apartment blocks. The spires of hundreds of towers were packed tightly through the city, the metal and plastic and glass exteriors glinting in the light of a thousand sparkling neon signs.

Slots.

Girls, Girls, Girls.

All-Night Stims.

Golden Hand Pachinko.

Eddie smiled and drew in a deep breath. The smell

of broken air filters and desperation and cheap beer and spices and hair dye and broken stim vials and sweat and come and pussy. This was it. This was the life.

He looked up and down the viewing platform. The denizens of dozens of stations and colonies were pouring out of the spaceport and flowing through the streets, looking for action, looking to experience the thrill of apocalypse. A swooping dress with a high collar and thick makeup bounced past him. Eddie had chosen a simple white shirt and a dark grey waistcoat for his outfit. It'd get him into most of the high class casinos, but he'd still fit in if he decided to slum it in a back-alley bookie's.

Heavy, familiar footsteps clanged behind him. You live long enough with a person on a ship the size of the *Solitude*, you get to know pretty much everything about them. Everything they can't hide, anyway. Their ticks, the little noises, their toilet habits, their footsteps.

"What's the time?" Eddie said as he leaned against the platform railing.

Dom appeared alongside him and checked her tab. "Just after two p.m. local."

He looked up at the false sky. "It's night."

"They're down to thirty percent of their solar collectors. They're on light discipline to save energy."

"Perpetual night," Eddie mused. It suited Temperance. Why hadn't they thought of it before?

Dom inspected her tab. She was still wearing her ridiculous duster, like she thought it could hide the submachine gun tucked under her arm. She was dreaming if she thought she was going to get to a high-roller table dressed like that. Oh well, she could suit herself.

While he was eyeing her outfit, she looked out over the city and pointed. "Reverend Benjamin Bollard's supposed to have his church somewhere in the starboard districts. We should find a train."

Eddie straightened and tucked his hands in his pockets. "You go ahead. I'll catch up with you later."

"What?"

"I feel like seeing if I can find some action."

"We've got a bloody job to do."

Eddie rocked back on his heels, trying to take in the whole city with his eyes, trying to imprint it on his memory. "You've got a job to do. It's your contract. Call me when you need some help."

"I need your help now."

"You'll be fine, Freckles. He's a preacher. What's he going to do, throw holy water at you?"

And with that, Eddie turned and strolled down a set of stairs leading into the thick crowds of the city streets. He whistled to himself to cover the sound of Dom's swearing.

Eddie threw himself into the hot press of the crowd. The street narrowed for twenty metres as he passed beneath a tall, garish archway. The neon lights across the arch should've spelled out the words *Welcome to Temperance*, but all the "e"s had been knocked out. To the right, there was an old man with one leg. His head was shaved, except for a ponytail emerging from the crown. He leaned against a wall, next to a spraypainted declaration: *The End is Nigh, Muthafuckas.*

With a roar of hot air, a grav train screamed past overhead, temporarily drowning out the excited hubbub of the crowd. Eddie pushed in between a knot of businessmen as the street widened into a long central strip that ran the length of the station. Revellers and gamblers and scant- ily clad men and women weaved across the strip in every direction, diving through massive entranceways of casinos that glittered with light and sparkle. Someone screamed far away, a scream of broken fingers and unpaid debts. But no one took any notice. Eddie was already stringing together the words that would bring Temperance to life when he wrote the tale of Roy Williams and the keen-eyed stalkers who brought him to justice. This was going to be a good one. He could feel it.

A topless woman with rings through her nipples and a short bob of blue hair pushed a pamphlet into his hands as he passed. An advertisement for some titty bar. Eddie tossed it aside.

A thick scent of spice tugged at his nostrils from a side road. His stomach growled. Dom was a lot of things, but she was no cook. And he was no better. He fished his wal- let out and thumbed through his cash. Still plenty there between the last royalty payment and their most recent bounty. He owed himself a treat.

With one last glance at the lights, he abandoned the glitter of the strip and ducked into the side road. The bus- tle of the strip faded. This had clearly once been part of the tourist district, but now it was nearly deserted. Spherical lanterns were strung up overhead between the buildings on either side of the street. Most of the shops he past were barred, their windows broken and their innards looted.

But there was a light on at a small noodle stall nestled between a pair of hookers. Eddie smiled as the smell drew him in. He handed over his notes to the young man behind the counter.

"You don't look much like a local," Eddie said to the man, eyeing his red-brown skin and thick curls of hair.

The man shook the wok back and forth over the small blue flame. "Not. Came here six months ago for a bit of fun. Same as you. You know how it is. But I had a bit too much fun. Got into a poker game, high stakes. Two pair, all black, aces and eights."

"Dead man's hand," Eddie said.

"Ain't it so. Got stupid. When he raised, I put up my travel pass. I was so sure he was bluffing."

"And now you're stuck here."

"And now I'm stuck here," he agreed.

"I didn't think travel passes were transferable."

"They ain't. But there's people that can do the forging. You want any peppers?"

"Surprise me," Eddie said. "So why don't you find yourself another travel pass? Get someone else to do the forging."

"That's the plan. 'Cept there's still the issue of money. Which is why I charge extra for the soy sauce."

"Wouldn't think there'd be much profit in a place like this."

"Probably not. Helps that I don't own the place. Just found it abandoned and got working. Keeps the overheads down."

The young man scooped the noodles into a box, shoved

a pair of chopsticks in, and slid it across the counter.

Eddie took a taste. "Pretty good for someone who can't cook noodles."

"I never said I couldn't cook. Just said I didn't own this place. I opened this place back up because it was something I'm good at. And because I'm sure as shit no good at cards."

Eddie dropped a tip on the counter and wandered away, shovelling the noodles into his mouth. A block down the road he looked up and found a man who'd decided he didn't want to sit around and watch the station die. He'd decided it by tossing himself out a fourth floor window and letting the electrical cable wrapped around his neck catch him. He obviously hadn't been the man who'd won the noodle kid's travel pass.

The Feds had stepped up their control of travel in the last five years as the stations started to break down more rapidly. If the denizens of a doomed station fled to other stations, those stations would die all the faster with the added pressure on the life support systems. So it was a lottery. You sat in your apartment and stared out the window and prayed to whatever god you thought gave a shit that the solar collectors would hold out, that the water reclaimers would keep grinding away. That some other bastard on some other station would be the one to face their certain death, not you.

Unless you were one of the lucky ones. Someone who served some role deemed vital to the machinations of the Federation bureaucracy. Like a pair of killers contracted to save a convicted murderer from a cold death in a dying station. To capture a man like Roy Williams and bring him back to justice. So he could live out his life in a cell while eighty thousand innocents faced their own personal apocalypse. Eddie was sure it made sense to some high-up official poking numbers on a tab. And in truth, he didn't mind the absurdity. It assured him that no matter how bloodstained and lurid and insane his little tales got, at least they weren't as bad as reality.

He was two blocks down and halfway through his box of noodles when he heard the footsteps behind him. Not normal footsteps, not the stumbling steps of a drunk or the excited stride of a tourist. The footsteps never got quieter or louder; they always stayed just the same, keeping pace with him.

He glanced in the reflection of a broken window and saw a shadow in a hat and a grey coat. Maybe it was nothing. For the hell of it, Eddie slowed a little. The footsteps slowed. He sped up. The footsteps quickened. A tail already. He couldn't believe it. He'd only been on the station an hour. Not even that.

The streets were narrow and quiet here. Apartment buildings rose on either side of him, dotted with abandoned restaurants and motionless escalators to underground markets. Eddie finished off the last of his noodles, tossed the box into an overflowing rubbish bin, and ducked quickly down a narrow alleyway. There was an intake of breath behind him. The footsteps picked up speed.

Eddie pressed himself into the shadow of an alcove made by a pair of dumpsters. The shadow in the hat hurried into the alley. His footsteps made a pitter-pat of panic.

The figure moved past Eddie, not seeing him. Eddie took a step after him and cleared his throat. "What's the story, Jack?"

The figure gasped and spun around. A flash of blond hair peeked out from beneath his hat. He was round-faced and red-cheeked. With white eyes he stared at Eddie. His coat fell open. Soft sheen of a handgun at his belt. The man's hand twitched.

"Don't," Eddie said. "Jack—"

The shadow's hand went to his belt. Fingers closed on the butt of the gun. Fumbled. Panic drained the colour from his cheeks.

Eddie fired. He hadn't even noticed himself drawing the pistol from his side. He never did. Muscle memory. The crack of the shot echoed back and forth in the tight alley. Maybe it would echo there forever, until the last of the oxygen drained out of the station and it finally went quiet. Eddie's ears rang.

The shadow clutched at the wound in his throat as he went down. But only for a moment. He barely made a sound.

Eddie lowered his gun. His mouth was suddenly dry.

"Shit."

He edged over to the shadow. Only a couple of metres separated them. He nudged the man with the tip of his shoe. The body didn't move.

"Shit," he said again. He holstered his pistol, turned, tightened his hands into fists, turned back, looked at the slumped figure. "What did I say, Jack? I said 'Don't'. Don't do it, you stupid son of a bitch." He shook his head. "Why'd you do it? Huh? Why'd you make me pull?"

But the man said nothing.

Eddie pushed air through gritted teeth. He settled down on the cold metal ground outside the widening pool of blood. No one had screamed, no one had come running. Probably gunshots weren't a big deal on Temperance. But still. But still.

He stood up, sat down again, stood up once more, and pulled out his tab. Unlike Lieutenant Pine's tab, Eddie's was held together with electrical tape and epoxy glue. One corner of the screen had cracked a few decades before he was born and every year another few pixels died. With a few taps on the ancient device, he bleeped Dom. A moment later, she picked up.

"What's the situation with the law on Temperance?" he said.

"What do you mean?"

Eddie chewed the inside of his cheek. "Is it illegal to shoot someone here?"

"It's illegal to shoot someone anywhere."

"Yeah, but how illegal?"

"Eddie, what's going on? Don't tell me you've shot someone."

"All right, I won't."

"For the love of Man." He could hear her grinding her teeth through the tab. "We only just got here. We're supposed to be scouting."

"I didn't go looking for it. I had a tail. Probably been following me since we landed. Someone knew we were coming. I stopped to have a chat. He got spooked."

"How badly did you shoot him?"

Eddie looked at the blood slowly oozing from the throat wound. "Well, he won't be complaining about it."

"Ah, fuck me," Dom said. "Did anyone see?"

"I managed to be discreet. I need your help."

"You're a real piece of work, Gould."

"That's what they tell me."

Dom grunted. "Deal with it. Get the hell out of there. No one's going to bother to look too hard."

"The law won't. This guy's bosses might."

"Deal with it," she said again.

Eddie exhaled. His breathing was beginning to slow. The shakes would come soon. But he had a few minutes, that blessed space between the panic of sudden action and the time when the adrenaline withdrawals began.

"Okay. I'll deal with it. Keep an eye on your six, Freckles. If there's one, there might be another."

"Bloody hell," she said. Then she cut the connection and he was listening to the low beep of a lost signal.

He slid the battered tab back into his pocket and rubbed his jaw, staring down at the body. No one had come running to investigate. He had time. With a quick glance up and down the alley, he crouched and turned out the man's pockets.

The man's fingers were still wrapped around the gun he hadn't managed to pull from his belt. No wonder he'd fumbled it, the thing was a hand cannon. The barrel must've tickled his balls every step he took. Stupid kid had let it get tangled in the folds of his trousers.

Aside from that, he was running light. No tab on

him. A billfold held a thin stack of cash and his ID card. Name read Javin Lindeman. He wasn't smiling in his picture. Probably thought it made him look tough. He was twenty-two and a Temperance native. He wasn't getting off the station. So what if he'd died a couple weeks ahead of schedule? So what?

The only other thing on him was a silver poker chip in his inner coat pocket. Eddie spun it back and forth in his fingers. No value written on it, no casino name, no nothing. Just a whole lot of nothing. And that was that.

Eddie pocketed the chip and slipped the cash out of the billfold and pocketed that as well. "Payment for the stress," he told Javin. Javin didn't seem too happy about it, but to hell with him.

Eddie stood. "Who the hell were you? And why the hell'd you make me pull? Stupid fucking kid." He shook his head. "Shouldn't speak ill of the dead. That's what my mother always said. All right. It's okay, Javin. I'm going to leave you here and no one's going to give a shit, but I'll remember you. I'll write something up. Javin Lindeman. Blond of hair. Loud of foot. Slow to draw. How's that? Huh?"

Javin lay there and said nothing.

"You're right. Needs work. Give me a break."

Eddie inspected his fingernails for blood, wiped his hands on Javin's coat, and walked out of the alley in search of a stiff drink and some answers.

3

Dom kept her hand on the compact submachine gun under her duster coat as she took the grav train across town. She had her eyes open, but she didn't spot anyone following her. That didn't mean they weren't there. It just meant they weren't as clumsy as the tail Eddie had shot. A good tail could blend into these crowds with ease. It could be the old man in the corner of the carriage leering at the cleavage of the woman sitting next to him, or any of the trio of rich young women with their faces pressed against the window as the city rushed by. Dom watched them all from her spot by the doors.

How could Williams be onto them already? There had to be a leak in the Feds. They were the only ones who knew why she and Eddie were here. Damn it all. If she found out Pine was furnishing his salary by selling them out to their bounties, she was going to take a knife to his belly and see what colour his insides were.

The train decelerated and pulled into a station near the starboard edge of the city. When the doors slid open, only a handful of people pushed their way out of the train along with Dom. She kept her eye on each of them, but none paid her any attention. All of them were hunched over, defeated. They shuffled away and disappeared into the twisting warrens of the city. She soon saw why. This part of town looked all but deserted. In one of the shattered windows of the surrounding apartment buildings, lights flickered from a drum fire. Dangerous, trying to heat yourself like that in a space station. Especially on a space station where all the firefighters had either fled or were drinking and gambling and fucking their last few days away. But with half the heating services down and the station-wide atmosphere regulators periodically taking a break, she supposed some people didn't have much choice.

Dom consulted the shoddily copied map she'd bought from a desperate huckster at the train platform and tried to orient herself. She held it up, looked around at the streets, tried to find a sign. She wasn't even sure she'd got off at the right station.

"Waste of bloody money," she said to herself. She screwed up the map, tossed it on the ground, and strode off down the most likely street in search of St Reynolds' church.

It turned out to be less a church and more a converted pachinko joint with delusions of grandeur. It was built into the ground floor of a tower block with two lopsided crosses screwed into the wall on either side of the security glass doors. She walked past it twice before she realised that yes, this was the place she was looking for. Roller doors were pulled shut over the windows, but the doors were ajar and the hand-painted sign above the entrance claimed that sanctuary and redemption were waiting inside. Dom wasn't looking for either. She went in anyway.

The door creaked open as she pushed her way inside. A hushed silence filled the church. Mismatched chairs were arranged in rows facing towards a small raised platform at the far end of the room. Half the lights were blown and the other half cast the room into a gloomy semi-darkness. Shadows lurked in the corners. A carved statue of Christ the Luminary hung from the ceiling, one hand outstretched towards the empty pews. The workmanship was nothing to write home about—Christ had fingers like slabs of concrete and a face that could've been carved from a potato. Where machines had been ripped out of the walls, the hollows left behind had been converted into alcoves draped with curtains for private contemplation. Dom's heavy footsteps echoed from the low ceiling as she moved down the centre aisle, eyes on the shadows. Nothing moved.

All churches made her uneasy, but the Luminarians most of all. The Church of Christ the Luminary was the religion sponsored by the Federation, or at least that's the way she'd learned it growing up on New Calypso under Federation rule. It was an outwardly bland religion, simple symbols for the simple-minded. An easy mechanism to keep the populace content even in the face of impending apocalypse. A religion of denial, a quiet voice assuring the populace that there was nothing to worry about, that God would never abandon his children to a lonely doom far from the rest of humanity. The leaders of New Calypso's insurgency had been quick to point out the Church's flaws in quiet meetings held in the sewers and bars and abandoned warehouses of the colony. The Church's links to the

Federation were clear, anyone could follow the money trails, the political support. So Dom had bombed Luminarian churches as readily as she'd bombed Federation supply stations and police headquarters. For the greater good.

Until she won her war. Until she spent three days watching the man she'd helped put in power order members of the deposed government and the church one by one into the bio-waste reclaimer, turning their bodies into slurry to fertilise the colony's farms. Until the leader of the insurgency proclaimed himself a prophet, a doomsayer, and traded the Church of Christ the Luminary for the church of the House of Man. She learned a lot about people in those few days.

A voice spoke from behind her. "Have you come to pray, my son? As you can see, the congregation has dwindled somewhat in the past few weeks. You might prefer to find salvation elsewhere."

She turned. The man stood to the side of the chapel, hands clasped together in front of him. He had a plump frame beneath his flowing black cloak. A pointed hat with a wide brim cast his face into shadow, all except his mouth which was split in a wide smile. His top teeth were crooked.

Dom glanced back and forth to make sure the man was alone. Satisfied, she relaxed her grip on her gun and withdrew her hand from under her coat.

"Benjamin Bollard?" she said.

He inclined his head. "I apologise. From your size I took you for a man. You're correct. I am Benjamin Bollard."

"I have some things I need to discuss with you."

"I'm afraid I'm a little busy—"

"This is important, Reverend."

He hesitated, then gestured to the row of chairs closest to the pulpit. "Please. And call me Ben."

She gave the chapel another scan as he moved to the front and sat down. She hated the smell of these places. The smell of dust and self-righteousness. But she couldn't sense anyone else moving around. She walked to the front and sat down a few chairs over from Bollard, positioning herself so she could watch the door and have a hand free if trouble came.

"This isn't much of a church, Reverend," Dom said. "Are you really a preacher?"

"I really am," he said, apparently without taking offence. "I didn't take my training here, of course. Temperance isn't big on modesty and quiet contemplation. I came here three years ago from Babel and took over a church from an ageing colleague. Not here, of course. A real church at the end of the strip. When it was announced that the station was expected to soon become unable to sustain life, some fearful individuals attacked the church."

"You seem awfully understanding about it, sir, if you don't mind me saying."

"Time and the approaching end have given me some perspective. At the time, well, I certainly had a few Old Testament thoughts about appropriate ways to punish those responsible for the church's destruction." He smiled. "But enough about me. Your accent—New Calypso?"

"Yes, sir."

He tipped his hat back, letting the light catch his face. His eyes were a deep blue. "Then I suspect you're not a follower of the Luminary?"

"No, sir. I'm not much of a follower of anything these days. Except those people who hold my leash."

"Yes? And who would those people be?"

"The people looking for a man named Roy Williams."

A twitch at the corner of his mouth. "And why do they want to find this man?"

"Because he is a murderer and a fugitive."

"If he is on Temperance, he will be dead in a matter of weeks. His sins will be between him and God. He cannot leave the station. What point is there in capturing him?"

"So he can face justice," Dom said.

Bollard studied her face. "You don't believe that."

"It doesn't matter what I believe. I have the contract on Williams. I'll find him. I'll find him and I'll turn him over to the Feds and they'll say that's justice and that's good enough for me."

"Why? Why do this for them? I can see into your heart. I can see you do not love them. So why do this?"

"Because I have no choice. Not if I want freedom. Because I'm a killer of men and a traitor to the Federation. Because I'm a traitor to my own insurrection. Because the only way to be free is to pay back my debt to the Federation, and the only way to pay back that kind of debt is with this." She pulled back her duster coat to reveal the Marauder-pattern submachine gun pressed against her side like a lover.

He licked his lips. Nervous for a preacher. "You cannot repay blood with blood."

"We'll see, sir. Until then, I'm going to need you to tell

me everything you know about Roy Williams."

"I'm afraid I can't do that, child."

"You can, preacher. You contacted the Feds saying you had knowledge of Williams."

"I didn't…." He looked at her and changed what he was about to say. "I was mistaken."

"You're a bad liar, sir. Tell me."

He shifted in his seat. "I can't. I think it's time you left."

"I'm not going anywhere, sir." Dom rested her hand on her gun.

The preacher's eyes flickered around the chapel. A drunk shouted outside, screaming for doom and the end of the world. Bollard leaned forward in his seat and lowered his voice.

"All right. Listen, child. Perhaps I can help you. But first, you have to help me."

"I don't have to do anything, sir."

"If you want Williams you do. He has people. Not many, but a few. When I…I contacted the Feds I thought… it doesn't matter. It doesn't matter. Luminary protect me. You have to get me out of here."

"Out of where?"

"Here. This chapel. This district. I know someone who can help me get off the station. But you have to get me out of here before they come back."

Dom eyed him. "Before who comes back?"

"I'll explain everything later. But please, we have to go. If we go fast, we can take them by surprise. Look at you. You can take them out. You kill them and I'll tell you everything I know about Roy Williams."

The chapel door creaked open. The preacher's big blue eyes went wide and wet. Dom threw herself to her feet. Her gun was in her hands. She aimed down the sights as three figures filled the doorway.

"Benjamin, Benjamin, Benjamin." The voice echoed through the chapel. "I can't believe you faltered now, this close to the end. Whatever shall we do with you?"

4

Eddie ascended a set of stairs plastered with glitched-out vid screens advertising casinos and shows with singers that must surely have died decades ago. At the top he was greeted by a closed door and a thin trickle of soft music. He pushed open the door and went inside.

The bar had once been something nice. A wide floor was separated into three sections by low railings and strips of red lights along the floor. Chairs were clustered around two dozen tables. A jukebox at the far end ported quiet music through speakers set around the walls. A vid screen above the bar showed a game of gravball, green and red uniformed players leaping from platform to platform in low grav, tossing a small black ball between them. As Eddie approached the bar he studied the game. He thought he'd seen this match—yeah, there was Rodriquez being a pussy after he got shoulder-checked by Temperance's winger. That was the last time Temperance won the cup, maybe five years ago. He supposed they had the right to remember the glory years. They wouldn't be winning any more games.

There were a handful of people in the joint, a few in

small groups but mostly alone. Eddie sat down at the bar. A grim-faced man contemplating the froth of his beer was Eddie's next-door neighbour. A few seats down on the other side sat a black-haired woman who was beautiful and knew it but had decided to pretend she didn't, just for fun. The bartender was a middle-aged woman with an easy smile and hands like frying pans.

Eddie still didn't understand why some of these people stayed in their jobs even now. The bartender didn't have a retirement to save for. Maybe this was all she'd ever known. Maybe she was lonely. Or maybe it was none of his goddamn business.

"You look like you need a drink, bud," she said.

"I knew I came in here for a reason. I'll take a beer. And put something cheap and nasty next to it."

She flicked the cap off a bottle—looked like the taps were down—and set up a double shot glass. "A little bottom shelf whiskey?"

"Lower than bottom shelf. Wipe it off the floor with a rag and wring it into a dirty glass."

"You got it, bud."

She poured the whiskey and Eddie knocked it back with shaking fingers. The heat burned down his throat and smoothed out the jagged edges of his insides. That was better. He screwed up his face at the taste, then took a sip of beer to wash it down.

"Nasty enough?" the bartender asked.

"You trying to kill me?" He slipped the dead kid's silver casino chip from his pocket and set it down on the bar. "You happen to know where this is from?"

The bartender frowned and picked up the chip. "A casino?"

"A wise guy, huh?"

She turned it back and forth in front of her face. "Strange style. No markings. I don't recognise it. I don't go to the casinos much anymore." She set it down and slid it over to him. "Sorry," she added as she headed back down the bar to serve another customer.

He shrugged. "Worth a try."

"The Crimson Curtain," said a soft voice to Eddie's right.

He took another slug of his beer and glanced over at the black-haired beauty a few seats down. She met his eyes over the top of her cocktail glass.

"Say again?"

She slid off her chair and flowed towards him, two fingers wrapped around the stem of her glass. Eddie pushed a coaster onto the bar beside him. The woman set her drink down, then set herself down in front of it.

"It's a casino. The Crimson Curtain." She reached out a finger tipped with a black-glossed nail and hesitated with it poised above the chip. "May I?"

"Go nuts."

Delicate fingers lifted the chip by the edges and turned it around. "See. Here, on the edge." She leaned in to show him. A rich musk of cinnamon and vanilla followed her. More intoxicating than the whiskey. He looked closely and saw a minuscule "CC" engraved on the edge of the chip.

"You must have binoculars for eyes, seeing that from all the way over there," Eddie said.

Her lips curved like they were made for it. "I just know my casinos. I'm Meryl."

She held out a hand. He took it as softly as he knew how. He shouldn't have worried; her grip was strong.

"Eddie," he said. "You're another out-of-towner. How'd you get to know so much about Temperance casinos?"

"I own a merchant ship. It takes me interesting places and makes me enough money to flit away on temporary thrills."

"Lucky for some."

"It's too corporate. You wouldn't enjoy it."

He quirked an eyebrow. "What makes you think that?"

She smiled and gestured to the gun strapped to his leg. "Just an assumption. Gunslingers don't usually take to the corporate life. Was I mistaken?"

"Spot on. Tell me about this casino."

"Centre of the strip, starboard side. Crimson tower, grav train runs right past the upper floors. You can't miss it."

"You go there often?"

She made a gesture with her hand, a slow unfolding of her fingers. "On occasion. When I have the paper to spare. The Curtain mostly caters to the high rollers."

"And how much would this little thing be worth?" He picked up the chip and flicked it into the air with his thumb. She kept her eyes on him as it flipped up into the air, stopped, and tumbled back down into his waiting palm.

"Nothing."

"Damn." He spun the chip in his hand. "I thought I'd

got rich."

"I've seen people carrying chips like that before. It's not for betting. It's a token. There's some sort of private elevator that goes somewhere else in the tower. Like a private member's club."

"Huh. Then I guess that means I'm now a member."

Meryl rested her chin in her palm and studied him. Her eyes were long and narrow, the irises so dark they were nearly black. He decided her ears were her best feature on a body full of good features. He couldn't say he'd ever really paid that much attention to a woman's ears before, but there was something about these ones. They were perfect.

She lowered her voice almost to a whisper. "Can I ask you something? How did you get that chip?"

He broke her gaze and took another long sip of beer. He was nearly finished and he could still feel the frayed ends of his nerves brushing his mind.

"Sorry," she said. "I shouldn't have asked that, should I?"

"You can ask what you like."

"I'll ask something else then. You don't look much like a tourist. And you're not a local. So why are you on Temperance? What do you do?"

"I'm a writer."

Her eyes lit up. "A writer with a gun."

"I'm not a very good writer. If someone tries to bump me off to get back at me for my lousy stories, I need to be able to defend myself."

"I can't tell if you're joking."

"I get that a lot," he said.

"What do you write about?"

"People at the end of their rope."

Her eyes danced at that. "True stories?"

"Depends on your definition. They're not always factual. But they're all true."

"Tell me the names of your books. I might know them."

"I doubt it."

"Try me."

"*The Reaper's Last Mark*. No, no one read that. *The House of Man Was Built with Bones* was the last one."

She tapped a finger against her lips. "You know, that rings a bell. It's one of the dimes, right? Those aren't the full titles. You always have two titles. Like: *The House of Man Was Built with Bones; or, The Fires of New Calypso*."

"Looks like I was mistaken. I apologise for doubting you."

"Don't act like you're not pleased with yourself. I can see you trying to hide it."

"Maybe I'm a little pleased."

"I always wondered," she said. "Why the two titles?"

"I can never get it right the first time."

He drained the last of his beer and tossed a few of the dead kid's notes on the counter.

"You're going?" Meryl asked.

"Places to be." He slipped the silver chip into his pocket.

She bit her lip with calculated precision. "If you have an hour to spare, perhaps we could spend a little more time together."

"What did you have in mind?"

"I have a room." She paused. "Why are you smiling?"

He checked the time on his tab. "This city. Nowhere else in the system can a man get so much excitement within a couple of hours of leaving his ship."

"It's because everyone is here for the same thing," she said. "I'm staying for a week. I'm planning to spend the days at the casinos and the nights visiting the brothels. The male prostitutes on Temperance are all hand-picked from across the system."

"You're liable to break something if you don't pace yourself with all that," Eddie said.

She smiled. "I thought maybe you could help me warm up."

He grinned back and shook his head. "This city. Christ, I'm going to miss it when it's gone. Thanks for the tip about the chip." He slipped a 1000 vin bill across to her. "Your next drink's on me."

"Are you sure you wouldn't rather drink it with me? Last chance."

He stood and waved. "Make sure you stretch before you hit those brothels. Maybe I'll see you around."

He was still chuckling to himself as he crossed the bar and pushed open the door to the stairs. What a girl. He might've been interested if he hadn't just had to shoot a man. He'd head to the Crimson Curtain and stake the place out. If it'd been Roy Williams sending a clumsy hitman after him, the casino seemed a good a place as any to investigate. And if it wasn't Williams, well, Eddie wanted to find out why the hell he'd had to leave that damn kid lying in an alley with a hole clean through his neck.

He rolled the chip between his thumb and forefinger in

his pocket as he descended the stairs.

Out of the corner of his eye he saw one of the vid screens flicker to a new advertisement. He went two more steps, then froze. *No. It wasn't. That's not possible.*

He licked his lips, staring straight ahead at the door at the bottom of the stairs. No point looking. He was mistaken. He hadn't seen what he thought he'd seen. And even if he had—which he hadn't, because it was impossible—what did it matter? He had enough on his plate. That was the last thing he needed. No need to dig into the past. Not now. Not ever. *So keep walking.*

But he didn't. He couldn't. Not until he was sure. He turned and looked at the vid screen.

Grime had gathered around the edges of the screen, bordering the garish rainbow background of the image. The words *Lady Luck Gentlemen's Club* scrolled along the bottom of the picture. In the centre of the screen, three bare-chested women waved enticingly at him from between the busted pixels. The image was grainy and the figures jittered as they moved, the old vid file long corrupted. Two of the women meant nothing to him. Just tits and vacant smiles. But the third woman, the third woman was different.

Eddie leaned close to the screen, straining his eyes to study the woman. Rust-brown hair fell in curls around her narrow face. Longer than she'd ever worn it when Eddie knew her. Her nose was upturned and her eyes were half-closed and smeared with makeup, but he could see the flash of green in a couple of pixels. She was older, she'd filled out a little, become a woman. But it was her.

The screen labelled her Daisy. That was a lie. Her name was Cassandra Diaz. And she was supposed to be dead.

He'd mourned her. He'd almost forgotten her. Except those occasions, maybe once every couple of months. Those times when she'd stray into his head, linger for a moment, and leave, as if she'd never been there.

But none of that mattered now. As soon as he saw that vid, all the feelings came rushing back. She was alive. She'd escaped. She was on Temperance.

A city that was about to die.

His mind was racing so fast he didn't hear the footsteps coming down the stairs after him.

"Oh, you're still here," the voice said.

He blinked and turned and found Meryl watching him, her handbag dangling from her shoulder. A stray lock of hair had fallen across the corner of her left eye.

Her eyes rounded. "What is it?" she asked.

He took two steps back up the stairs, wrapped his hands around her cheeks, and pressed his lips against hers in a bruising kiss.

For half a second, she was stiff. Then she melted into him and he pressed her against the stairway wall and tasted her lips and dragged his hands down her side and sank his teeth into the soft flesh of her shoulder while Cassandra Diaz's face flickered on the vid screens around him.

He broke the kiss. "Your room. Where's your room?"

She took his hand and dragged him onto the street and into the hotel opposite. As they rode the elevator up she told him exactly what she needed, every movement and sigh and sweet hurt. And when they got to her room he did it all, and more.

Afterwards, when he untied the necktie that bound her wrists to the bedpost and massaged the glowing pink handprints from the flesh of her bottom, she traced the scratch marks on his chest with her lips and asked him what had changed his mind.

And he began to tell her about Cassandra Diaz.

5

Dom aimed down the sights of her submachine gun as the three figures stepped into the chapel.

"Lookie here," the front man said as he emerged into the light. His face was criss-crossed with a perfect grid of deep scars. "Ben's got himself a girlfriend. And look at the size of her."

The other two grinned. One was a woman, small and spry. Two scars ran across her right eye and turned it milky white. The other was a bruiser of a man clad in a heavy coat. His bald head shone, reflecting the overhead light.

"Hands, all of you," Dom shouted. "I won't ask twice."

The front man raised his arms. His left ended in a stump at the wrist. "You heard the lady. Show her we mean no harm. Go on."

The other two smirked and raised their hands. The woman gave a fake tremble and stared at Dom with wild eyes.

"Kill them," Reverend Bollard hissed next to her. "Kill them now, child."

"Shut up," Dom said. She raised her voice. "That's close enough, ladies and gentlemen. Who are you?"

"Will you listen to that?" The man with the criss-cross scars laughed. "Ladies and gentlemen. When was the last time you were called a lady, Daz?"

The woman grinned. "Six and a half years ago. My fiancé said it. I remember, because I cut his tongue out later that week. He didn't say much after that."

"Ouch," the front man said. "Daz has a few issues. But don't mind her. This big fella is Greg. And I'm Bones. On account of this." He waved his stump back and forth. "Spend enough time in solitary and it gets to a man. It's the boredom. I was a gambler, home-grown Temperance lad, in fact. So when I was eight months into my solitary stretch, I had a thought. To keep myself occupied I'd shoot some craps. Only I didn't have any dice. And that's when I got the idea, you see. One of the guards smuggled me in a knife, and I started cutting. Right here." He pointed to his stump. "There's still a few scars from where I cut the wrong place. You can't imagine how much it hurt. How much it bled. But I got the hand off in the end. And then I started skinning it, stripping all the flesh off, right back to the bone. It was hard, trying to do it with one arm. But I got better. And when I had the bones, I started carving them. Whittling them down. And pretty soon I had a whole collection of dice to play with. Handmade, so to speak."

He laughed, a crooked, uneven laugh. The back of Dom's neck went cold.

"You know the funniest thing?" he said when his laugh subsided. "The very next day they let me out of solitary. And they took my dice. One of the guards, he laughed his fucking arse off when he saw what I'd done. I watched him take my dice and toss them into the trash chute to be shot out into space. Laughing the whole time. Laughing, laughing. I very much enjoyed dislocating his shoulders so he'd fit in the trash chute all those months later." He licked his lips and stared at Dom. "There, now we're all introduced. Best friends now. So why don't you tell us why you're trying to get poor little Ben to tell you about Roy Williams?"

"None of you are my concern," Dom said. Her hands were steady on her gun. "If you're fugitives from the Bolt, your records are lost. Maybe some stalker out there wants your head. Not me. I will shoot all three of you down if I have to and the Federation will thank me. But I have no desire to do so."

"Ain't that magnanimous of her?" Bones took a step forward, arms still raised. "You wouldn't think of killing us in God's house, would you?"

"I'm looking for Roy Williams. That's all. Where is he?"

Bones shrugged. "What makes you think we'd know where the old bastard is?"

"You broke out of the Bolt together. You hijacked a shuttle and station-hopped to Temperance with him. You know where he is."

The preacher edged close to her. "Please kill them, child. Now. Now, before they kill us both."

"What's that, Ben?" Bones said. "You're not asking her to shoot us down, are you? I don't think we'd be very happy about that. Not after we've had so much fun together, robbing the poor bastards who came in here looking for God." He turned his smile back to Dom. "Do you know much about Ben? He does pull off the preacher act quite well, I'll give him that. Tell her when you found your precious Luminary, Ben."

"We have to go," the preacher hissed.

"Shut the hell up," she said, keeping her eyes on Bones. The scarred convict was still edging forward. His comrades blocked the only exit she could see.

"Fine, I'll tell her," Bones said. "Ben here, he's been looking for the Luminary his whole life, or so I hear. What's the principle of the Luminary? Purity. And what's the purest thing in the universe? Any guesses?" He held his arms out. "Why, it's children, of course. So Ben went looking for the Luminary in children. How many counts of rape were you convicted of in the end, Ben? Forty? Fifty? That was only the ones they could prove, of course. I bet it didn't even scratch the surface."

"Stop moving," Dom demanded. "One more step and I shoot."

Bones stopped and his smile dropped from his face. "I'm trying to explain things to you. Why do you have to be so fucking rude, huh? I'm trying to explain things. I'm trying to explain that you've got one chance to leave this chapel, stalker. You put down that gun, empty your pockets, and then you walk out of here and leave Temperance. One little chance. Or Ben's precious Luminary is going to get a blood sacrifice."

"I'm not leaving this chapel without the whereabouts of Roy Williams, sir."

He shook his head. "A shame. A real shame." He brightened suddenly, his grin slipping back into place. "What am I saying? It's always fun seeing a Fed dog die. Ben, I'm very disappointed in you. But I'm also a very forgiving man. If you want to live, well, you know what to do."

A knife sang behind Dom. Out of the corner of her eye she saw a flash of silver.

"Shit," she said, pulling her gun around as the preacher launched himself at her, a heavy knife slashing towards her face.

She squeezed the trigger. The Marauder submachine gun bucked and roared and screamed in her hands. Red flowers blossomed across the preacher's chest. His face caved in. The stink of gunsmoke filled her nostrils.

A round screeched past her, close enough to tug at her duster coat as it passed through. She dived away from the toppling preacher behind a row of seats as the three convicts fired the guns they'd pulled. Bullets pinged off the metal chairs, ricocheting around her.

The roar of gunfire in the closed space rang in her ears. She crawled along the ground as shots punctured the air around her.

Fucking Eddie. He should've been here to back her up.

Under the rows of seats she saw feet hurrying down the centre aisle. Dom rolled herself over and squeezed off a burst of gunfire. The ankles were ripped apart in a cloud of red mist. The figure toppled with a scream. The female convict's face dropped into view, twisted up in pain. Dom fired another burst and put her out of her misery.

Bones was shouting over the gunfire, but the words were muddy in Dom's ears. She scrambled onto all fours and dived aside as a burst of fire came crashing through the chairs, slamming into the ground where she'd been lying.

The gunfire ceased for a moment.

"Did you get her?" Bones yelled.

A grunt from the big one. Dom edged to the end of the aisle and peeked out.

A gun barrel stared at her from across the chapel. It flashed and she threw herself out of cover as the air was filled with the screams of gunfire once more. She fired back, blind, as she ducked into an alcove. Bullets chewed splinters out of the wall inches from her head.

The gunfire stopped again. The big one grunted and swore. Dom ducked and swung her Marauder out of cover. The bald bruiser struggled to hide himself behind a row of chairs as he slammed a new magazine into his assault rifle.

Dom lined him up and squeezed the trigger without a thought. He fell with a gurgling scream.

"Fucking hell!" Bones screamed from across the room. For a moment she couldn't make him out through the smoke. Then there was a wisp of movement and a flash of a pistol shot.

It scraped the air alongside her arm. She squeezed off an instinctive burst as she pulled back into cover. Her magazine ran dry. But not before she heard Bones cry out. She tossed the submachine gun, drew her heavy revolver, and strode quickly out of cover.

Bones leaned panting against a chair, sweat pouring down his forehead and trickling through the scars on his face. Blood coated his right thigh. He glared at her with gritted teeth and shakily raised his pistol.

Dom fired and two of Bones' fingers disappeared. He

dropped the pistol with a scream, toppling onto the floor in a pool of his own blood.

"Fuck you," he spat.

Dom planted her boot on his wrist and pointed her sidearm at his last three fingers. A groan bubbled out of his throat.

The air was thick with the stink of blood and smoke. It was almost choking. The gunfight had only lasted a few seconds. But she felt as exhausted as if she'd spent three days hauling crates around the *Solitude*'s cargo hold.

"Roy Williams," she said. Her voice sounded thick in her ears. "Where is he?"

He snarled up at her. "You're bleeding, bitch."

She touched her shoulder. Her fingers came away streaked with blood. Only a scratch. She shrugged. "So are you. Roy Williams. Tell me now."

"How the fuck should I know where the bastard is? He used our help to bring us to this dying shithole and then he went underground. He went underground with my fucking money!"

"You're lying. You know where he is. The preacher knew."

He gave a hacking laugh. "He's not a goddamn preacher. I told you that. He's a convict, just like us. And he knew shit. Little piss pot."

"He contacted the Feds. Told them he had information."

"You think a fugitive would be stupid enough to call up the Feds and tell them to send a stalker—" Something flashed behind his eyes. His jaw went stiff. "The augment." His head rolled back in a delirious smile. "The fucking augment. I'll kill him. I'll...."

He went still.

Dom growled and booted him in the head to make sure he was really out. He didn't make a sound. What augment was he talking about? If Bollard hadn't called the Feds, then who in the name of Man had?

The smoke was slowly clearing. Dom stepped away from Bones and found the other convicts. She checked them, but it was obvious they were all dead. None carried identification, nothing but a pack of smokes on the woman and a collection of knives on Bollard. She'd been careless to turn her back on him. She knew better than to trust someone who called himself a preacher.

Something creaked. Dom froze over Bollard's body, tuning her ears to the sound. It had come from the back of the church, to the left of the pulpit. There was silence for a moment. Then another creak. Footsteps. Footsteps trying hard not to be heard. She scanned the wall. Her eyes fell on a thick white curtain in the far corner. Just to the right of it she could see a crack in the wall panelling. A door. There was a mechanical chattering sound. Someone jimmying the electronic lock.

She slipped across the room as silently as she could and pressed herself into the alcove where she'd taken cover during the firefight. As the lock gave a quiet beep, she picked up her empty submachine gun and tugged the curtain closed around her.

Hinges whispered. The door opening. A long pause. Then scuffling footsteps. Someone light, small, like a rat. Dom pressed her revolver tight against her hip and held her breath.

A voice like a badly tuned synth-harp drifted from across the room. "Bones, you're not looking so good. How many of your fingers am I holding up? Huh? I can't hear you. Don't worry about it. You never could count, anyway. You always were a stupid cunt."

Dom slowly pushed the edge of the curtain aside with her revolver barrel and peeked out. A tiny man stood over Bones' unconscious body, peering down at him. He couldn't have been much more than a metre tall. With a stubby arm he was gripping Bones' face by the chin, shaking him back and forth. He had a head of silver hair, but he didn't look like he was past his mid-twenties. One beady eye was missing, replaced by some kind of old-tech computer panel that she didn't recognise. He wore a grey shirt that was much too big for him, the sleeves rolled up. A dozen wires dangled from his left forearm, each ending in a different coloured socket.

This had to be the augment Bones mentioned, Dom realised. But what in the name of Man was he doing?

The augment seemed to grow bored of playing with Bones' slack face. He stood and scurried over to the body of the woman.

"And Daz," he said. "Look at you, Daz. You were much too pretty for that place. Now I think you'd fit right in. Hey, remember that time you had Greg hold me down in my cell while you took your knife to my thighs? Ah, the fun we had together. I'm going to miss you, Daz, really I am. I just hope you're up there somewhere looking down on me, listening to me right now. I hope you're screaming.

I hope you know I won."

He patted what was left of her cheek and stepped away from her. He spread his lips in a grin. Metal teeth glinted from his sunken gums. With his remaining eye he scanned the church. Then his gaze came to rest on the alcove Dom was hiding in.

"Come on, stalker," he called. "Do I look like I'm much of a threat? You're not going to spend the whole day hiding there, are you?"

Dom pushed the curtain aside. She raised her revolver and aimed at the augment.

He put his hands in his pockets and grinned at her. "Jesus fucking Christ, you look even dumber than I imagined. Do you have a brain in there or is it just muscle all the way through?"

She took a step forward, silent.

"Speak up," he said. "You can speak, can't you?" He spoke louder and slower. "Speak? Words? Do you un-der-stand me?"

"If one more word comes out of your mouth that isn't telling me who you are and what you're doing here, sir, I'll cut you down and leave you here with your friends."

The augment raised his hands in triumph. "God in Heaven, the noble savage speaks!"

Dom fanned back the hammer of her revolver.

"Calm yourself, Tarzan," he said. "They call me Knox. 'They' being this lot." He gestured at the crumpled bodies of the convicts. "And I'm here for one reason. I'm going to help you find Roy Williams."

She decocked her gun. "Keep talking."

6

When Eddie first met Cassandra Diaz, she put a gun to his head and demanded his wallet.

It was six days after he'd abandoned his home station of Ophelia to escape his family's shame. After his dear father was arrested for embezzling from the university he lectured at, Eddie had used the last of his family's influence and liquid assets to procure himself a travel pass. He went to the spaceport and got on the first ship that would take him. It was headed for the asteroid mining colony of Fractured Jaw, so that was where he got off. It seemed a good a place as any to start a new life.

After spending half the day trying to convince a mine foreman that his pretty little delicate sixteen-year-old hands were capable of operating an electrodrill, he was on his way back to the shithole single-room apartment he'd rented. He'd taken a shortcut down a catwalk through a maintenance tunnel. Condensation dripped from the pipes overhead.

He never heard her approach, not until he felt the barrel pressed against his head and her soft whisper in his ear. "The wallet, rich boy. Quickly."

He hadn't yet developed the knack of dressing like the locals. Between his clothes and his clean skin and the lack of electricity burns on his arms, anyone on the colony could pick him as a rich off-worlder from a kilometre away. They thought that made him weak. But the rich of Ophelia enjoyed a great deal of leisure time. Time they could spend on other practical pursuits.

Pursuits that included knife fighting.

Eddie reached into his pocket and passed his wallet backwards over his shoulder. The woman snatched it from his hands. The gun left the back of his head. And Eddie spun, a knife slipping into his other hand from where he'd kept it up his sleeve.

He got barely a glimpse of her before he slashed. It wasn't a slash meant to cut; it was directed at her gun hand to make her recoil. And recoil she did. He snarled and planted his feet and launched himself at her, getting inside her outstretched gun arm. She backed up into the wall of pipes behind her. Trapped. He pressed the blade against her throat while he pinned her gun arm against the pipes.

"Bad day," he said to her. "I'm not in a good mood. Drop the gun."

She let the gun fall. He was close enough that he could feel her breath against his lips. She was a few years older than him, maybe in her early twenties. Cute rather than beautiful. Upturned nose, close-cropped curls. Her hair was dyed a white blond, but he could see the deep red roots coming through. She sneered at him to cover her fear.

"Good," he said. "The wallet as well. Drop it."

She dropped it. "Are we done?"

Her voice had a surprisingly melodious quality. It didn't match the harshness of her eyes.

"Now your wallet," he said. "Hand it over."

Her eyes widened. "I don't have one."

"Nice try." He pressed the blade against her throat a little harder. "Want to answer again?"

"What does a rich boy want with my wallet?"

"No such thing as too much money."

Her narrow lips quirked into a lopsided smirk. "How broke are you?"

"A little less broke now."

"You're pretty fast," she said.

"So it would seem."

"How old are you, boy?"

"Old enough, girl. I haven't seen that wallet yet."

"I have an alternative proposition."

"Those are big words for a street rat. Are you sure you know what they mean?"

Her green eyes sparkled above her sneer. "You're all alone here, aren't you?"

He said nothing.

"This is a small colony," she said. "I'd know if a whole family of rich snots moved in. The administrators keep tight control over anyone who might be a threat to their jobs."

"Get to the point before I get bored and open your throat to shut you up."

"Let me keep my money and maybe I can offer you the chance to make more money. Real money. And if you do good on that, maybe I can offer you something else. I run a crew here."

"A gang, you mean."

"If you want to call it that. There's a bunch of gangs on Fractured Jaw. Most of them powerful, most of them leeching off the mining trade, the unions. And we leech off them. There's only a dozen of us. All of us orphans or runaways. I can take you back with me. I can introduce you. If they like you, if you can prove yourself, maybe you can join us."

He grinned. "You really think I'm stupid, don't you? You think I'm going to walk into a room full of your friends and assume they won't just stick me the instant I get through the door."

"If we wanted you dead, you already would be. Marco's had a gun trained on you since you asked me for my wallet."

Eddie glanced to the side and saw a pair of eyes in the darkness. Below them was the gunmetal glint of a pistol.

"Shit," Eddie said. He released the woman and tucked the knife back into his sleeve. She massaged her wrist where he'd been gripping her.

"Don't forget your wallet," she said, pointing with her eyes.

He hesitated, eyeing her and the gunman carefully, then slowly reached down and picked up the wallet. His gaze drifted to the fallen gun, but the woman picked it up before he could make a move for it.

"Nice gun for a street rat," he said.

She examined it with disdain, shrugged, and tucked it into the back of her trousers. "It shoots."

She turned and strolled away in the direction of the gunman. The shadowy figure's eyes stared at Eddie. Eddie stared back.

The woman paused just before the shadow swallowed her. She turned her head. "Name's Cassandra."

"That's swell."

She smiled. A real smile this time.

"Are you coming?" she asked.

He said nothing.

Cassandra shrugged. "If you've got somewhere better to be…? Come on, Marco."

Marco's eyes disappeared. A moment later, Cassandra started walking again. She disappeared out of sight. But he could hear her footsteps in the corridor.

Eddie listened to them as they grew quieter. He licked his lips. He said, "Shit."

And he followed her into the darkness.

Eddie paused in his recount of his first meeting with Cassandra. Meryl the black-haired beauty curled against Eddie in her red-tinted hotel room, their flesh pressed together. "You fell in love with her?"

"Like a rock. We were pulling jobs together within a week, ripping off the syndicates and filling our pockets with cash from Fractured Jaw's corrupt administrators. Within two weeks her gang had accepted me as one of their own. By the third week we were sleeping together."

He flashed back to a moment not unlike this one. They were in an abandoned apartment building, not a hotel room, and he was young and stupid and bursting with feeling. But just like now there was the skin of a woman beside him, the scent of their sex hanging in the air. He pictured Cassandra reading aloud from a lurid dime novel on weathered paper as his fingers slid deep inside her, slick and hot. His education on Ophelia had stressed the value of good literature, classics from before the fall of the Gypsy Gates, thick tomes that promised to expand his mind and make him worthy—of what, he was never quite sure. It wasn't until he abandoned all that and found Cassandra that he learned of these other stories, stories written in the language of the working class, stories that were wild and violent and sexual and yet somehow truer than anything he'd read before. He felt like he'd spent his entire youth cut off from the universe, contained within some tiny bubble that had never fit quite right. And now he'd finally found the truth, here in this dark apartment on Fractured Jaw with this girl who was four years his senior, this girl full of harshly learnt wisdom.

"What happened?" Meryl asked.

"Ambush. Revenge. We were mosquitoes buzzing around the colony's syndicates, siphoning off what we could. We were nothing but an annoyance to them. But I guess you get annoyed enough, you want to squish that mosquito. A police raid hit us in our hideout. I say us, but that's not right. I wasn't there. I was out on a job. I was on my way back when I saw it. The police lining up the gang against the side of the building. I could see right away that something was wrong. I knew the law. I knew police procedure. But those kids, they didn't know shit."

"They weren't cops," Meryl said.

Eddie shook his head. "Syndicate members in stolen uniforms. They pulled out their guns and filled the kids full of holes. Just a roar, just five seconds, then it was over. They were all dead."

No. Not all. *Cassandra*. If she'd survived the attack, why hadn't she contacted him? Had she assumed he was dead like he'd assumed she was?

Forget it. None of it mattered. She was alive. He made his decision. He had to find her and get her off Temperance. It was all that mattered.

He sat up, gently pushing Meryl off him. He'd wasted too much time already. He'd enjoyed himself with Meryl. He needed it, after the boy in the hat, the boy with the hole in his throat. And the shock of that vid screen. But Meryl wasn't Cassandra.

Lady Luck Gentlemen's Club. That's where Cassandra was. That's where he'd find her.

"You're going?" Meryl asked as he stood and kicked through the clothes strewn across the carpet.

"Have to. Sorry. I have to find her. Enjoy your brothels." He picked up her dress and tossed it aside.

"Looking for these?" she said.

He turned and found her twirling his underwear on her finger.

He extended his hand. She snatched the underwear out of his grasp and grinned impishly at him.

"Once more. I enjoyed myself. I think I could do with a little more warming up before you leave."

She had stamina, he had to give her that. He sat on the bed, took her face in his hands, and kissed her full on the lips.

Her eyelids fluttered open as their lips parted.

"A goodbye kiss?" she said.

"Sorry. Any other day...."

"But not today." She nodded and reluctantly passed him his underwear. "Maybe I'll see you around sometime."

"Maybe."

He dressed quickly, her eyes on him.

"You won't find her, you know," Meryl said.

He pulled on his shoes. "And how's that?"

"You know why people come to this city. If she's alive, if she's here, she's not the woman you once knew. It'll all end in tears."

He stood, took her hand, and kissed it.

"Everything always does."

Eddie stared at the burned-out husk of Lady Luck Gentlemen's Club on the corner of Valentine and Wilcox. The neon sign above the door had survived, but not much else. He could see footprints in the blackened debris. The place had burned up months ago. He hadn't even been close.

The downer pill he'd picked up at a pharmacy on the way fizzed under his tongue. Calm was returning to him once more, focussing his mind. He let the drug flow through his blood, envelop his heart, slow its beats. His hands no longer shook, his neck no longer felt stiff.

But he could still feel the whisper of Cassandra Diaz's breath on his ear.

High heels clacked on the street behind him. "You're a little late, honey."

He glanced back. A tall man wearing a sleek dress and stiletto heels stood beside him, royal blue lips wrapped around a cigarette.

"Late for what?" Eddie said.

The cross-dressing prostitute gave him a smile. Unlike the rest of him, it was a reserved smile, quiet and conservative. "Late for Lady Luck. I knew the woman who owned the place. She ran into some debt when her mother took ill. The only money she had was tied up in the club. Temperance was already preparing for its demise. No one would buy a club on a dying station. So she came up with a Plan B."

"Insurance fraud," Eddie said, staring at the burned building.

"You got it, honey. And why not? What's a little casual insurance fraud between friends?"

"Uh-huh."

"So she hired a couple of toughs to come in splash a bit of liquid ship fuel around. Lit a match and whoosh." The prostitute spread his hands. "Up it went. I don't know how, but the insurance company bought it. Probably couldn't be bothered fighting it. The place wasn't worth much anyway."

"You sure seem to know an awful lot about it, Jack."

"Like I said, I knew the woman." He took a long drag of his cigarette. "You got any more Bluen?"

"Huh?"

"I saw you popping one before."

The downer continued to bubble in Eddie's mouth. "You must have good eyesight to recognise a pill from all the way over there."

The cross-dresser shrugged. "What can I say? Do you have any more?"

"Keep talking and we'll see."

"What's to tell? She got the money. Bought a forged travel pass. Hired passage off the station. The Feds scanned them as they were leaving and her pass didn't check out. That's what the forgers never tell you. If any Fed takes more than a casual look at your pass, they'll see it's forged. And they won't react kindly."

"Arrested?"

"Didn't get the chance. She wasn't the only one with a forged pass on board. The pilot tried to run the Fed blockade. The Feds locked weapons and blew them out of the sky. And that was that."

Eddie nodded. "I'm sorry about your friend."

"I never said she was my friend."

"I'm looking for someone who used to work here. A dancer."

"I might recognise her. Do you have a picture?"

Eddie shook his head. "Her name was Cassandra. But I thinks she went by 'Daisy'."

He thought about it. "Sorry, honey. A lot of dancers come and go from these sorts of places. She might not even be on the station anymore."

"Maybe not. But I have to try to find her."

The prostitute dropped his cigarette and crushed it under his stiletto heel. "Why? Does she owe you something?"

"No. She owes me nothing and I owe her nothing. But if I can find her, I will. I couldn't tell you why, Jack. That's just the way it is."

The man was quiet for a moment. Eddie studied the building's burnt facade. Music drifted out of the handful of strip clubs up and down the street. There'd be records on Lady Luck somewhere: ownership, tax, booze licences, all that. There'd be names and addresses. But he had no way to access any of that. He was nothing but a stalker, a concerned citizen with a gun and some flimsy legal justifications for hunting fugitives. Neither the Feds nor the local administrators would give a shit about his ex-girlfriend.

Finally, the cross-dresser spoke. "Most of the people who worked here are long gone. But I know one woman. A girl who ran the bar."

"You know where she is?"

"Sure. But I don't want to bring her any trouble."

"There won't be any trouble. I just need to talk to her. I just want to know what she knows about my friend."

He nodded. "I'm going to die on this station. A couple of weeks, they say. I'm scared."

"You could try to run."

"There's no running. The Feds have this place locked down. No, I'm going to die here. My last few weeks alive and I can't even enjoy it because I'm so scared." He looked sideways at Eddie. "Can you help me? If I help you, will you help me?"

Eddie stared straight ahead. He held no judgement. Everyone died differently. He'd learned that. Some cried, some blanked it out, some fought, some tried to run. Some watched the others dying, recording it, trying to understand it.

He dug the blister pack of downers out of his pocket and handed it to the prostitute. Five more Bluens remained. Enough for a couple of days, if the man was careful. Enough to blank out the panic as doom ticked closer.

The cross-dresser popped a pill out of the foil and slipped it into his mouth. The tension drained slowly from his shoulders.

"Thank you, honey," he said.

"The name and address."

"Victoria Palmer. Green Acres apartment building, five blocks that way. Apartment nine-oh-three."

Eddie committed the information to memory. "Tell me. What kind of place was Lady Luck? Did they treat the girls right?"

"Do you want the lie or the truth?"

"The truth."

"It was the worst kind of place. The kind of place even the most perverted bottom feeders would be ashamed to be seen going into. The kind of place you only worked when you had nowhere else to go."

Eddie nodded.

"Do you wish you'd asked for the lie?" the cross-dresser said.

"What would've been the point?" Eddie turned away in the direction of Green Acres and raised two fingers in a wave. "Thanks for your help."

"I hope you find who you're looking for, honey."

Eddie thrust his hands into his pockets and kept his head down as he walked away.

7

Roy Williams picked up the wrench once more and slammed it down on Scott Hudson's knee. The bound man screamed into the socks stuffed in his mouth, sweat pouring down his cheeks. The chair rattled beneath him as his body shook in agony.

Roy put the wrench down on the bed and stood over the man in the dim half-light of the abandoned apartment. He waited, breathing. In and out, in and out.

He had to remain calm during this. It was the only way he'd get anywhere. Be calm, be patient. He hadn't broken out of the Bolt and skipped halfway across the system to screw everything up now.

Slowly, Hudson's muffled screams subsided to coughs and groans and panting. His eyes drooped. Black bruises marred his normally feminine cheeks. Roy had been tempted to break the man's long and pointed nose, but he didn't want the gagged man choking on his own blood. That wouldn't do at all.

Roy stood between the overhead light and Hudson, casting his large shadow over him. Hudson kept his eyes on the floor. Roy grabbed the man's chin and forced his face upwards. Grunts escaped Hudson's throat. His nostrils flared.

"Three hours," Roy said. "That's all it's been, Hudson."

He hadn't known the man's name when he'd knocked him out and brought him here. Never seen his face before. He didn't even know if the name he'd pulled off the ID in the man's pocket was real. But that didn't matter. It'd do. Hudson was nobody. Nothing but an unfortunate pawn.

"It's going to keep going like this, Hudson. I don't get tired. I don't sleep anymore. Maybe a couple of hours a night. It doesn't pay to sleep in the Bolt. I had a lot of enemies in there. Plenty of guards willing to leave my cell unlocked for one of the other cons to come and stick me. Guess how many of them succeeded? Guess how many of them were flushed out the airlock with their own shank buried in their throat?"

Hudson tried to look away, but Roy gripped the man's damp chin tighter and tugged his face upwards.

"Temperance has perhaps two weeks. Say I keep doing this for, I don't know, twenty-one hours a day. Twenty-one times fourteen, that's…let me see…nearly three hundred hours. Three hundred hours for me to get the answers I want out of you. And you've only been through three. Three hours and you're already crying. Look at your knee."

He grabbed the back of Hudson's head and pulled it down to face the pulped and bloody mass that should've been his knee. Hudson went even paler.

"You're not going to be able to walk on that leg again, Hudson. You know that, don't you? But you've still got another leg and two arms and two eyes and a cock and a couple of balls. You're doing pretty good, all things considered. For the moment. Because make no mistake, I will take each of those things from you one by one until you tell me what I want to know. Do you understand? Hudson, listen to me. Do you understand what I'll do? Do you understand how far I'll go? You've heard tales about me? Those tales are nothing compared to what I've truly done. You'll talk. Everyone always talks."

He dragged his hand across the man's face and then brought his fingers to his mouth, tasting Hudson's fear sweat. The man's eyes spun wildly in his head.

"Are you ready to talk?" he said. "Are you ready to tell me how to get to Leone?"

Hudson twisted his head around as if looking for escape.

Roy stood up straight and turned back towards the bed. "Maybe you don't understand yet. Maybe you need another lesson."

He lifted the wrench and faced Hudson. His captive began to hyperventilate, eyes fixated on the wrench.

"You're bringing this on yourself," he said. He raised the wrench.

Music drifted through the damp air. Someone whistling a tune.

Roy froze and half-turned his head towards the apartment door. Footsteps in the hall outside. This apartment building was supposed to be near empty. And the few residents that remained didn't whistle.

Roy glanced at Hudson and tapped the man's cheek with the wrench. A little reminder to keep quiet. Hudson got the message. Holding the wrench down by his side, Roy crept to the door and pressed his eye against the peephole.

A figure strolled down the hall, hands in pockets. He was a thin man, skin a yellowish-brown with eyes so sunken he looked malnourished. His body became that of a gangly alien in the fish-eye lens of the peephole. He whistled a song Roy didn't recognise. His dress was simple: a shirt and waistcoat with dark trousers. A man who'd chosen to blend into the crowd. There was a pistol strapped to his thigh. Roy's hand tightened on the wrench.

A muffled cough came from behind Roy. He spun his head and bared his teeth at Hudson. The captive thug's eyes were wide in panic. His head jerked as he tried to suppress another cough. He looked up at Roy, pleading for mercy with his eyes.

Roy held the wrench up so Hudson would know what would happen if he didn't control himself. Hudson nodded quickly. Roy glared, then carefully brought his eye back to the peephole.

The sunken-eyed man was staring back at him. Roy held his breath. The whistling had stopped. The man couldn't see through the peephole. But he was staring at the door like he could. What the hell was a gunslinger doing in a place like this? He didn't look like a local. He wasn't one of the residents. There were no casinos or whorehouses in the apartment block. So if he wasn't a tourist and he wasn't a local, what was he?

Roy's gaze flashed to the man's gun. *Stalker.*

He knew it was true as soon as the thought came into his head. He could tell by the way the man carried himself.

The casual vigilance. The calm stare. This was a man prepared for the swift and cold application of violence. Not unlike himself.

They couldn't have found him. Not yet. He wasn't done yet! He glanced back into the room. A pistol lay on the bed. Three steps away. Half a second to pick it up and turn back. Would he be fast enough? He had to be quick. His muscles tensed.

But before he could move, the whistling tune returned. Roy looked out the peephole once more. The man was moving on. Roy watched him through the fish-eye until he was out of sight. His footsteps stopped again. The whistling continued, but quieter.

Then three sharp knocks on the next door along. Victoria Palmer's door. Roy glanced past Hudson at the wall that this apartment shared with Victoria's. And the hidden panel he'd installed to connect them.

Roy crossed the room silently, lowered the wrench onto the bed, and picked up the pistol. He brought his lips close to Hudson's ear.

"You don't know pain. Not yet. If you make a noise, any noise, then I will truly hurt you. You'll talk, you'll tell me everything about Leone, you'll tell me how many fucking pubic hairs he has. But it won't stop me. I'll hurt you and I'll keep hurting you until this station dies and you spend your last minutes gasping for the oxygen that just won't come. Understand?"

Hudson nodded.

"Good." Roy pulled back the pistol's slide as quietly as he could and aimed at the hidden panel.

Not today, stalker. I have too much left to do.

Three more knocks. And then he heard Victoria's door creak open.

Victoria Palmer was the prettiest thing Eddie had encountered since setting foot inside the Green Acres building, but that wasn't saying much. Like the apartment building, with its stained carpet and cracked walls, Victoria Palmer had been left an empty shell of her former self. She answered the door wearing a ripped shirt. Dark eye shadow surrounded her tired eyes. Her hair was cropped so short he could see her scalp.

"What?" she said.

Eddie glanced past her at the apartment within. "Victoria Palmer?"

"Why?"

"Because I'm looking for Victoria Palmer. I take it that's you?"

"I haven't got nothing I want to buy and I haven't got nothing worth stealing."

"Doesn't bother me," Eddie said. "I only steal from the dead. I want to ask you about a girl you might've known."

"I don't know anyone." She started to shut the door.

Eddie jammed his foot in the door. "No need to get hasty. I can pay for the information."

"What the hell do I need with money? Move your foot."

He ignored her. "You worked the bar at Lady Luck Gentlemen's Club."

"You've got the wrong woman."

"Someone says otherwise. And your picture was on the

vid screen advertising the place."

"And?"

Eddie slammed his shoulder into the door. She bounced back and he slipped inside, pulling the door closed behind him.

"What the fuck do you think you're doing?" Palmer said. "Get out of my house."

Eddie shook his head, crossed the room, and sat down in a broken couch with half the stuffing missing.

"Sorry, sweetheart. I'll get lost as soon as we've had a little chat. I talked to a friend of yours, he told me where to find you. I just want to know about another girl who worked at Lady Luck."

She glared at him from the door. "I'll call the law."

He cracked a smile. "Go ahead. Maybe they'll get here in a day or so. Then I'll tell them who I am and they'll be on their way and you'll be right back where you started. Trust me, sweetheart. The fastest way to get me out of here is to talk. This girl—"

"I didn't talk to any of the other girls. It was a job. I did it five nights a week for three months then left when it burnt down. I didn't know anyone."

"That's all right. Anything you can tell me will be helpful. This girl, she'd be about thirty-five now. Curly reddish-brown hair, green eyes, bit of a curve to her. The vid ad called her Daisy."

"I don't know. They've all got some stupid flower name like that. Daisy or Violet or Rose or Petal. It could've been any of them."

Eddie leaned back and spread his arms on the back of

the couch. "Why are you being so difficult? It's a simple question."

"I can't remember. Why can't you get that through your head?"

Eddie let his head loll to the side as he examined the apartment. It was a tiny shoebox, more of a cheap motel room than a proper apartment. The single bed was crammed into a corner in the back of the room. A tiny kitchenette was built into a hollow in one wall, alongside an open door leading to the bathroom. On the other side of the room were a couple of shelves holding a busted vid screen and a handful of synth-paper books. He turned his head to the side to read the titles. He grinned.

"What?" Palmer said.

Eddie pointed. "That book. That's one of mine. *The Fall of the Virgin Assassin*. What'd you think?"

"It's not mine. It came with the apartment."

Eddie stood and strolled over to the shelves.

"What are you doing?" Palmer said, her voice rising slightly.

"Easy, sweetheart. I just want to have a look. I didn't know they put this one out in paper. I forgot I even wrote it." He pushed a couple of other books aside to pick it up. The text was smeared slightly on the thin pages; always the trouble with this piece of shit synth-paper. He thumbed through a few pages and remembered why he'd forgotten this particular book. Not one of his best.

As he returned the novel to the shelf, his eyes caught on a thin seam running vertically down the wall at the edge of the shelf. Strange workmanship. He tried to follow the

seam. It looked almost like there was a panel there. Maybe
a storage cupboard. He reached out to find a handle.

"She's dead," Palmer said.

Eddie stopped. He turned to look at the woman.
"What?"

"The girl you're looking for. She's dead."

He studied her face. Her lips were tight. She was nervous. "You're lying."

She shook her head. "She was causing trouble at the
club. Stealing from customers, trying to get hold of a travel
pass. So her employer had her killed."

Eddie slipped his hands into his pockets. "Her employer? You mean the woman who burned her club down?"

She hesitated. "Yes."

"You're lying again."

"It was her. We called her the Witch. She had the contracts. The club was under her name. But she wasn't the
true owner. She wasn't the one who called the shots."

"Then who was?"

"The same man who calls all the shots on Temperance.
Feleti Leone."

The name tugged something in the depths of his memory. "White Hand syndicate?"

Palmer pressed her lips together and said nothing.
Eddie thought it through. The White Hands. Roy Williams'
ex-gang. Now that he thought about it, he remembered
reading somewhere that the White Hands were still operating on Temperance. Was that why Roy Williams came
here? Was he back in charge? But why here, on this dying
station?

And Cassandra. Why would she be working for a man like that? He turned back to his book lying on the shelf, touched the cover. It was because of Cassandra he'd discovered the kinds of tales he now wrote. Absentmindedly, his hand drifted away from the book, back towards the almost hidden crack in the wall.

Why was she dancing for this Leone? It made no sense. But if Leone had killed her....

His fingers touched the panel.

His tab beeped in his pocket, snapping him out of his thoughts. He turned away from the wall and answered the call. Palmer was still staring at him, but he couldn't read her expression.

"Yeah?" he said into his tab.

"You need to get back to the *Solitude*," Dom said. "We have to regroup."

"I'm kinda in the middle of something, Freckles."

"I just killed three people for sure. Maybe four."

He paused. "You've had a busy afternoon."

"This isn't funny, Eddie. Get back to the ship. Now. We've got a lead on Williams."

"All right, all right. I'll be there as soon as I can."

He ended the call and returned his tab to his pocket. He directed a smile at Palmer.

"Thanks for your hospitality. But I have to get going. No rest for the wicked."

She was silent as he went out the door. She knew more than she was saying, that much was obvious. Half of what she said was rubbish. But the bit about Leone, something in that rang true. Not the whole story, maybe. He wasn't willing to accept that Cassandra was dead. Not yet. But there was a connection there. Someone knew something. And he'd find out what.

He started whistling again as he strolled towards the stairs.

Roy Williams watched silently through the peephole as the stalker passed. His whistling faded as his footsteps echoed lightly in the stairwell. Finally, when silence returned to Green Acres, Roy allowed himself to breathe. The tension drained out of his shoulders. He put his gun down on the bed, gave the bound Hudson a cool glare, and eased open the panel connecting his apartment to Victoria Palmer's.

She was waiting for him, a glass of vodka in her hand and a cigarette between her lips.

"Is he coming back?" he asked.

Victoria blew twin streams of smoke from her nostrils. "I don't think so."

"He was a stalker, wasn't he?"

"A writer, he says."

Roy glanced towards the door. *A writer?*

Victoria pointed her cigarette at the shelf behind him, next to the hidden panel. "That's his book, so he says."

He picked it up. A cheap dime novel with a big-titted woman on the cover. "Eddie Gould." The name didn't ring a bell. "You've read this?"

She shook her head. "It was Lilian's."

He shot her a look, then dropped his eyes back to the novel. *Lilian.* What was she doing with that man's book? And why did a writer need a gun?

"He's looking for her," she said.

"What?"

"Gould. He's looking for Lilian."

A cold hand wrapped its fingers around Roy's heart. He tossed the book down on the shelf. "Find out everything you can about him. Who he is, why he's here, how he got to Temperance. Everything."

She sneered. "I'm not your secretary."

He straightened, hands curling into fists at his side. "You will be if you want your next fix. You're exactly what I want you to be until this is over."

She brought her cigarette from her lips with a trembling hand.

"If you don't like it," he said, "I can return you to the street in the condition I found you in. Is that what you want?"

Her eyes found his. "Fuck you, Roy. Fuck you."

He stepped forward. She cocked her wrist to toss the vodka in his face. But before she could, he grabbed hold of her wrist. He could feel her soft flesh bruise as she tried to twist away.

"Find out who he is," he said. "And make sure I'm not disturbed again."

He grabbed the glass of vodka out of her hand and poured the burning liquid down his throat. She glared and twisted her hand free.

"Yes, sir," she spat.

He shoved the empty glass into her hand and turned, crouching to pass through the hole separating their apartments. Hudson stared at him as he came back into the dim apartment. His stink filled the air.

"Now," Roy said as he pushed the panel closed and picked up the wrench. "Where were we? Ah, yes. You were telling me how to get to Leone."

Hudson began to sob.

8

Dom couldn't believe how much food the tiny augment managed to pack away. He'd already been through two bowls of egg fried rice and he was starting on his third. An empty pitcher of beer sat on the small ship table in front of him. Dom folded her arms as she watched him. He was going to eat them out of the damn ship.

"You wouldn't believe the shit they tried to get away with feeding me," Knox said around a mouthful of rice. "No meat, no vegetables. I don't even know what it was. Metal filings and cardboard, probably." He nudged his pitcher. "Fill her up, will you?"

"We're out of beer," she said.

"Come on, stalker, don't be stingy. I saw those bottles in the fridge."

"They're not mine. They're my shipmate's."

"He won't mind. Come on. We're partners now. Share and share alike."

Dom suppressed an urge to throttle the augment. She pulled a bottle out of the fridge and slammed it down on the table in front of him. "Here."

He held up his fingers, the implanted wires winding

around his palm. "Does it look like I've got a bottle opener on here?"

She gritted her teeth, jammed the edge of the bottle cap against the lip of the table, and slammed her hand down. The blow sent the cap flying across the ship's kitchen. Foam bubbled out of the neck of the bottle.

"Better?" she said, setting it down.

"Much." He grinned and picked it up. "Cheers."

The airlock hissed and familiar footsteps clanged on the catwalk. She'd never been so glad to hear Eddie come home. The writer stepped through the hatch into the kitchen with his hands in his pockets. He stopped and stared at the augment.

"Freckles, why is there a midget in my chair?"

Knox slowly lowered his beer and turned to face Eddie. "I take offence to that, friend."

Eddie gave Knox a bored glance, then returned his attention to Dom. "And now it's talking. You know how I feel about midgets sitting in my chair, Freckles." His eyes narrowed. "And is that my beer it's drinking?"

"Shut up and take my chair," she said. "We need to talk."

"That's your chair. I want my chair."

She rubbed her forehead. "Since when do you even have a chair?"

"Since this little can opener decided to sit in it." He waved his hands at Knox. "Go on. Move. Shoo. Don't make me get the bug spray."

Knox took a long pull of his beer and addressed Dom. "This is the writer? I thought he'd be a little more cultured.

At least more cultured than you. You stalkers are a boorish lot."

She was fed up. "You, shut up," she said, pointing at Knox. "Eddie, sit down before I make you sit down."

Eddie continued to glare for a moment. Then he shrugged, strolled around to the other side of the table, and plonked himself down in the seat. He leaned back and put his feet on the table, right next to Knox's bowl of fried rice. The augment scowled.

"Are you boys done?" Dom asked. She spread her arms questioningly. "Can we get started?"

Both men were silent.

"All right, then," she said. "So, it turns out that Reverend Benjamin Bollard never actually contacted the Feds with information about Roy Williams. Even if he had information—which he doesn't now, because I put three rounds through his skull—he probably wouldn't have been willing to pass it on to the Feds, because he was one of the convicts that broke out of the Bolt along with Williams. I encountered some more of them soon after."

"And you shot them all." Eddie gave her a thumbs up. "Nice job."

"Not all of them," she said, and she looked at Knox.

Eddie followed her eyes, then sighed and tilted his head back. "You know what's worse than a midget can opener sitting in my chair and drinking my beer? A midget can opener *convict* sitting in my chair and *if he doesn't stop drinking my beer I'm going to shove that fucking bottle down his throat.*"

Knox grinned, drained the last of the beer, and tossed

the bottle onto the floor. Eddie brought his feet off the table and glared.

"Enough!" Dom roared. "For the love of Man. Knox, just tell him what you told me."

"No problem, sugartits." He pushed his bowl away from him and tented his fingers as he locked eyes with Eddie. "Yeah, that's right. I escaped the Bolt with Williams and his gang. Not because I was one of their best buddies. Because I was the only augment in the joint. I was the one who hacked the databases and wiped the prisoner records."

"You're not doing a good job explaining why I shouldn't put a bullet in your head," Eddie said.

"How come, bud? If I hadn't wiped the databases, the Feds would've caught up with us somewhere in system space and there would've been no fat contract for the two of you."

Eddie shrugged. "That's the thing. There's always another contract. Seems some people just can't stop themselves breaking the law."

"And you wouldn't know anything about breaking the law, would you?" Knox said.

Eddie just smiled.

"Keep talking," Dom prompted.

Knox settled back in his chair. "Williams split from the others as soon as they landed on Temperance. You'll find the ship they used docked at airlock four-two-four. Not that it'll be much use. It was a cargo ship we jacked coming out of a dark road near the Outer Reach. Flushed the owner out the airlock and sold all his cargo to a passing black marketeer. Plenty of cash for everyone. Except as soon as we landed on Temperance, Williams took all the money and disappeared. As you can imagine, they weren't too pleased with that. Bones and his cronies had me working on some ancient piece of shit computer they found in that converted church, trying to track Williams. But he's gone off the grid."

"Hold on a second," Eddie said. "Let me piece this together. Your fellow convicts were making you work for them."

"Correct."

"And you didn't like that."

"Would you?" he said.

"So you contacted the Feds and told them that you were this Reverend and that you had information on Williams."

"Out of the aliases the others were using, the Feds were least likely to investigate Ben's. It's remarkably easy to impersonate a preacher and get away with it."

"You knew the Feds would be sending a stalker to investigate."

Knox spread his lips in a grin. Dom knew where Eddie was going with this, because it'd been burning away inside her as well. She hadn't planned to bring it up until she could be sure she wouldn't do something she'd regret to the augment. But it looked like it was coming anyway.

Eddie looked at her. "He led you into an ambush. Tell me again why you haven't killed him already?"

"It wasn't an ambush," Knox said. "I didn't tell Bones you'd be coming. Besides, if you couldn't handle Bones and his buddies, you wouldn't stand a chance against Williams."

Dom closed her eyes and tried to keep her anger in check. "It's fine. I dealt with it."

"Don't give me that bullshit," Eddie said. "He used us to save his own midget arse. You could've been killed. If I was there, *I* could've been killed."

"But you weren't there, were you?" Dom said. "You were off…where? Shooting guys in alleys? Getting drunk? For the love of Man, I can smell the pussy on you from here."

"Ah, fuck this." Eddie stood up and slouched over to the fridge. He popped open a beer and slugged it back.

"It's a delight to see such camaraderie in action," Knox said. "Truly a testament to the noble profession of the stalker."

"Let's turn him over to the Feds," Eddie said. "Maybe we'll get a few vin for him. Better than having to listen to him."

Knox shrugged. "Sure, you could do that. Good luck finding Roy Williams without me."

"You've been looking for Williams for weeks," Eddie said. "Guess what? You haven't found him."

"That's because I haven't had access to the proper equipment."

Eddie snorted and shook his head.

Dom sighed. "Just listen to him, will you?"

"He's screwing with us. He knew we were coming. Hell, he was probably the one who sent one of his buddies to tail me. Some dumb goddamn kid with a hand cannon and a stupid fucking hat."

"That wasn't me," Knox said. "And it wasn't one of the

other convicts. Miss Giantess over here dealt with all of them. All except me and Roy Williams." He tapped his chin. "Could be the big boss's men were following you. The Fed outpost is full of Feds willing to sell information on any interesting arrivals."

Eddie paused. He looked like he was thinking. "The big boss?"

"Feleti Leone. He practically runs Temperance these days."

Eddie's face went cold. Dom frowned at him.

"You know the guy?"

He didn't answer. His eyes were far away. What had got into him?

Dom shrugged and turned back to Knox.

"All right, tell him about the casino."

Eddie snapped out of it. "What casino?"

"The Crimson Curtain," Knox said. "It's Leone's central command. Right in the middle of the strip. He's got places all over the city, but the Curtain is where all the decisions are made. He chose it because it's big and looks fancy. But also because it's an ex-Solar Federation command centre from before the fall of the gates. The top floors are ancient Solar tech. Control systems for the life support, grav controls, planetary monitoring, intersystem comms. Stuff that only the station governor would know how to use in the pre-Fall days. You know, to make sure us Fringe-dwellers didn't get too big for our boots."

"Get to the point," Dom said.

"Leone uses some of the systems for surveillance and to monitor their businesses. Real surface-level stuff. But there's a whole infrastructure they don't even know exists. Half of it's probably busted by now. But I happen to know that the systems are still networked with the Fed databases. Everything I wiped when we broke out of the Bolt, it's all still there in the Crimson Curtain."

"So what, a few pictures, some fingerprints, a rap sheet?" Eddie said. "That's not much to work with."

Knox shook his head and grinned like a magician about to conclude his trick. "But that's not all. What the Feds probably didn't tell you—what most of them probably didn't even know—is that in the last twenty years the Bolt has been trialling some old tech. Tech the Radiance rediscovered. An implantable tracking device. The other convicts didn't even know they'd been implanted. Just thought it was part of their normal vaccinations."

"But you knew?" Dom said.

"I did. Because I was the only augment there. I grew up with the Radiance on Uriel. I knew the people who found the trackers and sold them to the Feds. Somewhere in that database in the Crimson Curtain are the identification codes to access the tracker information. If I can get into their systems, I can get hold of that information. Then the tracker will lead you fine stalkers right to Roy Williams."

Dom glanced at Eddie. "What do you think?"

He looked like he was chewing it over. There was something dark behind his eyes she couldn't read. He'd probably been taking too many Bluen again. He never could control himself.

"What's his price?" Eddie pointed his chin at the augment.

That hadn't come up yet, but she was bracing herself for it. She looked to Knox.

The augment picked at his nails. "I take all the money Williams stole from the convicts."

"A third," Eddie said immediately. "Freckles and I split the rest."

"All right. But then you give me passage off Temperance to a safe harbour."

"Are you kidding?" Dom said. "We're not risking getting shot out of the sky by the Feds to get you out of the city."

"You won't have to. If I can access those systems in the Curtain, I can issue myself a travel pass. It wouldn't even be a forgery. It's the same systems the Feds use. It'd be indistinguishable from a Fed-issued pass."

"I don't care," Dom said. "We're not a taxi service. You can have the money, but—"

"It's fine," Eddie interrupted.

She froze with her mouth open. "What?"

"We need him. If he can make himself a pass, we can take the risk."

She studied him carefully. "What are you talking about? You didn't even want to look at him. Now you want us to risk the ship for him? What changed?"

"Do you want Roy Williams or not?" he said. "You chose the contract. You brought this guy here. I come along and I help you out and I take my cut and I get what I need to write my books. It's your call. I'd love to hear any other ideas you have."

A muscle twitched in Dom's eye. Eddie was lying to

her. There was something else he wasn't telling her. He liked to pretend he was so cool and calm, but she could see right through him.

But fine. If he wanted his secrets, he was entitled to them. As long as they didn't endanger her or her ship.

"All right," she said carefully. "Fine. We'll try this." She looked at Knox. "If it doesn't work, we're handing you over to the Feds."

"Fair enough," he said. "We're all agreed then? No more complaints?"

She looked to Eddie. He sniffed and took another sip of beer.

"Okay," Knox said. "There's a few things we have to work out if we're going to get into the Crimson Curtain. Feleti Leone isn't fond of stalkers. He's not going to be too inclined to let us wander in and use his systems."

"Naturally," Eddie said.

"There'll be plenty of guards and plenty of tourists in the way if bullets start flying. That's just on the lower floors. I'll have to get to the upper floors to access the systems. As I'm sure you can guess, I'm not exactly capable of fighting my way up there myself."

"We can protect you," Dom said. "How do we access the upper floors? I guess it's not as easy as taking the stairs."

"I'm a little hazy on that point," he said. "I couldn't find much about the casino in the public records. I know there are private member elevators to the high roller lounges. That might get us closer. But I don't know how we get access."

Eddie pulled something from his pocket. "I might be

able to help with that."

He flicked something towards her. She caught it and held it up. It looked like a silver casino chip. "What's this?"

"Our membership card."

9

Roy Williams loitered outside the spaceport, smoking cigarette after cigarette as he sat watching the tourists pour in and out of Temperance. He was dressed like a tourist himself, wearing a heavy jacket over a silk shirt. Victoria had told him that this outfit was in fashion on Ophelia a couple of years ago. He felt like a fool wearing clothing like this after years spent wearing prison jumpsuits. Surely the people passing by must see right through the feeble disguise, see right through to the violence underneath. But no one gave him a second glance as he sat on his bench near the outlook over the strip. They were all blind.

He'd washed Hudson's blood off his hands before he got dressed. Leone's man was still alive, for now at least. Roy hadn't yet decided what to do with him. The idea of sending him back to Leone skinned and cut into chunks appealed, but that would be foolish. He didn't think Leone knew he was on the station. He'd been careful in his approach. He had to be.

He took a long drag on his cigarette and looked out over the strip. Halfway down, a huge tower stretched up towards the night sky, nearly brushing the transparent ceiling of the station. Even though the rest of the city was a mottled collection of greys and browns lit with neon, the tower had retained its crimson colouring. A huge fabric sign lit with spotlights hung over the entrance. It bore only three words: The Crimson Curtain.

Before he was arrested, Roy had run the White Hand syndicate. The organisation had stretched over eight stations and colonies and had fingers in a dozen more. Temperance had always been a lucrative station, but never the base of operations. Roy liked to keep some separation between himself and the business.

But it appeared Leone had no such qualms. Roy's muscles tensed at the thought of the man. His second-in-command. The man Roy had brought up from the streets and made rich and powerful. Roy had been like a father to Feleti Leone. And Leone had repaid that by betraying him to the Feds and bringing half the syndicate down with him. Just to put himself in the pilot's seat.

Roy would kill Leone for all that. That was the way of things in this business. His crimes would justify a swift death.

But Leone wasn't going to get a swift death. Roy savoured that thought. He'd been right. Hudson had eventually confirmed it when Roy took his eye. His wife was alive. Alive and in Leone's hands. The things that man had done to her, the way he'd degraded her....

He stubbed his cigarette out. For all that, Leone would suffer. Roy would have to be careful. He was one man with a couple of million vin and only Victoria for an ally. One man against Leone and all that remained of the syndicate. It'd be difficult. But he'd do it. He'd get Lilian out. He'd see Leone suffer before he died.

And he wouldn't let anyone stand in his way.

He glanced back towards the spaceport as a gangway door slid open. There were a hundred doors along this section of the platform, but he only cared about this one. A moment later, out stepped the stalker with the sunken eyes. The one who'd come to Victoria's. Eddie Gould.

Roy watched the man strut out of the gangway, hands in his pockets as he casually surveyed the crowd. Roy turned his head away to light another cigarette. But the stalker didn't look in his direction.

Gould had changed his outfit. He now wore a suit jacket over his waistcoat and a shoestring tie around his neck. He'd slicked his hair back with some sort of oil. The gun was missing from his hip, probably concealed beneath his jacket. He'd be slower to draw it. He was less than twenty metres away. How easily Roy could cross the distance, draw his own gun, put a bullet through the stalker's skull. His fingers itched.

Why is he looking for Lilian? What could a stalker want with her?

He could feel the cold metal of his gun beneath his coat. But he just brought the cigarette to his lips again. Not here. He couldn't afford the attention. Not until Lilian was safe.

Besides, the stalker wasn't alone.

Another figure emerged from the gangway. A woman, tall and broad. Long strides carried her across the platform after the thin man. She wore a handsome dinner suit, an older style than the thin man's. She wore it like it somehow offended her. A grey hat with a narrow brim sat on her head. Where the thin man wore leather shoes, she wore boots. Boots made for fighting in. He couldn't see a gun on her either, but he had no doubt she was armed.

Two stalkers, then. Their ship's records were correct. Victoria had done well, buying the information from one of the Port Authority officials.

He stood, put his cigarette between his lips, and thrust his hands into his pockets as he followed them. But as he turned away from the spaceport, movement from the gangway caught his eye.

Knox. What the hell was the augment doing with them? Were the other convicts working with the stalkers as well? No, Bones wouldn't let the augment go off with the stalkers by himself. Too dangerous. The augment was their most valuable asset, their best chance of getting off the station. *And finding me*, he reminded himself. He'd needed the convicts' assistance to make the escape from the Bolt. But he had never planned to stick around and put his trust in men like that. Men who would cut their own goddamn hand off just to carve a set of dice. He was safer on his own.

No, if Knox was working with the stalkers, that could only mean that Bones and the others had already encountered the stalkers and come out on the wrong side of the fight. That was one less thing for him to worry about. But perhaps he should have strangled the augment before he left with the money.

Too late to worry about that now. This settled it. The stalkers were after him. They thought they could get to him through Lilian. They'd see how well that turned out.

Knox fell in beside the female stalker, scurrying on his little legs to keep up with her long strides. The thin man ranged ahead of them at his own pace. They made their way down the stairs from the platform towards the strip. Roy tossed his cigarette and tailed them from a distance.

If he was careful and quiet, perhaps he could take them all out. But it would be a distraction he couldn't afford. The crowd of tourists and locals celebrating their last weeks on earth in drunken abandon swirled around him as he followed the stalkers. The woman's height made her easy enough to follow. The thin man would blend in almost anywhere, but the woman and the augment stood out, no matter how they dressed.

The grav train slid past overhead. From the side of the street, a deranged follower of the House of Man screamed about the coming doom. The religious nut waddled after Roy as he passed.

"Embrace it!" the man shouted at him. "Embrace your death and accept the Gospel of Dust."

Roy ignored him but the man lurched closer.

"Why do you fight? Why do you pretend to live? You were born dead, made animate by sin and the cursed machines that destroyed our ancestors. Surrender to the void. Surrender!"

"Be quiet, old man!" Roy growled, shoving the man away. The doomsayer tumbled to the ground and lay there, staring at the dark sky.

"The void comes! It comes to claim Man! Surrender!"

Roy pushed his hands back into his pockets and returned his attention to the street. For a moment he thought he'd lost the stalkers in the swirling crowd. Then he spotted the woman. He headed towards them. They'd stopped near a looted stim store opposite the Crimson Curtain. The thin man was peering through the broken window of the store, picking through the remains of the display stand. But the other two were casting glances towards the Curtain.

Did they know Lilian was being held by Leone here? An idea took form in his mind. A way to take care of one problem and possibly draw Leone out into the open.

He backed up down the street, keeping the stalkers in his sight, until he came across a public comm terminal with an intact screen. He fed a couple of notes into the machine. It binged happily. Among the many bits of information Hudson had spilled to try to stop the pain, there had been a particular comm number Roy had made sure to take note of. Roy fished the number out of his memory and punched it into the terminal. He brought the handset to his ear.

There was a moment of crackle as a tab picked up, but no one spoke. Light breathing whispered in his ear. He rubbed his palm against his cheek, feeling the scratch of stubble.

"Mr Leone," Roy said through a closed fist, trying to disguise his voice.

"Who is this?" The voice on the other end was smooth. It reminded him of an oil slick. Just like he'd remembered it.

"A friend with sources inside the Federation. I have

some information for you. For your safety."

For ten seconds there was only the sound of Leone's breathing. But when he spoke, his voice was as calm and smooth as ever. "And why would I need information like that?"

"I know that some inside the Federation consider you a protected individual. But that protection is not absolute. The Federation is a large organisation. You can always use more sources. I wish to prove my usefulness to you."

"Do you, now? How did you get this number?"

"A mutual acquaintance," Roy said. He watched the street as Knox and the female stalker split away from Gould, crossing the street and heading for the Curtain's main entrance. "I hope that in future we can do business together. But to do that, I need to ensure you remain free. Two stalkers are about to enter the Crimson Curtain. They have a contract on your head."

More silence. "I know of no such contract. What would the Federation want with an honest businessman like me?"

Roy smiled. The man said it like he almost believed it.

"Your friends in the Federation may not care about you as much as you believe. The stalkers will be entering the Curtain any moment. Perhaps they are only scouting the casino. But make no mistake. Before Temperance falls, they will attempt to apprehend you."

"You must be mistaken. No one has mentioned this to me."

"If the Federation was sending stalkers after you, they wouldn't warn you first. Find them. Watch them. See what they do. If I'm lying, you only have to deal with a little unneeded stress. If I'm telling you the truth, I'm saving you from a lifetime in a supermax prison station. I'll be in touch."

"Wait—"

Roy cut the link and Leone's voice disappeared. He glanced around, drew a knife from beneath his coat, and prised open a panel on the side of the comm terminal to sever a handful of wires. The screen died.

He slid his knife back into its sheath and strode casually away from the terminal, rejoining the crowd. Across the street, Knox and the woman walked past the bouncers at the entrance to the Curtain and disappeared inside. A few moments later, he caught a glimpse of Gould slipping quietly after them.

He'd shaken the tree. Now to see what fell out.

Roy followed.

10

Dom stepped through the grand entranceway of the Crimson Curtain, the sea of revellers breaking around her. Crimson carpet underfoot led the way through the entrance lobby and trailed down wide halls. Ahead, a short set of stairs led to a gaming floor. The walls were white plaster hung with red curtains. Staff in red uniforms smiled through red lips at the waves of oncoming gamblers. She walked past red leather couches and tables covered with red laminate.

Whoever designed this place really knew how to follow through with a theme.

Dom resisted the urge to tug at the suit she'd stuffed herself into as she passed security officers who didn't even try to pretend they weren't gangsters. She'd left her Marauder on the *Solitude*, but she had her revolver strapped directly to her thigh. A hole in her trouser pocket was her only access to it. But it was better than nothing.

Knox buzzed at her side like an insect. "This place is a goddamn eyesore," he said.

"Good thing you've only got one eye then," she said as she scanned the crowd.

"Oh, you're a funny one now, are you? I can see why all the boys can't keep their hands off you."

Dom ignored the augment. They came around the side of a stained glass dividing wall—red glass, naturally—and the main casino floor opened up. The place was gigantic. Row upon row of slot machines and gaming tables stretched out into infinity. There was a slight curve to all the red-carpeted pathways that ran between tables, so once you were inside the exit was never in sight. She could see three bars from where she stood, each crowded with young men and women mostly dressed in the sleek, pointed fashions of Babel and Ophelia.

In amongst the rich foreign socialites, a woman paced and drank and slid a stack of chips onto a green felt mat, all with the nervous twitch of a habitual stim user. To the tourists, she was invisible. To the floormen dealing cards and supervising games, she was a walking pile of vin.

"A lot of staff around," Dom noted. "Why are they still working when they're all about to die?"

"That'd be Mr Leone's doing," Knox said. "Word is he has a way off the station. And he has a reputation for taking care of his own. All these poor saps are praying to the Great and Just Lord Feleti Leone to save them. And all they have to do is put on a red suit and a smile and take these tourists' money."

The universe really was filled with fools. Or maybe desperation just bred foolishness. She was no exception.

She put the thoughts aside. She had a job to do.

"Where would this private elevator be?" she asked Knox.

"My bet? Central column." He pointed to the centre of the wide casino floor. A silver pillar a few metres in diameter rose from the floor to the ceiling's highest point. There were two mezzanine floors above them, and the uppermost one extended all the way from the wall to the column.

"Entrance up there?" Dom said.

"Your guess is as good as mine, darling," Knox said.

The two of them found the stairs and headed to the upper levels. Up here, the guests' clothing became more expensive. Dom became even more self-conscious.

As they ascended to the upper mezzanine, a set of doors came into view on the central column. They were flanked by a pair of red-suited security. Dom let her gaze slide past them. She was conscious that Knox was drawing occasional glances, and she wasn't doing much better. Nothing particularly suspicious about a dwarf or a large woman, but they'd be remembered if something happened.

She settled herself on a stool at a slot machine shaped to look like an old battle cruiser. Knox looked it over with a sneer.

"It's supposed to be the Nador Three," he said. "Solar Federation vessel. The Fringe forces tore these things to pieces by the dozen during the Gravity War. The fucking crates couldn't turn. Fringe fleet would just open up a Gypsy trail, jump in behind them, and broadside them with grav beams. Then jump away again before the fleet could mount a response. Typical Solars. Big dicks, all right, but they didn't know how to use them."

"Delightful," she said. "Is that what they teach you about in the Radiance? An old wars that no one remembers?"

"It's a shame, really. I wish I'd got the sort of practical education I hear you New Calypsans got. What did they teach you? How to turn an empty beer can into an improvised explosive? The delicate art of applying Molotov cocktails to a line of police recruits?"

She set her jaw and turned away from the augment so he wouldn't see how close he'd hit. She grabbed hold of the slot machine's lever and tugged it down. The dials didn't spin.

She felt—rather than heard—Eddie come up behind her. By now she could recognise his thick aftershave anywhere.

"You'll need some chips if you want to have a spin on that," he said, his voice barely distinguishable above the excited rumble of wins and losses and whirling colours echoing up from the lower floors. He pushed a small crimson sack into her hand. When she opened it, it was filled with low denomination casino chips. She took one out and put it in the machine. Pulled the lever. Lights flashed and the dials spun. They died with a sad beep. A bust.

"Security's all packing," Eddie said. "And the pit bosses are on alert."

"So don't try to cheat any games."

"Too late," he said. "Where do you think all those chips came from?"

She couldn't tell if he was joking. She wasn't sure she wanted to know.

"Elevator's over there," she said, pointing with her eyes. One of the guards on duty beside the elevator doors pulled out his tab and answered a call. The other yawned.

"Seen anyone go through yet?"

"Not yet."

"Well, we've only got one of these here fancy silver chips," Eddie said. "I'm guessing that means only one of us is getting upstairs. And since you two are dressed like a couple of bums at a job interview, it's probably going to have to be me."

"I resent that," Knox said.

Eddie shrugged. "Resent it all you like, Jack. Who wants to spot me half a million vin?"

"I can tell you exactly where you can stick your head to go looking for it," Dom said.

"Come on. I'm dressed the part to get up there, but I need the cash. They're not going to let me gamble in the high rollers room with my pocket lint."

"Take this, then." Dom shoved the sack of chips back into his hand.

"Are you kidding? That wouldn't even buy me a martini up there. Look, anything I bet, I'll make back."

"By cheating," she said flatly.

"Not if I get lucky."

She sighed. "You're going to get us both killed one day. It won't even be exciting. Some pit boss is just going to walk up behind us and put one in each of our heads."

She dug her cash card out of her wallet and held it out. He grabbed it, but she didn't let go.

"Two hundred thousand," she said carefully. "Not a single vin more. Not if you want us to have enough left to pay for fuel off this damn station."

He grinned. "Whatever you say, Boss."

She reluctantly released the card and he strolled over to a chip exchange desk on the wall behind them. With a scowl on her face, she watched him swipe the card across the desk. The woman behind the counter slid a stack of chips to him.

"That's a lot more than two hundred thousand," Knox observed.

"I know," she said.

"Does that make you mad?"

"Would you like me to show you how mad it makes me?"

"I don't know." He gave her a leer. "Maybe I would. You might be sexy when you're angry. It can't make you any worse, anyway."

She regretted not shooting him in the chapel.

Eddie returned with his sack of chips, took one look at her face, and smiled at her.

"Sorry. Couldn't resist." He shook the sack and closed his eyes in bliss. "But would you listen to that clink. Sounds like heaven, doesn't it?"

She snapped her fingers and he handed her back the cash card.

"I saw a security station down on the ground floor when I was walking around," he said. "If you want to make yourself busy while I'm upstairs living it up."

"I might be able to access the building plans on their systems," Knox said. He smiled like he was thinking of something.

"What?" she said.

"What?"

"Why are you smiling?" she said.

The smile vanished and he shrugged. "I was just thinking we might be able to find their central servers that way. Maybe even find us a way in that doesn't involve gambling away all our money in the high rollers room."

"*My* money," Dom said. "Not ours. Mine. You get your share of whatever's on Williams when we find him." She directed a glare at Eddie. "No cheating." She looked at Knox. "And no hacking the casinos computers to steal their money."

The augment frowned. "Were you reading my mind? What sexual position am I thinking of right now?"

"I've spent plenty of time around criminals. I'm familiar with the stupid things they think of. I don't want us to come to Feleti Leone's attention. We stay quiet, we get what we need to, and we find Roy Williams. That's the job. Okay?"

Knox put his hands up in surrender. "Fine, fine."

"Eddie?" she said.

"You're the boss. Are we done?"

"Keep the line open on your tab. You have your glasses?"

He pulled a pair of thin-rimmed spectacles out of his pocket and slipped them on. She brought up her tab and connected to the speaker hidden in the spectacles' earpiece.

"Can you hear me?" she said into the tab.

"Loud and clear, Freckles."

He leaned over her, slipped a chip into the slot machine, and pulled the lever. Three Gypsy Gates spun into place. The machine chirped delightedly. Chips poured into the cash tray.

"If I kill you, do I absorb your luck?" she said. "Is that how it works?"

He grinned, took one chip out of the tray, and left the rest. "Don't get into too much trouble without me."

He strolled away towards the elevator, pocketing the chip as he walked.

Knox cleared his throat. "So, if he doesn't want all these…" He gestured to the chips. "…can I have them?"

"Touch them and I break your neck," Dom said.

He looked mournfully at the chips. "At least buy me a drink, then."

She sighed and shoved the chips into her pockets.

11

Eddie stopped in front of the goons wasting oxygen next to the elevator and gave them a good look at his teeth.

"Good evening, sir," the one on the left said. Eddie got the feeling he'd only just started using words like "sir" and hadn't quite got used to it. "Do you have your token?"

Eddie flicked the silver casino chip at him. The man caught it with both hands and examined it. Satisfied, he slipped it into a thin slot above the elevator call button. The doors hummed open and the slot spat the coin back out.

"Will you have any company joining you tonight, sir?" the man said as he handed Eddie back the chip.

"Not tonight," he said, stepping into the elevator. "A man's got to have some alone time. And what the wife doesn't know won't hurt her." He winked at the guard.

The man just nodded. "Yes, sir. Enjoy your evening."

The doors slid closed and the elevator began to move.

Eddie whistled to himself, checked his reflection in the mirror, and slicked back his hair. Then the door opened and he stepped out into a room of classical music and the smell of vanilla.

Something warm and young pressed itself against his arm.

"Good evening, sir."

A pretty girl all of about sixteen smiled up at him with perfect teeth and blue eyes so big you'd need a nav console and a grav drive just to get from one corner to the other. Her red gown plunged so precipitously at both the front and back he wondered why she didn't just go topless and be done with it.

"Evening," he said. She remained attached to his arm. "Am I under arrest?"

She giggled a giggle that was as annoying as it was vapid. No wonder she was pressing her breasts against him so tight—they seemed to be the only thing she had going for her. "I'm Brittany. Would you care for an escort this evening?"

Escort? He glanced behind her and finally noticed the small crowd of beautifully boring men and women in red outfits waiting to ambush lonely high rollers. He guessed they must be playing the odds, shoving this schoolgirl at him instead of one of the well-muscled men.

"Is this your first time with us, sir?" Brittany said. She wrapped her fingers around his hand and gently pulled. "Come, let's get you a drink. What's your name, handsome?"

Handsome? Bloody hell.

"Mr Black," he said.

"Lovely. Follow me, Mr Black."

She practically skipped through the tiled entrance hall. Wide arches opened up into rooms on either side of him, each revealing gaming tables thick with black suits and cigar smoke. A cheer erupted from a blackjack table, the dealer smiling along with the winners.

Three more red-gowned pretties passed them. Each had a businessman or woman on their arm. The female escorts all shared their luscious smiles with him. Oh, how the rich lived.

The entrance hall ended and opened up into a wide, high-roofed chamber with three platforms of tables and chairs sloping progressively downward to a red-curtained stage at the far end. A handful of suited men and women nibbled on tiny portions of steak and chicken while seated at the tables. On the stage, a lone microphone stood on a stand against the crimson backdrop.

"When's the show?" he asked.

"In about thirty minutes. Are you a music lover, Mr Black?"

"On occasion."

"Then I'm sure you'll enjoy the musical talents of Miss Mayweather."

She led him over to a wide bar to the right of the main doors. If he wasn't mistaken, the bar top was made of real wood, stained and polished.

The barman stood patiently with his hands behind his back. "What can I get you, sir?"

"Lotus blossom." He paused and put on half a smile. "And a Bluen if you have one handy."

"Certainly, sir." The barman went to work, filling the shaker with ice and vodka and liqueurs. He shook the shaker with the kind of poised assurance that earned fifty thousand vin tips, then strained the liquid into a cocktail glass and garnished it with a leaf of mint and a small flower. When he'd prepared the drink to his satisfaction, he placed it on a napkin in front of Eddie. Next to it he laid another napkin and dropped a Bluen pill into the exact centre. That done, his hands slid behind him and he probably gave himself a little pat on the back for a job well done.

It'd been a long time since Eddie had been anywhere like this. He'd grown up with money—most of it embezzled by his father, of course, although he didn't know that at the time. But he'd forgotten what it was like to be surrounded by this kind of extravagance. It didn't feel right. Where was the grit? He wanted to feel some kind of texture when he ran his finger along the bar top. Even the Bluen tasted too clean when he slipped it under his tongue.

He hoped he had enough money to pay the tab when it was time to leave. He should've taken even more off Dom's card.

As if on cue, a short crackle hummed through the earpiece of his glasses.

"Are you in?" Dom's voice came through. "Cough if you can't talk."

He brought his fist to his mouth and gave a small cough, following it up with another sip of his cocktail.

"Just listen, then. We're about to make our move on the security station. Knox says if he can plant some sort of gizmo he can access the basics from his tab. If we get the plans, we can guide you from here. And if you find the systems room, we'll see about sending Knox up to access it. Tap twice if that's okay."

He made to scratch his ear and tapped twice on the side of his glasses.

"Roger," she said. Then she was gone.

Eddie sat for another couple of moments with Brittany the escort casting him blank, pleasant smiles over her own drink. Every few seconds, she'd try some more small talk. As the last of the Bluen dissolved, he smiled back and picked up his cocktail.

"I feel like a little blackjack. Would you show me the way?"

The girl wrapped her arm around his and beamed. "Certainly, Mr Black. I can tell you're a man with a lot of luck."

"You have no idea."

12

Dom eyed the security station over her barely touched cocktail. "I hate being sneaky. I don't do sneaky."

"Really?" Knox said dryly, looking her up and down. "But you seem so spry and nimble."

"Shut up." From her position a couple of metres behind a roulette table she could see through the reinforced glass windows into the security station. There was only one staff member inside the room in front of the bank of security monitors, but plenty of security guards walking the floor nearby. They'd see her if she tried to force the door.

"Looks like we need a distraction," Knox observed.

"Preferably one that isn't going to put the place in lockdown. Some of these guys look a little jumpy. I don't want to kill anyone I don't have to."

"A noble sentiment," the augment said. "I've got an idea. Follow me."

He moved around to the side of the security station, heading for several long rows of slot machines. Only a handful of gamblers played, each pulling the levers of two or three adjacent machines at a time. She followed Knox down the row until he reached the end.

"Is anyone watching us?" he asked.

She glanced around. They were in a blind spot between a couple of security cameras. This section was too deserted to receive much staff attention. "We're clear. What are you doing?"

He bent down next to the last in the row of slot machines and pulled a thin metal panel off a box affixed to the side. "All these casinos control the slot machines centrally. That way they can adjust the odds up or down as they need to." He rolled up his sleeve, revealing the cables disappearing into his skin. He selected a pair of them and plugged them into two jacks inside the box.

"That's disgusting," she said.

"Typical Luddite from the House of Man."

"I don't follow the House."

"But you were raised by them. And that counts for a lot."

He pulled a chunky grey tab out of his pocket and plugged a third cable from his arm into it. The monochrome green screen lit up. The machine clicked rapidly as it powered on.

"Nice tab," she said.

He shifted slightly, like he was embarrassed. "Shut up. It's a hunk of shit piece of new tech. I used to have an Engage 4, pristine condition, latest model from before the Fall. Except the Feds seemed to think I shouldn't have it anymore when they arrested me." He pressed an analogue button on the side of the tab and shuddered as if he'd been shocked. "Christ, it's like jacking into a toaster."

She didn't know much about augments, only the urban legends the Fed-controlled media couldn't suppress. Most of them came out of the Radiance, the fringe group of Pre-Fall tech hoarders that made their home on Uriel. The Feds made them out to be some sort of cult, worshipping old tech and trying to coax new life out of it. She'd heard rumours that human augmentation used to be fairly common in the Core systems before the Fall. Not so much out here at the Fringe, where the Solar Federation hadn't trusted its citizens with more advanced technology. That didn't make it any less disturbing watching Knox plug into the tab, connecting it to himself on some level she couldn't even begin to understand.

She swallowed her unease. "You still haven't told me what you're doing."

"Adjusting the odds." Knox's fingers flew across the tab, faster than she could keep track of. His remaining eye stared blankly ahead, while the electronic replacement hummed quietly. "You still got those chips Skinny gave you?"

She glanced down the row of slot machines and got the idea. "Want me to start playing some slots?"

"See, all the other kids say you're slow, but I knew you'd catch on eventually."

"Gee, thanks. I'll leave you and your department store tab alone."

His cheeks flushed. "It's a temporary tab. Temporary. Get on with it, Tarzan."

She moved down the row and fed chips into three different machines. With a glance back, she saw that Knox had unplugged himself from the panel and was slinking slowly back towards the security station. He met her eyes and gave a quick nod. She licked her lips and pulled each of the slot machine levers, one by one.

The dials spun and spun. She backed up a little bit, away from the machines.

The first machine burst out with a victorious melody of beeps. "Jackpot! Jackpot!" it yelled.

Eyes glanced towards the slot machines from nearby. Flashing lights lit up the machine as chips began to pour into the tray, overflowing onto the floor.

The next slot machine over stopped its spinning and joined in the victory song. "Jackpot! Jackpot!"

Then the next one. "Jackpot! Jackpot!"

Gamblers were drifting away from the roulette table now, coming to see the commotion. A couple of red-suited security guards spoke urgently into their tabs. None of them looked at her as she quickly slipped away.

One of the women further down the line of slot machines gave a delighted shriek. "Jackpot! Jackpot!" her machine declared.

There was a moment's pause as every nearby gambler stared at the rows upon rows of slot machines. The overlapping shouts of "Jackpot!" and whistles and pouring chips rang in Dom's ears. She could see the flashing lights reflected in the gamblers' stares.

Then the stampede started all at once, as if it'd been choreographed. Men and women dressed in tuxedos and gowns elbowed each other out of the way in a rush to fill the slot machine seats. Soon the cacophony was accompanied by shouts and the clunk of slot levers being pulled and dials spinning.

"Jackpot!"

"Jackpot!"

"Jackpot!"

Security guards and staff members ran around wildly, yelling into tabs and trying to tug gamblers away from the machines. Dom smiled to herself and slipped away through the growing crowd, heading for the security station.

Knox moved alongside her, using her bulk as a buffer against the crowd. "Did I do good, Mummy?"

"That is the creepiest thing I've heard you say yet. Never ever call me that again." She pushed her way out of the crowd and glanced at the security station. The staff were all distracted, but she could see one security guard still inside the station, standing up and watching the chaos on his monitors.

"That security booth's door is locked," Knox said as they approached the station.

She brushed past a security guard hurrying towards the chaos. When he'd passed, she held up the electronic key she'd swiped from his belt.

The augment gave her an appraising nod. "I'm impressed. They teach you that in between *Poisoning Public Water Supplies* and *Propaganda 101*?"

"Yeah, right after *How to Twist the Legs Off Annoying Augments*. I got an A in that one."

"Still a guard inside," he said. "Got a plan to deal with him as well?"

"Just the one."

She glanced around once more. No one looking her

way. Inside the booth, the guard rubbed his forehead as he stared at the monitors. Dom slid the electronic key into the lock and pulled open the door.

The guard started to turn. Dom kicked him in the back of the knee, wrapped her arm around his neck, and squeezed.

"Jesus Christ," Knox said as he came in after her.

"Close the door, for the love of Man," she said through gritted teeth. The guard's fingers clawed at her face. She had ten kilograms and a head's height on him. He could claw all he liked. He wasn't going anywhere.

She heard the door click as the electronic lock reengaged. The man's face was going purple in her arms.

She glanced at Knox. "Can anyone see?"

The augment peeked out the window. "I don't think so. You're going to kill him."

"I'm not going to kill him." The guard's struggles grew sluggish. His tongue protruded grotesquely from his mouth. His legs faltered and then she was taking all his weight. He went still.

She lowered him carefully to the floor and released him. His breathing started again, but his eyes remained closed.

"See," she said. "He's fine."

"Yeah. He looks just dandy. Get on lookout."

She positioned herself near the door and divided her attention between looking through the window and watching the casino's security feeds on the bank of monitors. She could still hear the calls of "Jackpot!" drowning out everything else.

When she glanced back at Knox, he was lying on the floor under the security computer, plugging himself into some hidden port. Like Knox's tab, the computer here was new and bulky. Mechanical clicks chattered from the machine as he hooked some sort of plastic chip into place.

"What are you doing?" she said.

"Computer stuff. You wouldn't understand."

"This'll let you access their security remotely?"

"That's why I'm doing it, isn't it?" He kicked the limp body of the security guard. "Move him out of the way, will you? I need to get over here."

She put her boot under the guard and rolled him so Knox could shuffle over. He pulled his tab out and plugged in another cable.

"Seems a bit strange," she said as she returned her attention to the window.

"What does?"

"Someone like you ending up in the Bolt. Most hackers don't end up in a supermax."

"Most hackers don't jack into the prisoner transport vessel they're in and vent the crew compartment's oxygen into space."

She grunted.

"What?" he said. "You don't approve of killing Feds, New Calypsan?"

"When I killed Feds it was war."

"I'm sure that's a real comfort to them." He glanced at her while his fingers continued to poke rapidly at his tab. "You know the real difference between you and me? When they caught me, they saw a midget and an old-tech cultist.

So they threw away the key. When they caught you, they saw a weapon. So they figured out how to use you."

"Well, now I'm using you. And you're using me."

"Ain't this one big happy family?" he said. "What's the skinny guy's deal? Why's a writer hanging around with you?"

"You'll have to ask him."

"Pass. I'm not in the mood to go making any friends." He unjacked himself and clambered out. "All done."

"You've got it?"

"I've got it all, sweetcheeks." He nudged the guard with his shoe. "What are we doing with him?"

"Leave him. Can you wipe any security vid feeds that might've recorded us coming in here?"

"Already done. Can we get out of here? I think this guy pissed himself."

She glanced out the window once more, waiting for a pit boss to pass, then pulled open the door. "After you."

"So polite, for a terrorist." He slipped through the door.

She held her tongue and followed him out.

Eddie tapped the table. The dealer slipped a card off the top of the deck and laid it on the table in front of him. Jack of hearts. Shit.

"Twenty-two," the dealer said. "Player busts. Sorry, sir."

He took Eddie's stack of chips and sequestered them in his tray.

"It seems like your luck is turning bad, Mr Black," Brittany said as she stood behind him, her hands resting on his shoulders.

"Doesn't matter. It's not my money," he said as he set up another bet. He was the only one at this table now. The middle-aged woman he'd been sharing the game with had started bleeding chips and went off in search of more booze a few minutes ago.

As the dealer dealt him his cards—a queen and an eight—his earpiece crackled back to life. Dom's voice whispered in his ear.

"We're in. Floor plans say there's another private elevator behind a staff door off the main corridor. It's locked electronically, but Knox says he can override it. That should take us to the upper floors. Leone's offices and the central command room. See if you can find the elevator. Then we'll see about getting Knox up to you. Cough to confirm."

He cleared his throat as he signalled to stay. The dealer revealed his own hand: fifteen. He took another card. Eight of clubs.

"Dealer busts," he said. "Well done, sir."

Eddie pushed his chips across the table and stood. "Too much excitement for me. Colour me up."

The dealer nodded and traded in his chips for higher value ones. Eddie slipped them into his pocket, leaving one on the table. "Buy yourself a drink."

"Thank you, sir." The dealer smiled as he took the chip.

Brittany clung to his arm as he turned away from the table and returned to the entrance hall. He put his hand on hers.

"If you'll excuse me, I need to use the facilities. Can I meet you in the restaurant for the show?"

"I'll save us a table," she said, releasing him and bouncing away. He headed towards the bathroom until she disappeared out of sight. Then he turned aside, nodded to a pair of elderly high rollers, and went searching for the staff door.

He found it a few moments later. He hadn't noticed it on the way in through the tiled hall. It was constructed to blend into the wall as just another panel; the only thing giving it away was the small gold handle. As he strolled past, he put a finger out and tested the handle. Locked. Hopefully the midget was as good as he claimed he was.

He headed back towards the bathrooms and pushed open the door. Shining white surfaces gleamed at him from every direction. It was a far cry from the grimy little bathroom on the *Solitude*. He checked the toilets; both were empty.

"Freckles, you there?" he whispered.

"I don't answer to that name," Dom said in his ear.

"You just did. I think I found the door. Locked, like you said. But it's not well guarded. If the can opener can unlock it and get up here, I think we'll be able to get through. Any idea what we'll be facing upstairs?"

"Shouldn't be too many goons. Looks like security's focused on the casino floor itself. But the records say Leone's on site tonight, so expect at least a couple of bodyguards and whatever non-syndicate staff they need to keep this place running."

From outside the bathroom, the sound of a saxophone drifted in. He was missing the show. What a pity.

"Piece of cake. Think you can get the midget up to me?"

"We're going to need that silver chip. Head back down

and we'll do something about the guards on the elevator."

"But I'm having so much fun blowing all your money," he said. "Give me another ten minutes to spend the rest and I'll—"

A woman's voice sang out over the call of the saxophone. Piano music tinkled in the background. The woman's song tugged at him. There was something familiar about it.

"Eddie," Dom said. "Are you there?"

"Hold on." He took off the glasses and tucked them away in his pocket, cutting off Dom's protestations. His heart hammered in his chest, fighting off the sedating powers of the Bluen and the alcohol. His mouth felt dry. He pushed open the bathroom door.

The voice came down the hallway, clear and sharp like a knife. His legs carried him forward. The doors to the restaurant were open. It was dark over the tables, but lights illuminated the stage. The band played on, fading into the background.

And in the centre of the stage, hands wrapped around the silver microphone pole, stood Cassandra Diaz.

13

"Eddie?" Dom hissed into her tab. "Eddie, talk to me, for the love of Man."

Knox raised his eyebrow at her from his seat alongside. "Trouble in paradise?"

"Shut the hell up," she said through gritted teeth. "Eddie. Eddie, come in."

The augment just sipped his drink and stared at the gamblers going about their business. He didn't seem concerned that this whole sorry plan would go tits up if Eddie didn't hold up his part. She bared her teeth at him.

"Your neck's on the line as well, you know."

"Sure," Knox said. "But there's no point getting worked up about it. Want me to get you a drink, sweetcheeks?"

She ignored him and gave her tab a few sharp taps on the table. Piece of shit was older than the *Solitude*. She couldn't even tell if she was still connected to Eddie's tab.

"Take it easy," Knox said, his voice rising for the first time since they'd sat down. He snatched the tab out of her hands. "This is a relic of Pre-Fall tech, here. Manufactured by the Perna Corporation in the Ash system circa three hundred and fifty years ago. It's delicate."

"It's not working." She tugged it out of his hands.

"It's working fine. It's your partner who's not—"

He cut off with a sharp intake of breath as a man slid into the seat across the table from them.

Dom hadn't seen the man approach. She stopped abusing the tab to study him. He seemed…not familiar, exactly, but there was something about him that pulled at her gut.

He was a big man, broad-shouldered and packed with muscle. He wore a thick jacket and a silk shirt that wouldn't have suited him even if it hadn't been out of fashion. A dark shadow of stubble coated his cheeks and chin. In his forties at least. Eyes hard like steel. The eyes of a man who had seen a lot and done more.

The gears in her mind ground to a halt. She knew who this was. She slipped her hand into a pocket and gripped the revolver strapped to her thigh.

Something metallic tickled her knee under the table. A gun barrel. The man shook his head.

"Don't try it, stalker." His voice was almost guttural. "Hands above the table."

"No thank you, sir," she said. "I think I'll keep my hand right here." She tightened her grip on her gun. "Roy Williams, I presume."

"In the flesh."

Knox was staring open-mouthed at Williams, his face rapidly turning grey. Williams nodded at the augment.

"Knox," he said.

The augment said nothing.

Dom glanced around without moving her head. She couldn't see anyone who wasn't a gambler or a staff member.

"Don't worry, stalker," Williams said. "I didn't bring backup."

"Then you've saved me a lot of trouble tracking you down, sir. If you'll be so kind as to put your gun away, I'll have you cuffed and handed over to the Feds in no time."

He didn't smile. "I enjoy being free, and I intend to remain that way. You can consider this a warning."

A red-suited waitress smiled and slowed as she passed the table. "Can I get anyone a drink?"

"We're fine, thank you, ma'am," Dom said without taking her eyes off Williams. Out of the corner of her eye, she saw the waitress's smile slip ever so slightly as she took in the cold tension surrounding the table.

"Of course," she said, already backing away. "Call if you need anything."

Dom waited until the woman had passed out of earshot before speaking again. "You're staying quiet. You don't want to bring attention to us. That tells me you're not much liked around here. Otherwise you would've already told your old pal Feleti Leone about us. And we'd already be dead."

"Feleti Leone is no friend of mine," Williams said. "Then again, he is no friend to stalkers either. If he recognised me, he would find out who you were. And we'd both be buried in the basement."

"Then it seems we are at an impasse," she said. "Seeing as I need you alive and you can't afford to draw attention to yourself by killing me."

He nodded. "That was the intention behind this

meeting."

"This warning, you mean."

Williams' gun barrel scraped her knee. "I have no desire to kill you, stalker, but I have no particular concern about doing so. I've killed a lot of men and women in my pursuit of freedom. One more makes no difference."

"Then why so chatty?"

"I want to make a deal."

"Usually when gentlemen make deals, they don't aim guns at each other under the table."

"Then I suppose neither of us are gentlemen or gentlewomen."

Dom let a grim smile creep across her face. "I suppose that's the case. Let's hear it, then."

"There's something I need to do on Temperance. A goal I must achieve before this station dies. I will not leave this station until I achieve that goal. If I fail, I have no reason to continue living."

"Something important to you."

He nodded. "The most important."

"A woman," she guessed.

"You look surprised."

"Not surprised. Amused. I've seen this before when I've chased fugitives. They break out of the joint and the first thing they think of is getting back to the piece of pussy they last fucked before they went away. They think it's love. True love. Eternal. As if everything stands still on the outside when a man's behind bars. As if that woman hasn't moved on, hasn't completely forgotten the son of a bitch she threw a pity fuck at. As if she hadn't found out exactly who that man really was. Sound familiar?"

"You can think what you like. My point is that there are things I have to do here and I can't afford the time or attention necessary to remove you forcefully. So I'm taking another approach. I'm going to pay you to leave the station."

She raised an eyebrow. "Do you think you can afford to buy me off?"

"Twelve million."

"You're worth seventeen."

"That includes hazard pay," he said, leaning forward. "Leave now. An easy twelve million. I can have it delivered to your ship by morning."

She drummed her fingers on the table, meeting his cold eyes. The swirl of movement and laughter and panicked excitement hummed around them, but she blocked it all out. Knox had gone still and pale. He looked like he didn't know whether to run or wet himself. He'd been scared of Bones and the other convicts, but he was terrified of Williams. She chewed it over.

"No deal," she said.

A muscle tense in Williams' cheek. "You're a fool if you don't agree to this. A dead fool."

"No. I'd be a fool to take your money. Assuming you actually have that much—which I don't believe you do—it's still not worth it. Sure, twelve million for getting on a ship and leaving? It's a good deal. But then what? I have a contract on your head. A contract with the Federation. The same Federation who has me by the neck until I've paid back a debt to them. How many contracts do you think a stalker gets when they fail to capture their bounties? How long do you think a stalker lasts when they allow themselves to be bought off?"

"You're under the Federation's thumb because you allow yourself to be," Williams said. "There are plenty of places the Feds hold no power."

"I was a wanted woman once. I will not be again. I reject your offer, sir. You are a murderer and a fugitive. I will apprehend you and turn you over to be detained at the Federation's pleasure. I will collect my reward and put it towards my debt. And one day, years from now, I will be a free woman. And you will be living out your days in an isolation cell in the void."

He stared at her for thirty seconds, eyes cold. She stared right back.

"Very well," he said. "When you're lying on the ground with my bullet in your chest and the last of your lifeblood leaking out, I hope you remember this conversation."

He stood, quietly slipping his gun into his waistband and pulling his jacket out to cover it. He turned his back and started to walk away. Dom didn't release her own gun.

"I can't allow you to leave here, Mr Williams," she said. "Don't move."

He paused and glanced back. "You can't afford to waste time apprehending me now."

"I have all the time in the world." She rose, her hand still in her pocket, grasping her revolver. "You have to leave this casino sometime. And when we're outside, away from Leone's eyes, you're mine."

He kept his back to her. "No. You have a clock, stalker.

Leone's men are watching your partner. Mr Gould, isn't it?"

Her gut turned cold.

"He's upstairs in the high roller lounge," Williams said. "Leone knows he's a stalker. Only he thinks the two of you are after him. In minutes he will be captured."

"You're lying."

Williams half-turned and gave her a hard stare. "They will take him to an unused section on the port side of the fourteenth floor. He will be interrogated. Harshly. He will be asked about you. They will come for you next. You do not have much time, stalker. You can't do both. You can't rescue Gould and apprehend me at the same time. If you wish to save your friend, you have no choice but to let me walk out of here."

Her lips peeled back. "You son of a bitch. You set us up."

"And you declined my deal. Farewell, stalker. I'm sure we'll be seeing each other soon."

He turned and started walking away. Dom watched him go, grinding her teeth together. She had every legal right to capture Williams right here. But in this place, in Leone's den, she doubted the law counted for much. Williams was right. Men like Leone didn't take kindly to stalkers disturbing the peace in their businesses.

If she could just get Williams outside, get him away from all these prying eyes, she could disarm him and cuff him. It would only take a few minutes. He was lying about Eddie. It was all a bluff. It had to be.

Williams' back grew smaller. Then he disappeared behind a crowd of gamblers at a craps table. He was gone.

"Shit." Dom whirled around. Knox was downing the last of his drink, sweat pouring from his cheeks. "Anything on the security system?"

The augment blinked and brought up his tab. "Uh, not yet. Not that I can see."

Dom pushed back her hat and rubbed her forehead. It was a lie. She took a step after Williams.

"Wait," Knox said. "I just found something. An alert." He turned the tab towards her. A pixellated vid feed image of Eddie half-hidden in darkness. He was staring at something off-screen. "They're preparing to apprehend him."

Shit. Shit. Damn it, Eddie. She cast one more glance towards the craps table where she'd last seen Williams. *Forget it. He's long gone.* She finally released her gun.

"Stay here," she said, turning towards the exit. "Wait for my instructions."

"Hey, where are you going?" Knox said.

"I'm going to need a bigger gun."

14

A black gown clung to Cassandra, glittering softly in the light. She'd dyed her hair a deep brown. Heavy makeup bordered her eyes; a stripe of black across her face. But it was her. It was undoubtedly her.

Eddie stopped in the doorway, letting the shadow fall over him. His tongue was stuck to the roof of his mouth. He'd never heard her sing before; he didn't even know she could. But her song reverberated in the depths of his chest, making it hard to breathe. He wasn't listening to the words. All he could hear was the sadness in her voice, in her song.

He didn't know how long he stood there, trance-like, letting her music wash over him. One song stopped and the next started. Gamblers and escorts were seated throughout the restaurant, their faces hidden in the shadow, but for him it could have been just Cassandra and himself alone in this cavernous room, just the two of them and her sad song. The barman approached him, offering him a glass of wine on a silver platter. But Eddie just waved him away with a twitch of his hand.

And then it was over. The song stopped and no other song began to replace it. The last notes died in his chest.

With her eyes downcast, Cassandra turned away and disappeared out of the spotlight, vanishing behind the curtain at the side of the stage.

The spell was broken. Eddie jerked alive again. The audience gave a smattering of polite applause as the lights rose and the mumbling sound of conversation filled the silence. He saw Brittany looking at him from a table off to the side, a confused look on her face. Probably wondering why he was just standing there, why he hadn't sat down. He didn't give a shit what she thought.

First the gentlemen's club, now Cassandra was singing here. Why? It didn't make any sense. She wasn't a stripper and she wasn't a musician. She was a fighter, a thief, a leader.

But she was alive. He hadn't believed it when Victoria Palmer said she was dead, not truly. He'd been right. She was still alive. She was alive, and she was here. He'd been close enough to call to her. She was here, in this building.

He had to get to her.

All thought of Dom and Roy Williams and the private elevator fled his mind, pushed aside by that one thought, focused like an anti-ship beam. Find Cassandra.

He took a few breaths to cool himself down, then went back to the bar and took a seat in front of the barman.

"You've removed your glasses, sir," the barman said.

"They were straining my eyes. I'll take a lager. And, I know this might be an unusual request, but I was taken by that woman's singing. Could you send a bottle of champagne to her dressing room? You can add it to my tab."

The barman's forehead creased slightly. "I suppose that

would be all right, sir."

"Fantastic. Do you happen to know her name?"

The barman set the tall glass of beer down in front of him. "Miss Lilian Mayweather, sir. But I'm afraid I don't know much more about her. She only began singing here recently."

"Mayweather," Eddie said, rolling the name around on his tongue. He didn't think it suited her. But then, nothing she'd been doing lately suited her.

The barman pulled out a bottle of champagne. "Will this be suitable, sir?"

"That'll be great. You're going to deliver it now?"

"I'll have one of our escorts take it to her." He slid the bottle into an ice bucket and looked past Eddie. "Perhaps Brittany would oblige." The escort was approaching from the table. "Brittany, would you mind delivering this champagne to Miss Mayweather's dressing room on behalf of this gentleman?"

She gave him a smile that didn't touch her eyes. "Of course. Shall I give her your regards, Mr Black?"

"Not necessary. Just tell her it's from a fan."

She nodded and took the ice bucket. "I'm sure she'll be delighted." She turned and walked back across the restaurant, disappearing through a door to the left of the stage.

Eddie thanked the barman and took his beer on a walk through the restaurant. The spices and smells of the meals being eaten around him turned his stomach. He sat down at an empty table near the stage and waved for a waiter.

"I'm in the mood for a bit of chicken. What do you have on the menu?"

"Tonight we're serving a dish of pan-roasted chicken and squash served with a chard salad topped with bacon vinaigrette."

"Sounds delicious," Eddie said, not caring. "Give me that."

"Very good, sir."

The waiter disappeared. Eddie took a sip of his beer. He looked around the restaurant, making sure none of the staff were looking his way. Then he stood, straightened his jacket, and slipped through the door beside the stage.

The quiet hubbub of the restaurant died away as he closed the door behind him. He was in a simple synth-wood-lined corridor that bent and continued on, probably behind the stage. Someone was talking somewhere out of sight. He shrugged, felt the weight of his pistol in the holster strapped to the small of his back. If he got to Cassandra, how would they get out? He'd have to move fast. Stay unnoticed as long as possible. Shoot his way out if he had to. He knew this was a stupid plan. But he might never get another chance.

Dom was going to kill him for this. She wouldn't understand.

He moved quietly down to the corner and peered around. No one in sight. He kept moving. Every few metres there was a door. He passed one labelled *Storage*, another labelled *Furniture*, and another that said *Security*. Footsteps were coming from ahead of him, around another corner. High heels. Brittany coming back, perhaps. Too late to turn back. He straightened, preparing a lie that would keep her from calling security for at least a few seconds. Long enough for him to get to her and take her out.

And then he saw it. His heart hammered. The door ahead of him, where the corridor turned. A name written across it. *Lilian Mayweather.*

There was a light on inside, the glow leaking out under the door. *Cassandra.* Her name formed silently on his lips. He made for the door.

Brittany emerged from around the corner and stood in his path. Between him and the door. Between him and Cassandra. There was no surprise on her face.

He opened his mouth. But his prepared story died on his lips. She stared at him with dead eyes and raised her arm. She was holding a pistol.

"That's close enough, Mr Gould. Put your hands up."

Footsteps behind him. He glanced back, saw three more goons in red suits approaching along the corridor. Two were armed with handguns, one with a submachine gun. They pointed the muzzles at him and glared.

He could feel the cold metal of his own pistol against his back. It might as well have been on the other side of the system. And the same for Cassandra.

"Mr Gould," Brittany said. "I will not ask you again. Raise your hands and get down on the ground."

The gun was steady in her hands. She knew how to use it. At least she'd become marginally less dull, he supposed.

He smiled a mirthless smile and put his hands in the air.

15

Eddie stared through the wall-length windows that looked over the city. He could see the strip stretching away below him, all glimmering lights and excited movement. Eleda VI hung overhead, clouds still raging across the planet's surface. It was quiet. Peaceful. He closed his eyes.

The back of a hand crashed across his cheek. His eyes jerked open as his head snapped around. He spat blood onto the ground and grinned up at the goon standing over him. The man was round and heavy, eyes too close together.

"I asked you a question, Eddie." Another man's smooth voice behind him. "You don't mind if I call you Eddie, do you?"

For the thousandth time, Eddie tested the bonds that held him to the pillar. They weren't getting any looser.

"Go right ahead, Jack," he said. "I guess you're calling the shots right now."

The man stepped into view, the soft leather of his loafers whispering on the bare concrete of the floor. This room appeared to be under renovation—the walls were stripped out, carpet removed, leaving only a bare skeleton littered with plastic sheets and rusted tools. Eddie guessed the renovation had stalled a few decades back. The concrete he sat on was stained, some of it his blood, some much older. He wasn't the first person to be brought here and roughed up.

As for the man with the loafers, he was a skeleton as well, but a better dressed one. He had a youthful face, but his long-fingered hands were wrinkled and veiny. Not that Eddie could see the man's hands now, clasped behind his back as they were, but he could sense them there. He'd seen those hands as the man sipped a glass of red wine while his three goons softened up Eddie's innards. The flesh hung loosely from his fingers, like they were rotting. Eddie could picture it even now. He decided that there was nothing worse than ugly hands. The man could dress himself in imported white dinner suits as much as he liked. He could oil up his hair and tighten his tie and slip on his fucking loafers. He'd still have those hands. He probably cried himself to sleep thinking about how ugly his hands were. The piteous life of Feleti Leone.

Leone looked down at him, a faint smile playing at his lips. But there was a nervousness in his eyes that betrayed him. Eddie didn't like nervous people. Not when they thought a gun or a few goons could keep them safe. Those people were dangerous.

"So?" Leone said.

"So what?"

"What's your answer?"

Eddie licked his lips and tasted blood. "I've forgotten the question. Remind me."

Leone nodded and turned to the biggest of his boys, the one with the dimwit eyes.

"You heard him, Mr Hume. Remind him."

The thug smiled around the gap in his teeth, gave it a good windup, and slugged Eddie across the face. Stars danced in Eddie's eyes.

"Oh yeah," Eddie said, licking the blood from his teeth. "Thanks, pal. Now I remember. You wanted to know why I came to apprehend you. Is that about right?"

"Exactly, Eddie," Leone said. "That's exactly right."

"Well, you're gonna laugh when you hear this. You ready? Here's the gag: I'm not here for you, Jack. Don't give a damn what you've done and who you've done it to. Isn't that a laugh?" He chuckled to prove it.

Leone stared at him with his big eyes and his fake smile.

"Come on, Eddie. We're old friends now. You don't expect me to just believe something like that, do you?"

"I'm not jerking you off, Jack. You'd know if I was. I'm here for someone, but it ain't you."

Leone signalled to one of his other boys, a plain-faced man who had decided to take care of Eddie's pistol. He was practically fondling it.

"Nick," Leone said.

The man came forward and slammed the tip of his shoe into Eddie's solar plexus. The air rushed out of his lungs and he sat there for a moment, gasping into a vacuum. His eyes watered.

Leone knelt down in front of him and slapped his face.

"Eddie, Eddie. It's not nice to lie like that. I got a call not two hours ago. This friendly chap with sources at the

Fed outpost." He pointed out the window, towards the sky. "Do you know what he said? He said he had some information for me. He said a couple of stalkers were coming to arrest me. I wasn't sure whether to believe it at first. So I did a little digging into the stalker ship that docked earlier this afternoon. There were two names on record. One of them was Eddie Gould. And a few minutes later one of my staff spotted a new guest entering our Members' Lounge. Sneaking around. And what do you know?" He held his hands out. "Eddie Gould. In the flesh."

"I hope you didn't pay for that information yet, because whoever sold it to you was…." He trailed off, thinking. Then he smiled. "Ah, shit."

"What is it, Eddie?"

"Just thinking. My quarry, the man I'm after. He made me. Let me guess. This source of yours, you'd never heard from him before, right? And he just offered you this information about me out of the kindness of his heart. How's that?"

Leone didn't say anything.

Eddie nodded to himself. "Thought so. Where'd we slip up? Something my partner did must've tipped him off."

The midget. It could be him. He'd set up this whole casino job. Eddie hadn't seen him making any calls, but that didn't mean anything. An ancient tech system that could track Roy Williams? What a joke.

He'd told Dom. He told her not to trust a midget who sits in another man's chair and drinks his beer. Ah well, live and learn. Or not, as the case may be.

Leone stood and turned his back on Eddie, facing the

window. "Tell me about this partner of yours."

"Didn't you hear me, Jack? I'm not here for you. You might as well either let me go or kill me. I'd prefer the first one, honestly, but like you said, you're calling the shots."

Leone flicked his fingers again. Old Gap-tooth approached Eddie, cracking his knuckles.

"Say, pal," Eddie said. "How about we settle this over a game of checkers? I'll even let you go first."

Gap-tooth laid two punches into him, one after another. Like hitting a sack of meat. Eddie coughed and groaned.

"Not so funny now, huh, funny guy?" Gap-tooth said.

"Pretty funny. You fell right into my trap. I'm terrible at checkers. Reverse psychology, see?" He gave a hacking laugh.

Leone turned back. "Your partner, Eddie. Souza, right? That's her name. Tell me about her."

"Can't do that, Jack."

"I don't appreciate stalkers running around my station interfering in my business, Eddie. I mean that. But I would have let it slide if you'd kept to yourself. I sent a man to follow whoever left that ship of yours when you landed. But now I haven't heard from him for several hours. Do you know what happened to him, Mr Gould?"

Eddie said nothing. But in his mind's eye, he saw the kid with the black hat and the hand cannon stuck in his pants.

Leone stared into his eyes. "Temperance is my station. It doesn't belong to the Feds or the stalkers or anyone else. It belongs to me."

"Well, I got to compliment you on the place," Eddie

said. "Real nice. Pity about how it's going to be a dead husk in a couple of weeks, but until then it's got a special charm. And I'm not just saying that because we're friends."

Leone stroked his chin with his hideous hands for a few moments, studying Eddie.

Gap-tooth spoke up. "Want me to hit him again, Boss?"

Leone shook his head. "I think I'm beginning to understand our friend here. Really getting to know him."

"Soul mates, you might say," Eddie suggested.

"There, that's what I'm talking about. These jokes. That smile. Even here, even with us…" He gestured to his three goons. "…he's still got his confidence. He's still got his dignity. He's cocky. Don't you think, Nick?"

Nick stroked Eddie's gun. "Yes, sir. Very cocky."

Leone strolled away a few steps and bent down. He took hold of a rusted sledgehammer and lifted it. "Strip his clothes."

The three goons stepped forward and ripped at Eddie's clothes. Two buttons snapped off his shirt. Gap-tooth grinned as he unbuckled Eddie's belt and started pulling his slacks down.

"If I knew this was the way the night was going to end, I would've put on my good underwear," Eddie said. But his heart rate kicked up a couple of notches as he watched Leone drag that sledgehammer along the ground.

The way he was tied to the pillar, they couldn't pull his shirt and jacket off completely. But his trousers and underwear were soon lying a few metres away. The cold of the concrete floor beneath him bit so hard it hurt.

Leone nodded. "How's that dignity, Eddie?"

"Not bad. Okay, now you strip. We can compare."

"Still cocky." Leone hefted the sledgehammer. "Let's do something about that. Grab his legs."

Gap-tooth and Nick each took an ankle and dragged Eddie's legs apart. The blood rushed in his ears. The muscles of his legs strained, but the thugs held tight.

Leone gave a few practice swings of the hammer. "What do you reckon will happen to your balls when this hammer lands? I always wondered that. Will they pop like balloons? What do you think, Mr Rodriguez?"

The third thug shrugged. His hands loosely gripped a submachine gun. "One way to find out."

"My thoughts exactly," Leone said. "Let's try talking one last time, what do you think? Eddie, tell us about your partner. Tell us what she looks like and where we can find her. I can't have a stalker running loose on my station. Not now. You know that. So tell me. Tell me and I'll give you your pants back. What do you say?"

Eddie stared at the hammer, then at Leone. His shoulders slumped.

"All right. All right. Jesus."

"Tell me, Eddie."

"All right. Just, just don't use the hammer, all right? I'll tell you." He licked his lips, stared at the concrete floor. "My partner…."

"Yes?"

"My partner." Eddie swallowed. Met Leone's eyes. And smiled. "My partner is your partner. My partner in all things is our Lord Jesus Christ the Luminary. Have you heard His gospel? He is come to save us from the endless night, from the threat of the void. He is come to reunite us with our brothers and sisters of the Solar Federation. Praise Him, for He is the light in the endless night who will show us the way back home!"

Leone just smiled. "Eddie, Eddie, Eddie. You've made a very poor choice."

He grinned back through bloodstained teeth.

"It's the only kind I know."

Leone raised the hammer. Eddie closed his eyes and braced for the pain.

An intercom crackled overhead, static echoing off the concrete walls. Eddie opened his eyes to see Leone and his goons staring at the ceiling. They let go of his legs and stood. Rodriguez gripped his gun tight.

"Attention," a woman's voice boomed over the intercom. "This message is addressed to Feleti Leone and the three gentlemen with him on the fourteenth floor of the Crimson Curtain. Nobody move."

"Who the fuck is that?" Leone hissed.

Eddie grinned. "That? That would be my partner."

16

The intercom spoke.

"The first and most important thing I have to say is that if any one of you makes a move from this point on without my order, you will die. If you try to run, you will die. If you raise your weapons, you will die. If you try to harm the man tied to that pillar, you will die. You will die fast and without warning. I hope you gentlemen understand how serious I am about this point."

Leone bared his teeth at the ceiling. "She's got access to the broadcast system. Where the hell is she?"

"My name is Dominique Souza," the intercom continued. "I am a stalker, charged with the apprehension of a fugitive from the Federation. Neither Mr Leone nor any of you on the fourteenth floor is that fugitive. I repeat, I do not intend to apprehend any individual in that room. However, you have detained and assaulted a fellow stalker. My partner. And if he is not released, I will kill each and every one of you."

"Call security," Leone said to the goon carrying Eddie's gun. "Find that bitch and shut her up."

"I'm going to need each of you gentlemen to put your

guns down and take three steps away from my partner," Dom said. "You have two seconds to comply."

A second passed. Eddie grinned up at Leone. The syndicate leader glanced around, sneered, and took three steps away. Rodriguez dropped his submachine gun and backed up alongside Gap-tooth.

But the third goon hesitated. His hand wrapped around the grip of Eddie's gun.

The left half of his head disappeared in a spray of blood and broken glass.

A moment later, the boom of a gunshot rang out. Eddie spotted the neat hole in the window. He traced the bullet's path to the roof of the adjacent casino.

The bloodied goon took a step. Then he collapsed. Blood pooled rapidly around him.

Leone and the goons ducked and made to scramble for cover. But Dom's voice roared across the intercom.

"Nobody move! The next person to move ends up like him."

Leone and the two thugs grew still. The syndicate leader bared his teeth at Eddie.

"Let me be very clear," Dom said. "I'm not fucking around, here, gentlemen. I'm in a very, very bad mood. I do not take kindly to people who harm my colleagues. Now, I have a few simple instructions for you to follow. If they are not followed, I'm sure you can guess what will happen."

Gap-tooth was staring ashen-faced at the dead thug. He didn't look so pleased with himself anymore.

"Mr Leone," Dom said. "I want you to take out your tab and make a call. Another colleague of mine will be coming up to collect the man tied to that pillar. He will be allowed complete access to the necessary doors and elevators. Arrange it. You have twenty seconds to comply."

Leone's eyes slid to the dead thug. He took his tab out of his pocket and touched the screen.

Dom spoke again. "Note, sir, that any additional words you speak to your security teams will end in your death."

Leone gave a curt nod and brought his tab to his ear. "Security. It's me. Disable the elevator locks and stand by. Someone will be coming to level fourteen. Escort him in. Just do it." He lowered his tab.

"My colleague will confirm you've followed my instructions in a moment," Dom said. "In the meantime, I want the large gentleman to untie my partner. And give him his clothes back, for the love of Man."

Rodriguez nudged Gap-tooth, who was having trouble keeping his eyes off the downed thug. He blinked and glanced nervously out through the bullet hole in the window.

"Yes, sir," Dom said. "I'm talking to you. Untie him."

Gap-tooth's tongue darted out, licking his lips, and then he scurried behind Eddie.

"Stay in sight," Dom said. "Unless you want to see if this rifle can put a hole right through that pillar."

Gap-tooth took a few steps to the right. Eddie could feel his fumbling fingers tugging at the knots in the rope. A few moments later, the bonds came loose. Eddie let out a sigh that burned his bruised ribs. He massaged his stomach and pointed a thumbs-up out the window.

"The clothes," Dom said, "then back over with your

friends, sir."

Gap-tooth shuffled away, grabbed Eddie's trousers and underwear, and tossed them to him.

Aches throbbed through Eddie's stomach as he bent over to pull his trousers on. He tried and failed to stifle a groan. A dazed cloud was coming over him. He needed a sleep and a drink. But he wasn't getting either yet. He rolled over and fished his gun out from under the dead thug.

"All right, my colleague's on his way," Dom said. "Stand by, gentlemen. You're so close to getting out of this alive. Don't screw it up now."

As he waited, Eddie ejected the magazine from his pistol and checked it. Still full. He slid it back into the gun and smiled up at Leone. "We should do this again sometime."

He scowled. "If you weren't here to apprehend me, then why did you come? Why were you skulking about?"

He thought for a moment. He'd never get a better chance than this to ask the syndicate leader why Cassandra was here. He could threaten the man, get her out. But the moment Dom took her sights off Leone, he'd want revenge for this. Cassandra was safe for now. If Leone knew that Eddie wanted her….

Eddie shook his head. "Never mind, Jack. Play ball and you'll stay a free man. That's all you should be worrying your little head about."

A door opened at the back of the room. Light spilled across the bare concrete. A small shadow approached.

"Oh, Jesus," Eddie said. "She sent the midget. That's fantastic."

"You should keep quiet if you want to get out of here alive," Knox said as he carefully approached. He was eyeing Leone and the thugs. A thin sheen of sweat coated his forehead.

"What is this?" Leone said, staring at the augment with a sneer. "Who are you?"

"Delivery service," Knox said. "Here to pick up a package." He glanced at Eddie. "Come on, get up. We haven't got all day."

Eddie sighed. "Christ. Give me a hand, will you?"

The augment came over and put an arm around Eddie. He grunted as he pulled on him. "You look better this way," the augment said, eyeing his bruises. "More colourful."

"Shut it," Eddie said through gritted teeth. He exhaled noisily and put his gun hand on his side to keep his guts in place as he slowly rose. "Bloody shit fucking tits that hurts."

Leone growled. "You'll hurt a lot worse by the time this is through."

"Don't give me any more reason to kill you than I already have, Jack."

The intercom crackled once more. "Well done, gentlemen," Dom said. "You've held your rage in check nicely. Now there's just one more thing. My partner is going to escort my colleague to your central command console, Mr Leone. They're going to access it. And then they're going to leave. There will be no harm to you or your business. We just need some information. During that time, you and these other two gentlemen will remain in this room where I can keep an eye on you. If my friends are detained or attacked, you will be the first to die, Mr Leone. Nod if you understand."

The syndicate leader gritted his teeth and nodded. His eyes were cold.

"Very good," Dom said. "Make it so."

Knox tugged on Eddie's arm. "Let's go. If you pass out, I'm leaving you."

Eddie nodded and shuffled towards the door, trying to remain standing while using the augment as a completely inadequate crutch.

"Mr Gould," Leone called as they reached the door. "I'll see you again, friend."

Eddie winked and made a gun with his fingers. "Bang bang."

They pushed open the door and shuffled into the light of the corridor. Knox huffed with Eddie's weight, one arm around Eddie's waist while the other scanned a map displayed on his tab.

"Does my partner know what she's doing?" Eddie asked as they moved towards the elevator at the end of the hall.

"Clearly not, otherwise she would've left you for dead."

"You know, I thought you might've been a traitor. Did you sell me out to Leone?"

"I should've done. It would've paid better than this bullshit." He gestured down a corridor. "This way. I'm guessing you'd prefer the elevator to the stairs."

Eddie grunted his assent and they got into the elevator. Knox punched the button and the elevator rose.

"So," Knox said. "How's your day going?"

"Swimmingly." He prodded the bruises on his face.

It felt like his nose had grown three sizes. He'd kill for a Bluen right now.

The elevator doors slid open, revealing a corridor running left to right. The augment consulted his tab. "Down here."

Eddie hobbled after the augment. There were doors on either side of the corridor, name plates attached below windows set in the doors. Shadows moved inside, wide eyes staring out. Eddie made sure they all got a good look at his gun. The eyes disappeared.

"We won't have long," Eddie said. "Leone's people will be organising a counterattack."

"That's why you're here. You're my bodyguard."

Eddie breathed out his pain and frustration as they reached a pair of double doors in the corridor. An old-tech security lock was built into the side of the door, but when Knox pushed, the door swung open. The augment paused, glancing around, then scurried inside. Eddie took up the rear.

"This is it?" he said. He sniffed and looked around. The room wasn't much bigger than the *Solitude*'s common room. A small bank of old-tech computers were set in a circular array, paper-thin monitors rising out of them. Statistics and graphs and numbers filled every screen. "I was expecting something bigger."

"You know what they say about small packages." Knox licked his lips. He stood there, lusting eyes roaming over the command console.

Eddie shook his head. "You're a weird little man, you know that?"

"And you're as much a Luddite as your partner." The augment clambered into a chair in front of the computers and started plugging cables from his arm into the machine. "Keep an eye out, will you?"

"Gladly."

Eddie limped back to the door and glanced out. This place made him uneasy. Limited exits. If Leone sent security teams, their only choice would be to shoot their way out.

He leaned his head against the door. He'd been so close. He'd seen Cassandra. She'd been right there, right in front of him. He could feel her now, in this building. There had to be a way to get her out. He could ask Dom to demand she was released in exchange for Leone's life. But they were already pushing their luck. And if it went wrong….

His tab chirped. He shook aside the queasy feeling in his stomach and answered.

"Eddie," Dom said. "Are you alive?"

"If it isn't my saviour. Jesus Christ with a sniper rifle."

"Drop it. What's happening?"

"The can opener's giving the computer a handjob. Still got your sights on the big boss?"

"For now. What the hell happened?"

He smiled to himself. "Roy Williams. He tipped off Leone that I was there."

She was quiet a moment. "He's been following us. He talked to me."

"You getting soft, Freckles? We don't talk to our marks. We apprehend them."

"He got the slip on me." It sounded like it physically

pained her to say that.

"Yeah, well, he got the slip on all of us." Eddie glanced back at the augment. "Hey, can opener. Are we done?"

"Give me a few more minutes."

On the computer screen, an image of Knox's face flashed up, accompanied by screeds of text.

"What the hell are you doing?" Eddie said.

"Getting my ticket off this station."

"Williams first. Then get your goddamn travel pass."

Knox shot him a glare. "We're doing this my way. It's my neck, so it's my way. Williams comes later. You want me to get on with it? Or should I sit here arguing with you?"

Eddie growled and gestured impatiently. "Get on with it." He spoke into the tab again. "You hear that?"

"I did."

"I don't like him, Freckles."

"Cry me a fucking river. Keep the line open and let me know when you're on your way out."

He slipped his tab back into his pocket and shot another glance at the augment. His face had disappeared from the screen, replaced by an image of a strong-jawed man with grey eyes and weathered skin. He stared out of the screen with a look of barely contained rage.

"Is that him?" Eddie said.

"That's him." Knox scrolled through the data. "Roy Williams. It's...huh."

"What?"

"Maybe this console wasn't as well-preserved as I thought."

Eddie's head throbbed. "What are you saying?"

"Some of the data's corrupted. I might be able to patch it up, but—"

"Do you have to do that here?"

"I can transfer it and work on it from another computer."

"Then do it," Eddie said. "I want to get the hell out of here before trouble shows up."

"You know, I think we've found the one thing we can agree on. We're becoming fast friends."

"That's one way to put it," Eddie said.

17

Dom breathed easy, putting Feleti Leone's head in the crosshairs of her rifle's scope. She knelt at the edge of the roof of the Forbidden Casino, her rifle resting on its bipod on the low wall surrounding the edge of the roof. The air stank of exhaust fumes from the busted atmosphere regulator off to her right. It was making a shitty situation even more unbearable.

"All right, the can opener says we're done here," Eddie's voice hissed through her earpiece. "Heading out now."

"Make it snappy," Dom said. "This bastard's getting agitated."

Leone threw glares out the window in her general direction. She'd kill him if she had to. But she'd really rather not. As much as she expected Leone's wrath to come back on them, it'd be a hundred times worse if she gave his lackeys cause for revenge. Especially when Eddie and Knox were still inside the Crimson Curtain.

Damn it, Eddie. Why the hell did you have to go and get yourself captured? Williams' tip-off was only part of it. Eddie had deviated from the plan. And now she had to bail him out. He'd put the entire contract at risk.

Her shoulder was starting to ache where the rifle butt had slammed against her. The heavy rifle was a hell of a thing to lug around, even for her, and she hadn't had time to pick an optimal location to shoot from. Her legs were cramping up. Her eyes were also feeling the strain.

She brought her face away from the scope for a moment and rubbed her eyes with her left hand. As she lowered her arm, she caught a tiny flash of light coming from the eighteenth floor of the Crimson Curtain.

Shit.

She threw herself to the roof as a bullet slammed into the low wall in front of her. The surface crumbled and flung jagged chunks through the air as the round tore through. White dust puffed up. A moment later, another bullet whined above her head, followed by the boom of a rifle shot.

She grabbed the rifle, held it against her, and rolled away, using the low wall for cover as two more shots hit. A fragment of concrete bounced off her duster coat.

"Taking fire," she yelled into her microphone. "They've got a sniper on me." She stuck her head up, bringing her rifle with her. She looked through the scope. Leone and his goons were gone from the room. "Shit, Leone's run for it. Get the hell out of there."

She ducked again as the sniper took another shot. She couldn't get her head up long enough to line up a shot on him.

Knox's swearing trickled through her earpiece, but it was just background noise. As the boom of the last sniper shot faded, she heard the clang of bootsteps on the service stairs behind her.

"I'm bugging out," Dom said. "You're on your own. Meet at the rendezvous. Out."

She stared at her rifle for a split second, growled, and tossed it. It was her best rifle. And her most expensive. Fucking Eddie. She was going to kill him for making her save his sorry arse.

She snatched up her Marauder submachine gun and popped her head up for a second. Another shot rang out as she ducked. *Now.* She stood and sprinted for the service stairs, weaving as she ran. A bullet slammed into the ground at her feet. Chunks of concrete exploded outwards, slicing open a cut on her calf. She ignored the burn and ran.

Without slowing, she lowered her shoulder and slammed into the door to the service stairs. The lock splintered and she flew inside, colliding with the wall on the other side. She stared down the dimly lit, narrow stairs at the surprised faces of four red-suited goons clasping pistols and shotguns.

She squeezed the trigger of her Marauder, spraying from the hip. The front three thugs fell in spurts of blood and red mist. The fourth, saved from the worst of the hail of lead by the bodies of his friends, only took one in the shoulder before he raised his pistol and returned fire.

Burning pain cut through her jaw. She stumbled back as another bullet slammed into the wall behind her. She snarled through the pain and opened fire. The staccato flash of the muzzle strobed in the dark staircase. Through it she watched the fourth man fall with his mouth open, red wounds opening in his chest. The magazine ran dry and darkness returned. Her ears rang with the echoing sound of gunfire. The familiar scents of blood and gunsmoke mingled in her nostrils.

Wetness dripped from her jaw. She touched the side of her face and jerked her hand away as electric pain lanced through her. The cut was deep, going to the bone. She wasn't going to be attending any balls for a while. What a shame. She pushed aside the sickening pain, slammed another magazine into her gun, and stumbled down the stairs around the bodies of Leone's goons.

18

Eddie swore and stepped into the elevator, dragging Knox in with him.

"What'd she say?" the augment asked.

"Trouble." He jabbed the elevator button. The doors slid closed and the elevator began to descend. "Where's the rendezvous?"

"Get me out of here alive and I'll tell you."

Eddie bared his teeth and opened his mouth. Then the elevator jerked to a halt. An alarm blared overhead. *Shit.*

"They're locking the place down," he said. He pressed the button a couple more times, then slammed the butt of his gun against it. Nothing. "Can you do something about this?"

"Give me a second." Knox ripped a panel off the wall and jacked himself in.

Boots stomped outside the elevator. They stopped. He heard voices muffled by the thick doors and almost drowned out by the alarm. The doors slid open a crack. Fingers wrapped around the edges and pulled. Someone was prying the doors apart.

Through the gap, Eddie spotted two pairs of legs and

the black sheen of a couple of guns. The elevator was suspended between two floors. Not enough space to wriggle out the bottom as Leone's people slowly pulled the doors apart.

Eddie jammed his gun into the widening gap and squeezed the trigger. The crack of the gunshot was followed by a yelp of pain. The fingers disappeared. A shotgun boomed and pellets slammed into the elevator wall behind him. Gritting his teeth against the ringing in his ears and the ache in his ribs, Eddie angled his gun and fired a couple more shots. Shotgun blasts answered.

The elevator whirred to life again. Eddie tugged his hands inside the elevator as it began to descend. He leaned back against the wall, breathing heavily. Knox was licking his lips, eyes wide.

"You all right?" Eddie said.

The augment didn't answer.

"Hey." Eddie grabbed Knox's shoulders. "Look at me. Are you hit?"

Knox blinked a few times, his remaining eye focussing on Eddie's face. He shook his head quickly. "No. No, I don't think so." He put his finger in his ear and opened his jaw wide, like he was trying to make his ears pop. "Can't they make these guns quieter?"

"Don't ask me, I just shoot them." Eddie glanced up at the floor indicator. "How far down does this thing go?"

"Uh…back to the high rollers room."

Eddie nodded. There was a chance, if he was fast. A chance to get Cassandra out.

"I have to do something when we get there. There may

be shooting. Follow me and stay in cover. Is there another way out of that room? Besides the main guest elevator?"

The augment consulted his tab. "Through the kitchen there's a service elevator that goes to the storage room and the loading bay. I should be able to work it now I have access to their security."

"Perfect." The floor numbers counted down. "You ready?"

"No."

"Me neither. Away from the door."

Knox pressed himself up against the left wall while Eddie took the right. The elevator slowed. A quiet *bing* rang out. The doors slid open.

Nothing fired. Eddie peeked out. They were in a short corridor. Looked like something for the staff. No one in sight. He gestured to Knox and moved forward. There was a door at the end. It had to be the one leading out into the high rollers' main tiled hall. He couldn't hear anything on the other side. He tested the lock. Open. With a quick breath, he pushed open the door, leading with his gun.

Four red-uniformed guards waited in the hallway. But there were holes in all of them. They were dead.

What the hell? Eddie stared at the bodies for a second, watching their blood stain the white floor. He spotted a few cracked tiles on the wall where bullets had hit. The guards had been facing towards Eddie, but from the position of their wounds it looked like they'd been hit from the side. Someone had come at them from the main elevator.

No time to think about it. He gestured to Knox to follow him as he hurried towards the restaurant, one hand holding his gun ahead of him while he gripped his aching ribs with the other.

The place was deserted. They'd probably evacuated the high rollers. A couple more guards' bodies lay against up-turned tables, bullet holes punched through their surfaces. Who had done this?

"Where are you going?" Knox hissed as he hurried behind him.

Eddie ignored him as he passed the restaurant, heading for the door beside the stage. It was being held open by a slumped guard gurgling blood. Eddie stepped over him and made his way down the corridor.

Cassandra. I'm coming.

He spotted her door. It was open. His heart jumped into his throat as he hurried towards it.

He gestured to Knox. "Stay back."

The augment scurried out of sight. Eddie edged his way forward. Then he paused.

Footsteps coming around the bend ahead of him. Someone running. Eddie raised his gun.

A shot rang out. A female guard stumbled around the corner, dropping a gun from her blood-soaked fingers to better clutch at the hole in her stomach. She looked up at him, eyes glassy. Then she slumped to the ground.

Another figure appeared around the corner. Large, muscular. Stubble on his chin. A gun in each hand. He glanced up. Their eyes met. Eddie recognised those steely eyes. The man raised his arms.

Eddie snapped his gun up. "Roy Williams. Drop the guns."

Williams' gun boomed. Eddie threw himself through an open door to his left, snapping off a shot as he went. Two more of Williams' shots slammed into the door jamb alongside Eddie's head. Then there was quiet.

Eddie tucked his gun close to his chest. He was in a little storage room, no place to manoeuver. Around the corner he could hear Williams' heavy breathing.

"Mr Gould," Williams called out. "That was you, wasn't it?"

"That's me," Eddie yelled back. "Want to exchange business cards?"

No response. What the hell was Williams doing here? Eddie risked a peek around the door. The fugitive had ducked back around the corner—Eddie could see the man's shadow there. He didn't have a shot. He glanced past him at the open door to Cassandra's room. He could see a wardrobe and a small mirror inside. The mirror gave him a glimpse of Williams. Their eyes met in the reflection.

"She's gone," Williams said. "I already checked."

"Yeah? And who would that be you're talking about?"

"Don't pretend you don't know, stalker. You've been asking questions about Lilian."

Lilian. Eddie's eyes went to the open door. Lilian Mayweather. Cassandra. Word had got back to Williams that he'd been asking about her. That was how he'd found out they were tracking him. Christ, Dom really was going to kill him. At least he'd make a beautiful corpse.

"If she's not here, where is she?" Eddie said.

"They evacuated everyone."

"Where to?"

He ignored the question. "I thought I'd have more time." He sounded like he was talking to himself. His eyes met Eddie's in the mirror and his face hardened. "At least she's out of your reach, stalker. At least you can't use her."

Use her? Eddie couldn't work out what the hell was going on. His mind was too addled by beatings and adrenaline to puzzle this out.

"What now, then, stalker?" Williams called. "Do we come out shooting?"

"I'd rather not, seeing as I need you alive."

"That won't stop me. You're standing between me and my way to Lilian. That doesn't bode well for you."

Eddie's tab chirped. Without taking his eyes off the hallway, he put it to his ear.

"It's me." Knox was whispering. "I'm back in the restaurant. More guards coming in. Need help now, Skinny."

"On it. Hold tight." He put the tab back and listened. Footsteps, several sets. Some from the restaurant, but others from further down the hallway, past Williams. The fugitive must've heard them too.

"Leone's men are closing in," Eddie said.

"That they are," Williams replied.

"Come with me and I'll get you out of here."

Williams was quiet a second. Eddie watched him throw glances down the hallway towards the approaching footsteps.

"And then what?" Williams said.

"And then I take you in."

"You can try."

Eddie eased himself out of the cover of the doorway,

gun pointed towards the corner. A moment later, Williams moved into the open as well. They watched each other down their gun sights. Eddie smiled.

"You can't find her if you're dead, Jack."

Williams glared. From behind him, someone shouted. Williams snapped around and fired two shots down the hallway. Someone cried out. He brought his guns back to Eddie.

"Don't think this will save you, stalker."

"I'm not looking to be saved."

Williams slowly lowered his gun. Eddie did the same. They glared at each other down the hallway.

"All right, stalker," Williams said. "Let's go. Behind you."

Eddie spun as a thug appeared from the direction of the restaurant. He squeezed off a shot. The man fell with a hole between his eyes. His friends cried out.

"Nice shot," Williams said.

"Thanks," Eddie said over his shoulder, moving towards the restaurant. "But if we're done jerking each other off…."

A small silver sphere flew through the restaurant door, bounced off the wall, and rolled along the ground.

Grenade.

Eddie took three steps and kicked the sphere back in the direction it'd come. Someone yelled, "Shit!"

Eddie pressed himself against the wall and shielded his eyes as the grenade blew. A flash of blinding light pierced his eyelids. Static sang in his ears. Stun grenade. He blinked away the purple afterburn and limped out into the restaurant. Williams' heavy footsteps pounded behind him.

Two more of Leone's thugs staggered through the restaurant, hands over their eyes, retching. The furthermost one blinked and squinted at Eddie through open eyes. He began to raise his shotgun.

Eddie put him down with two shots through the chest. Williams' gun cracked behind him. The other thug slumped over a table, his groan fading into a hiss of escaping air.

"You look upset, stalker," Williams said. "Does this killing disturb you?"

"Unlike you, I didn't come here looking to start a fight."

"A stalker with a conscience. Surprising."

"And a murderer without one. Utterly, utterly dull. Where the hell is that can opener?"

"Back here," Knox said.

Eddie turned and found the augment emerging from behind the red stage curtain. Knox froze when his eyes fell on Williams.

"Why is he still carrying a gun?"

"We're all pals now," Eddie said. "At least for the next ten minutes. Come on, get down here before more of these goons show up." His eyes roamed over the dead thugs. Christ, what a mess. "How many does Leone have, anyway?"

"Less than he could have, but more than you could imagine," Williams said as he moved towards the kitchen. "This way?"

"Through the back. Service elevator."

Eddie followed, keeping one eye on the fugitive's back

while he scanned the kitchen. Something had turned black in an oven. Soup still bubbled in a huge metal pot on the stovetop. The scents mingled with the stench of his own blood and sweat, turning his stomach.

Knox stuck close behind him. "Is this a good idea?" the augment whispered.

Eddie gestured him to silence. Better to keep their target in sight than to have him running around this casino getting himself clipped by a lucky shot. Eddie wasn't going to let his paycheque drain away in a pool of his own blood.

And if the man had a link to Cassandra, Eddie wanted to know what it was. If he knew where she'd gone, well, he'd just have to follow him.

Eddie stuck close behind Williams as they made their way through the kitchen to a large service elevator with wire-mesh doors.

"That's it," Knox said. "That should get us to the loading bay."

Eddie glanced at the floor and saw footsteps outlined in blood. Williams noticed them too and met Eddie's eyes.

"They went this way," the fugitive said.

"Then we follow."

Roy jabbed the call button and a winch started grinding. From deep below, the elevator creaked upwards.

"Not exactly speedy, is it?" Eddie said.

Roy grunted. Then his eyes slid past him. Eddie threw a glance over his shoulder. A shadow moved behind the circular window in the kitchen door. The softest creak of leather against the floor.

Eddie grabbed Knox by the scruff of his neck and

shoved him to the floor behind a long kitchen bench. The kitchen doors flew open and gunfire roared. As scattered bursts of lead filled the air, he threw himself down. Williams dropped into cover beside him.

Metal pinged and cutlery dropped from overhead. Two leaks sprang from the soup pot, spilling thick orange liquid down the side. The soup turned black and smoky when it touched the stove flame.

"How many?" Eddie yelled over the cacophony of gunfire.

Williams held up five fingers.

"Shit," Eddie said.

He glanced over at Knox. The augment cowered with his hands over his ears and his eyes screwed up tight as bullets punched through the bench around him. A small gap in the benches separated Eddie from Knox. A cart of dirty dishes was parked in the gap, the ceramic smashing one plate at a time.

"Cover me," Eddie said to Williams.

Williams nodded. Stretched his neck back and forth. Then raised both his guns above the cover of the bench and fired blindly at the door.

The return fire slackened briefly. Thugs moving into cover. Eddie seized his chance. He peered around the edge of the bench, aimed between the racks of dishes on the cart, and started firing.

One thug went down immediately. Another saw his friend fall and darted back as Eddie's shot went flying past him, scraping along his forearm as he ducked around the cover of the door.

Williams' fire ceased. "Reloading," he said as he ejected his magazines.

Eddie fired at the thugs in cover until he ran dry as well. Gun barrels appeared again. He ducked back behind the bench and scurried out of the way as the dishes cart as a hail of lead smashed through it, demolishing what was left of the crockery.

"I'm out," Eddie said.

Roy glanced at him, forehead creasing slightly. Then he slid one of his guns along the kitchen floor.

"That's my last magazine. Make it last."

"Sure thing, Jack."

Eddie peeked out for a moment. Two of the thugs were laying down suppressing fire. And the other two… there, Eddie glimpsed one of them flanking around to the right. The other one would be on the left. He gestured to Williams to take the right. The fugitive nodded and slid across to the edge of the bench.

Eddie brought himself up onto all fours and scurried past the cart of dishes. A flurry of shots followed him. As he crawled past Knox, he shoved the augment down further.

"Lie down and stay down."

Knox only grunted in response.

There was a clang from the left, a shoe striking a fallen saucepan. Eddie pressed himself as flat against the bench as he could. A gun barrel appeared overhead, swinging down towards him.

Eddie pressed his own pistol against the thug's kneecap and fired. The thug toppled with a scream that trembled through Eddie's chest.

Before the thug could hit the ground, Eddie grabbed the man's gun arm by the wrist, buried his pistol into the man's gut, and fired twice more. The scream became a gurgle.

Breathing heavy, Eddie picked up the fallen man's gun and glanced across at Williams. The fugitive had dispatched the other flanking goon with a single shot to the head. Eddie could no longer hear anything except the ringing in his ears. He shuffled away from the still-moving thug beside him.

The elevator. He looked over as the mesh grate folded open.

"Williams!" he yelled. His own voice sounded thick, like he was underwater.

The fugitive glanced back and Eddie gestured at the elevator. He held up three fingers and began to count down.

Two.

One.

Eddie stood and blazed away at the kitchen doorway with both guns. Bullets ricocheted around him. Out of the corner of his eye, he saw Williams firing as well. The remaining thugs ducked back into cover.

Now was their chance. Eddie kicked Knox's shoe and gestured to the elevator. Shakily, the augment scrambled into the waiting metal box. As he moved, Eddie raised his guns and fired at the lights. One by one the room drifted into thin semi-darkness, concealing their escape.

Firing half-blind into the smoke as he went, Eddie hurried to the elevator. Williams reached it at the same time. They ducked inside as Knox pressed the button on the control panel. The gate creaked closed and the elevator began to rumble slowly downwards. Eddie continued to fire through the gate, keeping the goons suppressed.

One of Eddie's guns ran empty, then the other. Roy's was already dry. The return fire started again, but it was too late. The bullets pinged harmlessly above them as the elevator descended and the kitchen disappeared from sight.

19

Eddie breathed heavily as the service elevator descended. Next to him, Roy tossed his now useless gun on the floor of the elevator. Eddie tucked one of his empty guns into his pocket, but kept the other in his hand. He stretched his jaw to try to pop his ears and worked his little finger back and forth in his ear canal.

"I can't hear a damn thing."

Williams said nothing, just watched the concrete of the shaft grind past. Knox was jacking himself into the elevator control panel.

"What are you doing?" Eddie asked.

"Making sure they can't stop the elevator."

"Can you stop them calling the elevator back up when we hit the bottom?"

"Sure. For a while."

"Do it."

"None of this was part of the deal, you know," Knox said. "I wasn't supposed to get shot at."

"Bring it up with the union."

The elevator drew to a halt and the gate slid open onto a wide concrete box of a room. To the left were two rows of near-empty shelves. Beyond the shelves was a door. On the right side of the room, the wall opened up and tunnels disappeared in both directions. That'd be where the delivery train came through. Overhead, strip lights cast everything into a cold pale blue. There was no one in sight.

Eddie stepped out of the elevator, shoes squeaking on the slick lining of the floor. He could no longer see the bloody shoeprints of the evacuating staff.

"Where to from here?" he said.

Williams moved past him, heading towards the tunnel. "The train. The guard I interrogated said they commandeered a supply train. Leone has a standing agreement with the train company for such an event."

"Yeah? He does this often?"

"More than you would expect." Roy stood at the edge of the platform and peered up and down the tunnel. A low rumbling came from far away, but there was no telling if it was a train or the water pipes or a hundred other pieces of old-tech machinery struggling to keep the station alive.

"How long until the next train?" Eddie said to Knox. "Can you find out where they got off?"

The augment brought up his tab. "I can find out when the train runs, but they go all over the city. It could've stopped a hundred places between here and wherever they got off. It's all automated."

"Hm. So where'd they get off, Jack?" he said to Williams.

"Somewhere they think is safe."

"Is that so?" Eddie muttered to himself. He stretched his fingers and strolled towards the platform where Williams stood.

"Here we go," Knox said. "We're in luck. Next train in forty-eight seconds."

"Perfect," Eddie said as he slipped his hand into his inside jacket pocket and fished out his plastic zip-cuffs. "Williams, give me a hand with something."

The fugitive turned and Eddie slammed the butt of his empty gun into the larger man's face. His nose shattered with a spray of blood.

Williams stumbled back, growling. His eyes were unfocused. Ignoring his aches, Eddie closed in quick, raising the gun to deliver another blow. He had to do this fast.

He swung. But at the same moment, Williams charged forward. Eddie's blow went wide, striking the fugitive's shoulder. The blow jarred Eddie's arm. And then Williams was on him, wrapping his arms around him and slamming all of his weight into him.

The air went out of Eddie's lungs and he hit the floor, Williams on top of him. His gun and cuffs went flying. How was the fugitive this fast? He'd never seen a man his size move like that. He stared up into Williams' bared teeth as the man cocked back a fist.

With a flick of his wrist, Eddie dropped a short-bladed knife from his jacket sleeve into his hand and plunged it into Williams' thigh. The fugitive didn't even seem to notice it. Williams' fist descended, filling Eddie's vision.

He slipped to the side, feeling the tips of Williams' knuckles brush past his ear. Williams' bones crunched as his fist slammed into the floor where his head had been.

Williams snarled, momentarily recoiling from the pain. Eddie took his chance, pulling his blade clear of the man's thigh and bringing it up. Spitting blood, the fugitive brought his hand down again in an open-fisted blow.

Eddie got the knife up and drove it into Williams' palm. The force of Williams' own attack pushed the point of the blade deep into the flesh. The fugitive howled. The rumbling in the tunnel was growing louder. Knox was shouting something he couldn't make out.

Eddie twisted the knife. Williams' cry grew louder, his balance atop Eddie faltering. Eddie took his chance. Keeping one hand on the knife handle, he kicked out, rolling Williams onto his back and climbing onto his chest.

"Knox!" he yelled, his voice nearly drowned out by the roar of the approaching train. "Get the cuffs!"

"I won't let you take me, stalker," Williams growled through bloodstained teeth.

"You don't have a choice in the matter, Jack."

His arm trembled with the strain of holding the knife piercing the fugitive's palm. Williams' other arm darted out and snatched his wrist. The muscles of his forearm bulged as he struggled.

Knox came scurrying up, the cuffs in his hand. Eddie gritted his teeth as he strained to keep the larger man down.

"Get them on him," Eddie said.

"Me?" Knox said.

"Now!"

The augment hesitated, then reached out. Eddie shifted his grip on the fugitive's free arm to allow Knox to slip the cuffs over the struggling fugitive's wrists.

A rush of stale air blew into the loading bay. Eddie's

ears were suddenly assailed by the screeching sound of the supply train flying by.

Knox jerked back at the sudden sound. Eddie's grip on Williams' wrist slipped. The fugitive twisted, pulling free of the knife in his hand.

Shit.

Eddie tried to regain his hold on the man, but it was too late. Williams kicked out, his boot connecting with Eddie's knee. Sharp pain pulsed in time with the flashing lights of the passing train. He slipped.

With a final roar, Williams grabbed Eddie by the shoulders and slammed his forehead into Eddie's face.

Eddie's vision blackened for a moment. He felt himself roll aside, heard the sound of Williams' footsteps over the rattle of the train. *Get up. Get the hell up. He knows where Cassandra is. Get up!*

He pushed himself up onto his hands and knees and shook his head clear. The room spun around him. He squinted to make his vision focus. Williams ran towards the speeding train.

No. Eddie forced himself to his feet, stumbled forward two steps. Fell again with his head pounding. He couldn't do anything except watch.

As the rear of the train came into view in the tunnel, Williams leaped. He slammed into the railing at the back of the train, wrapping his arms around the guard rail as the train rushed on. He looked back, met Eddie's eye.

And then he was gone, carried away by the train.

Eddie closed his eyes, sat down on the cold floor, and exhaled heavily. Damn it. He'd underestimated how much fight the fugitive had in him. And he'd overestimated his own ability after the beating Leone's men had given him.

Stupid. Careless. He'd seen a chance and he'd taken it. But it hadn't been enough, and now he didn't have Williams and he didn't have a location on Cassandra. Shit!

"Hey, Skinny." Knox's voice dragged him out his head. "We've got company incoming. They're trying to get the elevator back online. We have to beat it."

Eddie sighed and opened his eyes. He touched his nose. He was bleeding a little, but at least it wasn't broken.

"Are you listening to me?" Knox said.

"Yeah, yeah. Take it easy, Jack." He planted his hands on the ground and slowly, painfully levered himself upright. "How long until the next train?"

"Too long."

Eddie nodded and limped towards the door at the other end of the loading bay. "Then I guess we're walking."

20

Roy clung to the back of the train as it whistled through the tunnel, passing loading bay after loading bay. He knew he was travelling beneath all the major restaurants and casinos on the strip and a good few smaller ones besides. The blood from his nose grew cold and sticky on his face as he was buffeted by the stale air. The stalker had hit true, even as injured as he was. Roy had to give him that.

But he wasn't going to be taken. Not now, not when he was so close.

The stalkers had managed to stir up the Crimson Curtain more than he expected. The chaos had got him in, but it'd been too late.

That didn't matter. He knew where he'd find the evacuated staff. Just one piece in a long list of the information he'd extracted from Leone's man back at the apartment. He imagined that in his position, Leone would've discarded the information as useless, or never even attempted to extract it from the source. That was always his weakness. To be a syndicate leader you had to be able to hold a thousand details in your head at once. You had to know how the whole picture fitted together. You had to know more about the enemy than he knew about himself. Roy had lost a lot during his time in the Bolt, but he hadn't lost that.

He was beginning to think the train would never stop, but then he heard the squeal of brakes and felt it begin to decelerate. He clutched the guard rail and waited as the train slowed and pulled to a stop in yet another underground loading bay. He released his death grip on the railing, edged around to the side of the train, and stepped onto the small platform. A scrawny kid barely out of his teens stared back. The boy pushed back his cap and wiped his hands on his overalls.

"Hey, pal, what the hell're you doing back there?"

Roy glanced around. The loading bay was much smaller than the Crimson Curtain's. A few scattered crates of beer and liquor were piled against the wall.

"Where is this?" he said.

"Louie's," the kid said.

"Who's Louie?"

"He's…I don't know, it's just the name of the bar. You can't be down here, pal."

Roy walked up to the kid. The boy's eyes rounded and his back went stiff. He didn't back away, but Roy could tell that was more from fear than bravery.

Roy had a head of height on the kid. He looked down at him and reached out his hand. The kid trembled. Roy plucked the rag out of the front pocket of the kid's overalls. Without taking his eyes from the boy, he dragged the rag across his face, soaking up the blood that had streamed from his nose. The rag was soon stained a deep red.

He tucked the damp rag back in the kid's pocket, his

fingers touching something plastic as he did so. He pulled it out. A small retractable knife, the kind used to open boxes. He extended the blade, checked the sharpness with his thumb. It would do. He retracted it and pocketed the knife.

"The exit," he said. "Where is it?"

The boy blinked and pointed to a small set of stairs. Roy grunted and patted the kid's face.

"Get back to work."

He stepped around the frozen boy and headed up the stairs, putting a cigarette between his lips and lighting it as he went. There was an open door at the top of the stairs. He came out behind a bar in some kind of dive half-filled with middle-aged locals bent over glasses, drowning their sorrows. The bartender, a woman nearly as wide as she was tall, stopped midway through pouring vodka into a shot glass.

"Who the shit are you?" she said.

He ignored her, moved around the side of the front bar, and found the bathroom, a dimly lit room that only held a single toilet and a sink. The door swung closed behind him and he snapped the lock.

He looked in the mirror. His face was a mess. Dried blood was crusted in his stubble. His nose was bulbous and angry.

He set his cigarette on the edge of the sink, turned on the tap, and put his hands under the flow. The icy water burned. He'd barely noticed the wound in his palm as he'd clung to the cold train railing. But now all the pain came flooding back.

He gritted his teeth and let the water clean away the blood and grime. The wound in his thigh would have to wait for later. The blade had been short; the stalker hadn't hit an artery. Roy snatched some paper towels from the dispenser and wrapped his wounded palm, tying them in place with a strip of cloth from his sleeve.

Someone hammered on the bathroom door.

"I don't know who you are, buddy," the bartender said. "But you've got to get out of here now."

He continued to ignore her. With his good hand, he splashed water on his face until the sink was red with his blood. His nose was crooked where the stalker had broken it. The little bastard. Roy had been intending to throttle him and leave him on the railway tracks. But the stalker had struck first.

The nose had to be re-set, there was no way around it. He stared at himself in the mirror, laid his thumbs on either side of his nose, and gave it a quick sharp twist.

He grunted and grabbed the basin with both hands, scraping his nails along the porcelain. *Fucking hell.*

The bartender banged on the door again. "I'm warning you, buddy, I'm armed. Get out here now."

He grabbed another handful of paper towels and cleaned the blood from his nose. The stalker was going to pay for that.

Returning his cigarette to his lips, he ripped open the bathroom door. The fat bartender stared at him down the barrel of a sawn-off shotgun. Her hands were steady, but her eyes gave away her terror.

He let his eyes drift past her. The kid from downstairs

was hiding behind the bar, watching.

"No sudden moves," the bartender said. "Just get out."

He pushed past her and walked towards the exit. The sullen eyes of the patrons followed him as he moved. He stopped at a comm terminal by the front door. A warning notice was displayed on the screen.

Attention all visitors to Temperance: In eight days, life support will no longer be guaranteed. The Temperance Municipal Authorities, in association with the Eleda Federation, advise all visitors to depart Temperance before this time to ensure your safety.

He dismissed the notice, fed a note into the slot, and dialled. He could see the bartender still pointing her gun at him out of the corner of his eye.

"Yes?" Victoria Palmer said when she picked up.

"I'll be returning with Lilian soon. If you want to get off this station, I suggest you get ready to leave. We won't have much time."

Before she could answer, he cut the connection.

He looked back at the bar. The hubbub had quietened into silence. A dozen pairs of eyes stared at him. The rest watched their feet or the table or the liquid swirling in their glasses. He took a puff of his cigarette, pulled his jacket closed over his bloodstained shirt, and walked out the door.

21

Dom's idea of a rendezvous turned out to be an abandoned hotel five blocks from the strip. With no staff around, the tourists staying there had apparently developed an honour system. They'd go behind the reception desk, take a key, and claim that room for however long they needed it. By the sounds of moans and thumping as Eddie walked down the corridor of the third floor, he guessed most of them only borrowed the rooms by the hour.

"Let's see," Knox said as he led the way. "Three-fifteen. This one." He reached for the knob.

Eddie put a hand on his shoulder and pushed him aside. He placed himself out of the direct line of the door and gave three sharp knocks.

"Freckles?" he called.

"I told you not to call me that," came the reply.

Eddie smiled. "You all right in there?"

"I'm alone. You can come in."

He heard her decock her revolver. The lock snapped open.

He eased the door open and took a look at her. She was holding a wad of gauze against her jaw. It was stained red, as was the fabric of her white tank top and the duvet cover where it looked like she'd been sitting. In her other hand she held her revolver.

Eddie waved Knox inside, closed the door behind him, and studied Dom.

"Bad trip to the dentist?"

She sat back down on the bed, next to the first aid kit she'd laid out there. "I'm not in the mood, Eddie. Did you get it?"

"That depends what you mean by 'get it'," Knox said. "You see, on the one hand, the data's all there. Everything we need to get to Roy."

"And on the other hand?" Dom said.

"On the other hand, well, there's some corruption. As it stands, I can't access the tracking information."

Dom growled.

"That's not to say it can't be done," Knox added quickly. "I should be able to patch the data. It'll just take me some time."

"We don't have time," Dom said. "We've stirred things up out there. Williams knows we're after him, Leone's probably got half the syndicate looking for us after what we did." Her eyes found Eddie's and went hard. "What the hell happened?"

Eddie hung his holster over the armchair beside the bed and lowered himself into the seat, clutching his ribs. On the other side of the room, Knox sat down by the room's computer console and hooked up his tab. Eddie left him to it.

"Take it easy, Freckles. Take a breath. We're not moving from here for a while, so we might as well relax." He gestured at the gauze pressed to her cheek. "Let me take a look."

"It's fine."

"Just let me take a look, huh?"

He leaned forward. Her lips formed a line, but she didn't resist as he peeled away the gauze.

The cut was deep. The flesh hung open, revealing a grisly mess of meat and blood. Any deeper and the shot would've struck bone. It ran from a few centimetres south of the corner of her mouth all the way back, nearly to her earlobe. The bleeding had slowed, but it still oozed from the wound.

"Will I ever play piano again, doc?" Dom said.

He grinned. "Did you clean it already?"

"Yes."

"Took something for the pain?"

"Didn't want to dull the senses."

"To hell with that. What've you got here?" He rummaged through the first aid kit and came up with a pair of small self-injecting disposable syringes. "Lie back and think of New Calypso."

He pulled the cap off one syringe and jabbed the small needle into the muscle of her shoulder. "One for you." A few moments later, the lines drained from her face. "And one for me." He took the cap off the other and plunged it into his thigh. Warmth spread through him, smothering the pain.

"There we go," he said. "Don't need a ship to fly, huh?" He prodded the flaps of skin around her wound. "Stitches or strips?"

"You're not coming near me with a needle and thread when you're high."

"Strips it is."

He found the wound closure strips in the kit and went to work, using them to bind the wound together. He could feel her eyes on him as he worked.

"What about you?" she said. "You look like hell. How badly did they hurt you?"

"Nothing some ice and time won't heal. Although you cut it a little fine. A few seconds later and I would've been taking up a new job as a choir boy."

"Might've stopped you being so cocky."

"Why does everyone think I'm cocky?" He pressed a fresh wad of gauze against the wound. "Hold this for a second."

She did so. "But you're all right."

He nodded. "Yeah. I'm all right." He paused. "Thanks."

"What happened in there, Eddie?"

"Like I said. Roy Williams figured out we were tracking him. He tipped Leone off." He peeled the backing off an adhesive bandage, took the gauze away, and pressed it onto the wound. "I...saw him in there, on our way out. He was using the chaos to get inside."

Her eyes flickered between his. He couldn't hold her gaze.

"You're not giving me the whole truth," Dom said.

"Since when have we ever told each other the whole truth, Freckles?" He wiped his hands on a towel, leaned back, and put his hands behind his head. "Why do you think I had to invent so many things about you when I was writing *The Fires of New Calypso*?"

"I'm still angry at you about that book, by the way. You could've at least warned me you were writing about me before you published it."

He shrugged and closed his eyes, enjoying the feel of the painkiller flooding through him. "If you were that mad, you would've kicked me off your ship long ago."

She kicked his shoe. He opened his eyes to find her glaring at him.

"Stop evading. What aren't you telling me?"

He hesitated. "I'm going to need you to trust me."

"I can't do that, Eddie. I know why you're here, why you do this. And it's not the same reason I do it. I have to know if whatever you're doing is going to interfere with the pursuit of Roy Williams."

He thought for a moment. Usually Dom could be brushed off with a few jokes and some apathy. But not today. "I don't know. It might. There's…there's a woman."

"For the love of Man. Not you too."

"What?"

"Williams. When he ambushed me in the casino he was talking about some woman he wanted to get back. He tried to buy me off so he could find her unopposed." Something in his face must've given him away, because she paused and studied him. "What?"

"You ever think about how small this system really is? It's funny, isn't it? So few of us out here at the edge of everything, floating alone through space. A few decades and we'll all be gone. And yet here we all are. Fighting for the tiniest things. Killing for them. Making the system a little bit smaller, one body at a time."

"It's what we've always done. Why stop now?"

He shrugged. "No reason to. Just funny, that's all."

"This woman," she said. "What are you going to do when you find her?"

"Talk to her. I have questions. Too many questions. Not that any of them matter. But I have to ask."

"And then?"

"I don't know. I hadn't got that far."

"Hm."

"What?" he said.

"Are you going to try to get her off Temperance?"

He looked around. "Is there any booze here?" Next to the computer console was a small fridge. Eddie gestured to Knox. "Hey, check the minibar, will you?"

"Eddie," Dom said.

"What?"

"You know we can't take her with us if she doesn't have a pass. And if she had a pass, she'd be long gone."

Knox pulled open the minibar. Empty. Eddie slumped back down in his seat.

"Eddie," Dom said.

"I'll figure something out. We'll find a forger and—"

"No, Eddie. The Feds would find her. You know how they watch us. They'd catch us before we got five thousand clicks from the station. They'd send her right back to Temperance. We'd forfeit the contract, probably end up in prison ourselves. They'd confiscate the *Solitude*. We can't bring her with us."

"No," he said. "You don't have to. But I do. You don't want to risk your own neck, that's fine. I get it. I'll find another ship. I'll take her myself."

"You can't afford a ship."

"I'll pay for it out of my cut when we catch Roy Williams."

"And you'll go off alone, is that it? Just take all your shit out of the *Solitude* and go? Go where? Where would you take her? To the Outer Reach? It's the only place you might be able to hide her away from the Feds. Or will you become a nomad? Just spend the rest of your days flying around the system, getting supplies shuttled in to you, just you and her together forever in the void. Is that what you want? Forget your stories, forget why you follow me around with a gun strapped to your hip. Just sit in space until your life support fails and the cold takes you."

He waved away her words and stood up. "Forget it. I'm going to find some booze."

"Like hell you are," she said. "Leone's men are out looking for us. And I have to contact the Feds and give Pine a report."

"Do it without me. Guy's a fucker anyway."

"Eddie, sit the hell down and put some ice on those injuries before you tear something."

He strapped his gun back on. "We have any ammo?"

"No."

"You're lying. I can always tell when you're lying."

She scowled. "Fine. There's a magazine in the bag." She waved at a duffel bag at the end of the bed. "It's all there was left of yours in the armoury. Now sit down, all right?"

He ignored her. He riffled through the bag, found the full magazine, and slid it into his pistol.

"Eddie, for the love of Man," Dom said.

He holstered his gun and went to the door. He paused, hand on the knob.

"You know what, Freckles?" he said. "I count you as one of my only true friends. Who else would've come to save me with such a ridiculous display of firepower? But you don't know me as well as you think you do."

"No," she said. "I think I know you better than you know yourself."

He didn't have anything to say to that. So he left the hotel room without another word and went down the hall-way, listening to the sounds of lovemaking all around him.

22

"Surly son of a bitch, ain't he?" Knox said when Eddie was gone.

Dom shook her head and said nothing. She'd never seen Eddie act like this before. He'd always been a man full of passion that he tried so desperately hard to hide. The monetary reward of the contract was always an afterthought for him, as much as he liked to pretend otherwise to the Feds.

But this—talking about leaving, trying to skip out with this woman—it wasn't like him. As much of a pain in the arse he was on the long trips through space, he was good at what he did. He was loyal. And even if you couldn't rely on him to always be there, he was there when it mattered.

They made an odd couple, they had ever since she found him in that bar on Pilgrim's Rest, so deep into his own stories he'd racked up a quarter million vin gambling debt with the loan shark Dom was tracking. He'd helped her then in exchange for a take of the bounty, and then he'd wormed his way onto her ship and proved his usefulness in contract after contract. After fleeing New Calypso and getting picked up by the Feds, she'd forgotten what it was like to have friends, comrades, people to count on when your back was against the wall and the predators were closing in.

Well, fine. She'd been alone before, she could be alone again if that was what he wanted. She wasn't his wife and she wasn't his mother and she had no desire to be either. Friendships ended, partnerships ended. It was the way of things. Eddie could do whatever the hell he liked. It was what he did best.

"How long until you can get that tracking information on Williams?" she said to Knox, a little more forcefully than she'd intended.

Knox looked up from the computer console, raising his eyebrow.

"You might want to try asking me a little nicer, sweetcheeks. I've already got the biggest part of what I went into that goddamn death trap for. I've got my travel pass. You're lucky I'm still here."

She stared at him for a moment. Then she rose from the bed, stretching to her full height.

"Listen very carefully. We made a deal. You get your pass. In exchange, you get me to Williams. If you choose to back out on that, I have very little use for a backchatting augment fugitive. And I may reconsider Eddie's proposal to turn you over to the Feds."

He put up his hands. "Easy, easy. Down, tiger. I'm not planning on abandoning you yet. I still want to get my hands on that bastard's money. I just don't want to end up back in the situation I was in today. Sending me into the lion's den to retrieve your friend went way above our original agreement. I just want a little compensation."

"Do you now? And what kind of compensation would that be?"

"Instead of a third of Williams' money, I get all of it."

She snorted.

"I'm serious," he said. "Do I look like a fighter? I got access to the security system, I got into the central command console to get his data, and then I helped get your friend out of that casino. While people were shooting at me. That wasn't the original deal. So I want to be paid."

It was getting more and more tempting to deliver him to the Feds. But she still needed him. And if she was honest, she'd known this was coming. She'd heard it in his voice as soon as she asked him to go in to pick up Eddie. *Damn it, Eddie.*

"Two thirds," she said finally. "I can't guarantee you Eddie's share of Williams' money. But you can have mine. Assuming you can keep the Feds from confiscating it."

He thought about it a moment, then nodded. "All right. Two thirds. In answer to your earlier question, I'm fucked if I know how long this will take. I'd say settle in for a long stay. Do we have any food?"

"I raided a vending store on the way in. We've got a fine selection of dried fruits, jerky, and highly processed gruel."

"My favourite. Bring me something, will you?"

She tossed a packet of jerky at the back of his head. It slapped against him and he turned to glare at her.

"Thanks," he said flatly.

"You're welcome."

She sat there for a few seconds, staring off into space.

Part of her wanted to head back out there, pound the streets, find Williams the old-fashioned way. But she knew all that'd get her right now was a bullet in the head. Stalking in tourist cities like this was always the worst. The criminal element was too powerful, the local law so greased up they wouldn't chase a murder if it happened to their own grandmother. And the population was too transient, too excited. The city was packed with too many people that didn't care that they were funding syndicate members as long as they could indulge their own vices. Like these people in the rooms around her, fucking away like they were trying to out-moan each other. No one had an identity here, just a persona that they slipped into like a suit. And Williams was the same.

No, she was stuck here in this room until the augment came up with something. That was her best lead. And it meant she was sitting here with nothing to do.

To keep her mind off the pain in her jaw, she dragged her submachine gun into her lap and started stripping it. The mindless task cleared her thoughts, let her focus. She hadn't brought everything she needed to clean the weapon, but she disassembled and reassembled it anyway, twice, three times. The tension never drained completely, but slowly she found herself able to think clearly again.

The job hadn't changed. Find Roy Williams. Apprehend him. Turn him over to the Feds. Everything had gone to shit, but the job remained. Knox was helping find him. But she still needed to apprehend him. And for that, she'd need weapons.

She was down to the last magazine of her submachine

gun. Another twelve rounds for her revolver in addition to the load it was already carrying. And that was all she had on her. She wished she hadn't had to ditch the sniper rifle.

Eddie was running low on ammunition as well. If he was still interested in helping. There wasn't much left in the armoury on the *Solitude*. And in any case, she'd decided to stay away from the ship until the heat died down. It wouldn't be hard for Leone or Williams to find the *Solitude*, if they hadn't already. No, the risk of walking into a trap was too great. But there had to be at least a couple of arms dealers left on the station. Somewhere they could go.

"Knox," she said. "Bones and the rest of your crew were all armed."

"I noticed."

"We need guns and ammo. Where'd they get theirs?"

"No idea," the augment said without looking up from the computer. "But why bother looking? I don't think Bones will be needing his guns anymore."

"They had a stash?"

"Not enough to outfit an army, but for all your personal defence needs, I think they'll have just what you're looking for."

"Where?"

"Upstairs from the chapel. There's a room that used to be the manager's office. The guns aren't hidden."

She licked her lips, stood up, and peered through the curtains at the street below. A couple of tourists bounced along, hand-in-hand. She couldn't spot any thugs in the perpetual semi-darkness.

"All right," she said. "I'll be back soon."

"Wait, you're going now?" The augment stopped working and looked at her. "What am I supposed to do?"

"Eat your jerky and get back to work." She hung her submachine gun in place beneath her arm and pulled on her duster.

"What if Leone comes?"

She shrugged, slipping her revolver into its holster. "Throw your jerky at him."

"This isn't funny, sweetcheeks."

"No one knows we're here. And if Leone does know, me being here isn't going to save your arse."

"You don't know that. He might go easier on me once he's taken his anger out on you."

She went to the door. "Lock the door behind me. And keep working. I want Williams' location by the time I get back. The sooner you get it, the sooner we find him, and the sooner we can all get the hell off this station."

"I'm aware of that. I'd just prefer to get off this station in a ship rather than being flushed out the airlock with half a dozen holes in me."

"Wouldn't we all."

He scowled at her until she closed the door and left him to it.

23

It took Roy a few minutes wandering the streets to get his bearings. Temperance wasn't a big town, but his need to keep a low profile had meant he hadn't had much time to explore it since he broke away from the other fugitives. In the end he had to find a public comm terminal and bring up a tourist map to find out where he was and identify the address of the place he was looking for.

Leone owned property all over the station, not just casinos but brothels and strip clubs and hotels and bars. According to the screamed confessions of Leone's man, Scott Hudson, he owned a small but classy hotel near the spaceport that was maintained to accommodate staff and visiting acts for his shows. In case of emergency, it was also used as an evacuation point for the more valuable of his staff.

Lilian would be there. Roy had no doubts about that. Leone wouldn't send her off to fend for herself in the chaos. He wanted to keep a tight hand on her, to continue to degrade her and use her for his own purposes. The thought made Roy's blood boil.

Leone's men were spreading through the streets as he

set off towards the hotel. As a pair of them walked past, one scanned him up and down. But they made no move to stop him. They were looking for the stalkers. He was just another tourist to them.

The wound in his thigh was aching irritatingly by the time he stopped down the block from the hotel. It was a quieter, more dignified looking hotel than the businesses surrounding it. No neon, no gaudy colours, just a simple white facade and an old-fashioned design that wouldn't be out of place on Babel.

The main entrance was a revolving door. Roy could see the lobby beyond, all thick carpets and warm lighting. A single guard was at the door, a grim-looking woman in a black coat that didn't hide the machine pistol hanging at her side. She stood in the shadow of the entranceway, the orange tip of a cigarette glowing between her lips. Her eyes tracked the tourists strolling past.

Roy dropped the butt of his own cigarette, ground it beneath his shoe, and put a new unlit cigarette between his lips. With his hands in his pockets, he headed down the street towards the hotel.

The guard eyed him as he closed. He could see her tighten her grip on her gun.

"Excuse me," he said. "Can I have a light?"

"Get lost, stranger."

"Just let me light it with yours." He leaned in towards her. Her gun twitched towards him.

He slammed her up against the wall with the full force of his body, pressing her gun back against her stomach so she couldn't aim it at him. Before she could cry out, he pulled the box cutter from his pocket and dragged the blade across her throat.

She stared at him through shocked eyes. The blood bubbled from her neck as she tried to speak. He stepped back quickly, taking her machine pistol with him.

She slumped down against the wall, clutching her throat. He reached into her pocket, took her keys and a spare magazine for the gun, and left her there.

He stepped through the revolving door. No one in sight. No one manning the reception desk or the bar. Most of Leone's people would be on the streets, searching for the stalkers.

He hurried across the lobby, wiping his box cutter blade clean on his sleeve. He punched the elevator call button and stood glaring at the floor countdown for a second before growling with frustration and heading for the stairs.

He'd waited years to get her back, and the years had turned into months and then days and then hours. And now he was so close he couldn't wait another second. This was the one thing that had kept him going through the long dark hours in that tiny box floating through the void. The one spark of hope and rage that had propelled him to freedom. Knowing that the demented bastard who he once counted among his closest friends had his paws all over Lilian. The only reason to not put a belt around his own neck and end it all.

Now he'd love to put that belt around Leone's neck and watch him go blue and then grey, smell his stink as he pissed himself when the last vestiges of life crawled out of that disgusting husk of a man. And maybe he still would, one day. But first he had to get Lilian off the station. Get her safe. Then he would have all the time in the world.

He emerged from the stairs on the first floor and ran down the hallway, banging on doors as he went. "Lilian! Lilian, it's me."

He could hear the nervous cries and whispers of people inside the rooms. But no answering call came. He ran back to the stairs and up to the next level and started down the hallway again. "Lilian!"

A woman's voice caught in a room as he passed. He stopped and turned back to the door. He hammered on the door with his fist. "Lilian. Lilian, is that you?"

He stepped back and kicked the door. It shuddered. He kicked again. Again. The synth-wood splintered. He growled and slammed his weight into it. The wood around the lock gave and the door flew open.

A female escort in a red gown cowered in the corner of the room, both hands and one bare foot lifted as if to ward him off.

Roy snarled and ran back down the hall and up to the next floor. And the next. And the next. Where was she? She had to be here. She had to be!

Top floor. He banged on door after door. Nothing.

"Lilian!" he bellowed.

He slammed his injured palm against a door, leaving a bloody handprint behind. The door creaked open under the force of his blow.

He stopped, stared at the door as it opened a crack. "Lilian?"

He pushed open the door and stepped into the hotel

room. A pair of high-heeled shoes sat lined up next to the front door. The curtains were pulled, but the lamp in the corner was on.

He brought the machine pistol up and moved through the central room. An open door led into a bedroom. The bedspread was dented where someone had been sitting on it. A tab lay forgotten on the bedside table. He picked it up, stared at it. Put it in his pocket.

"Lilian?"

He checked the bathroom. Empty. The whole room was empty. But she'd been here. He could smell her scent in the air. Even after all this time, he hadn't forgotten her smell. But where the hell had she gone?

A black mark caught his eye on the skirting board running along the wall next to the front door. He bent down. It was a mark made by a shoe. Not the high heels. A man's leather shoe. It could've been there for years for all he knew. But a place like this didn't leave marks like that on the walls. It was recent.

There'd been a struggle. Someone had come and taken her. Taken her without letting her get her tab or her shoes.

They knew he was looking for her. They'd heard him shouting. So she'd only just left. There was only one set of stairs, one set of elevators. He hadn't heard anyone running down the stairs. The elevator hadn't moved.

She could still be in the building.

He ran back to the stairs and took two steps back down. Then he stopped and turned back. Though the main stairs ended at the top floor, there was another door beside it. The sign on it read: *Roof Access.*

He tested the handle. Locked, but he could feel the flimsiness in the design. Once more he stepped back and aimed a kick at the lock. The door splintered and flew open, revealing another set of stairs. His heart pounded as he hurried up them.

He threw open the door at the top and looked out over the roof. The city spread out around him, all the way to the spaceport where he could watch the approach of tourist ships through the transparent panels that roofed the station.

But he didn't pay attention to any of that. He only had eyes for one thing.

Lilian Mayweather. Her dark brown curls framed her face. A black stripe of makeup ran across her eyes and the bridge of her small, upturned nose. The black gown she wore caught the light reflected off Eleda VI overhead, giving it a hint of blue.

There was a hand across her mouth and a pistol barrel pressed against her temple. Behind her, a skinny grey-coated man stared at him with bared teeth and wild eyes.

A roar of applause echoed from somewhere a few blocks away. But there was only silence on the rooftop. Roy couldn't take his eyes from Lilian's. His heart ached.

"Get the fuck out of here," the man in the coat said. "I've got backup coming. You better run, pal."

Roy took slow, steady breaths. "Listen to me, boy. You let her go. You let her go and you get to live. That's a promise. You don't let her go, you die. That's also a promise. And if you knew who I was, you would take that very seriously."

"Fuck you!"

The man aimed his gun at Roy and fired. Roy ducked back inside the stairwell as two bullets pinged off the doorway.

"You come any closer I'll fill her full of lead," the man yelled. "I'll do it. I'll do it, goddamn it."

Roy checked the machine pistol to make sure it was loaded and the safety was off.

"Okay," he said. "Okay. You win. Just let me talk to her, okay? I'll stay right here."

"Fuck off!"

"I just want to talk. I just want to make sure she's okay. Are you okay, Lil?"

A muffled grunt in response.

"Shut up," the man said.

"Listen," Roy said. "You really don't want to hurt her. And not just because I'm threatening you. Because your boss, Mr Leone, will be very, very upset if you harm her. Do you know who she is? Do you know why she's so important to him?"

"Just…just shut up. I'm not moving until backup gets here."

"She's important because, well, it doesn't matter why. You know she's important because otherwise she wouldn't be in this hotel. You know that, don't you?"

He was silent. Roy peeked out.

"Stay back!" the man yelled, pressing the gun barrel against Lilian's temple. "I told you to stay back."

"Look, I'm putting down my gun." Roy slid his machine pistol out and showed his hands. "See. I just want to talk to her. What's your name?"

"Don't you step out of there."

"I'm coming out. I just want to tell Lilian I love her."

"Don't come out!"

"I'm coming out."

He stepped out of the stairwell, empty hands out to his sides. He took two steps towards them.

"Stay back!" the man yelled. His eyes were wide.

Roy took another step.

"Fuck!"

The man brought the gun from Lilian's temple and aimed it at Roy. He thought he could see the tendons in the man's hand tightening as he began to squeeze the trigger.

Lilian bit down on the hand covering her mouth. The man screamed and fired. The shot went wide. Roy was already moving.

Before the man could squeeze off another shot, Lilian grabbed his left arm and pulled him down, teeth still sunk into the web of flesh between his thumb and forefinger. He cried out and raised the gun to bring it crashing down on the top of her head.

Roy drew the box cutter from his pocket as he ran and plunged the blade into the side of the man's neck.

The thug stared up at Roy with round eyes. The pistol dropped from his grasp as he clutched at the knife embedded in his neck.

Finally releasing the man's hand from her teeth, Lilian scurried out of the man's grasp and kicked the pistol away. Roy snarled and grabbed the man's head and pounded it against the ground. Over and over. Something cracked in the man's skull. His screams became slurred.

Roy didn't stop until the man's eyes went glassy. There wasn't much left of the back of the man's head by then.

He sat back, panting. Lilian stood over him, her face hidden in shadow by the glow of the planet hanging above her.

"Honey," he said, wiping the man's blood from his hands. "I'm back."

24

Leone's thugs weren't even trying to hide. Eddie watched from a doorway as a group of them swaggered past, coats swaying as they walked to reveal the guns holstered beneath. Tough looking guys and girls, but not very bright. Eddie traded jackets with a homeless man, hunched himself over, stole a shopping cart and filled it with trash off the street, and pretty soon not a single thug even glanced in his direction. Bunch of saps.

Most of the stores on Temperance were abandoned, but the one thing still in supply was booze. Eddie consulted a vid screen displaying a tourist map and followed its directions a few blocks towards the station's bow.

Below a neon sign proclaiming *Best Stims in Town*, he abandoned his cart and went down a set of narrow stairs leading off the street. He passed through a heavy door into a grimy liquor and stim store packed with equally grimy locals. With his tattered jacket—unwashed smell included—he fitted right in.

The place was more a gathering place than a store. Friends laughed and kissed and told each other lies that sounded like the truth. For a few moments he was immersed in the local culture as he picked up what he wanted and waited for the man behind the counter to get his tongue out of a plump woman's throat.

He returned to his cart a few minutes later with a case of imported beer—Carousel's finest dog piss. He popped the top and drank one straight away, then started sipping a second as he headed back towards the hotel. The booze mingled nicely with the painkiller he'd injected. He felt like he could sleep for a week. If it wasn't for the hunger battling it out with the nausea in the pit of his stomach, that was.

He went back and forth on the idea for a while, said, "To hell with it," and bought a meal from a street vendor off the strip. The meal consisted off some unidentifiable dry meat drenched in a savoury sauce and wrapped in limp lettuce and flatbread that tasted like cardboard. He took a seat in the alley beside a brothel—ribs aching as he sat—and choked down the meal with the aid of another can of beer. His stomach didn't thank him for it.

The details of the day swam in his head as he ate and drank. He knew he was missing something, but he didn't let it worry him. It would come. He just had to wait.

An off-duty stripper in a heavy coat went past the alley, head down. He listened to the click-clack of her heels fading away as she walked. The grav train screamed past somewhere overhead, shaking dust loose from the wall he was leaning against. He took out his tab and scribbled down some notes for himself, snatches of dialogue and descriptions. He pictured Roy Williams in his mind's eye. He would do as the villain of the story, although a few aspects would have to be exaggerated to make him more memorable. He decided to add a few inches to the man's height. It was a start.

For a few minutes he considered what he'd title the story, tossing ideas back and forth, but it was pointless. He didn't know how it ended yet.

That was another thought, one that made his heart tighten curiously. If he got Cassandra off the station, if he found a ship and they went off to live out the rest of their lives, then this might be his last book. There wouldn't be much adventure to be had floating around the Reach. No contracts to hunt down.

What would he do? He could continue to write, he supposed, just making up tales. But somehow that didn't feel right. He wouldn't know the truth of the matter if he wasn't there to see it. And if he didn't know the truth, then what was the point in writing it?

It didn't matter. They were just some scribbles. When the system was dying around you, what did his stupid stories matter?

He'd miss it, of course. As much as he and Dom fought, as much as they drove each other crazy on the lonely trips through space, he'd come to respect her. Once they left Temperance, he couldn't risk contacting her again if he smuggled Cassandra off the station. The *Solitude*, the contracts, they were everything to Dom. He couldn't risk that for her. So be it. She'd probably be glad to see the back of him.

He opened another beer, his thoughts turning back to Roy Williams. The fugitive had known he was looking for Cassandra. He'd recognised Eddie on sight. How had he found out so much about him in the short time they'd been on Temperance? Knox? But no, Knox didn't know Eddie was looking for Cassandra. All the questions he'd been asking must've got back to Williams.

The woman he'd slept with, she knew his name. But she wasn't a local. It didn't ring true that she'd fall in with someone like Williams. And the only other person he'd given his name to was….

Victoria Palmer. The woman at Green Acres. The woman who'd worked with Cassandra at Lady Luck. She'd been so nervous, so eager to get rid of him. She'd told him Cassandra was dead.

He sat up straight. *Williams was there*. As soon as the thought came to him, he knew it was true. Roy Williams had been there, hiding somewhere. He could almost recall a hint of the man's sweat lingering in the air as he'd stood in Victoria Palmer's apartment, fingers running along the pages of his book. The book Victoria said wasn't hers. The one she said came with the apartment.

What were the chances of finding his book—not even his best-selling book—in an apartment on Temperance owned by a woman who'd known Cassandra? Unless it wasn't her copy. It was Cassandra's. It had to be.

She'd known he was alive. She'd read his books. Why hadn't she ever tried to contact him?

He shook his head. It didn't matter. It'd all be explained when he found her, when he talked to her. And the key to that was Roy Williams.

The panel hidden behind the bookshelf in Palmer's

apartment. Had he been there? Had he been next door, listening in? Had he watched through the peephole as Eddie went past?

He put his back against the wall and pushed himself up, the booze tingling at the corners of his mind. Not drunk, just smoothed out. He'd walk it off on the way back to Green Acres.

He turned his back towards the street, took out his gun, checked the magazine. He was going to get an answer out of Roy Williams one way or another. No injury, no contract, and no partner was going to get in the way of that. He had a chance to make everything right, to erase the mistakes of his youth.

And he was going to take it.

He pulled his jacket around himself and took off down the street.

Leone's people were at the train station. Not wearing red—they weren't casino staff. But they were conspicuous enough in their grey coats and black hats. Four of them altogether. Dom watched them from an abandoned newsstand half a block away. They were grizzled, bulky. Not soft-faced security guards, but true syndicate thugs. Even the tourists went quiet as they moved past to board the train.

Dom chewed it over for a few seconds, but there was no way around it. She couldn't sneak past them and she couldn't take all of them out. Not without more ammo. And she didn't like the idea of going toe-to-toe with men like that in a public area.

So there it was. She had to walk halfway across the city. She sighed, turned away from the station, and got going.

She'd spotted three more groups of syndicate thugs by the time she was halfway to St Reynold's Church. They strolled down the street like they owned the place. Which they probably did. Each time, she ducked into an alley or an abandoned shop and waited until they'd passed. But sooner or later she was going to be spotted. She hoped Eddie was being careful. The bloody idiot was always reckless when his blood was up.

As she crept inside a ransacked market, hiding from yet another group of searching thugs, her gaze fell on a public off-station comm terminal near the checkout counter. Though the rest of the shop was torn to shreds, the standby lights were still on the unit. She slid onto the stool and touched the screen. The terminal came to life, flashing a welcome message at her from behind the smudged fingerprints on the old-tech screen.

She nearly stood up again and left, but she needed to make contact with the Feds at the outpost before they started getting antsy. Since she wasn't going to be getting back to the *Solitude* anytime soon, now was as good a time as any to make the call.

She steeled herself and slid her cash card into the machine's slot. It blinked her current balance at her—for the love of Man, how much had Eddie taken to gamble with? She could picture those chips now, sitting back in the Crimson Casino, pocketed by one of Leone's staff. Hell. She wasn't going to be seeing that money again.

Grumbling to herself, she accepted the charge and

punched in the Fed outpost's comm code. The machine deducted 450 vin for the off-station call and made the connection. She brought the handset to her ear as it picked up.

"Dominique Souza, stalker, for Lieutenant Pine," she said.

The receiver's voice came back distorted. "This call isn't coming from your ship, Miss Souza."

No shit. Who the hell did the Feds hire to take their calls?

"No, sir. This is a public terminal. Please connect me to Lieutenant Pine."

A crackle. "Very well. Stand by."

Dom drummed her fingers on the comm terminal's casing and kept an eye on the window. Through the dirty and broken glass she watched a homeless woman in a heavy tattered cloak hurrying away. A moment later, three syndicate men strode past, talking to each other in low voices. Dom kept still and quiet until they'd passed.

"Miss Souza," Pine's whiny voice came down the line. "It's a little late to be giving your report, isn't it?"

"Is it?"

She checked the time. Nearly four a.m. local time. And yet outside everyone was carrying on as they had since she'd arrived. A tiredness had settled into her bones, but not the kind of tiredness that brings sleep. The kind that only brings more tiredness.

"Sorry, sir," she said. "Time is difficult to keep track of with the light discipline."

"I'm disturbed by the reports I've been receiving from Temperance. I understand there have been firefights with local syndicate members."

"Yes, sir." She paused. "It was unavoidable."

"I doubt that very much, Miss Souza. Temperance is in a delicate state. If I wanted chaos, I would take a company of marines down there myself."

It was all bluster. Pine had no authority to initiate any sort of invasion or declare martial law over the station. But it made her uneasy to hear him make the threat. Men who wanted others to think they were powerful sometimes did stupid things to back up their boasts.

"That won't be necessary, sir. The situation is under control."

"You are close to apprehending Williams?"

"I believe we will be able to locate and isolate him in a matter of hours, sir."

He made a noise like he didn't quite believe her. "If you are unable to complete this contract, the Federation will have no choice but to revoke it and grant it to another stalker."

"I *will* capture him, sir. I would advise other stalkers to stay out of the way, lest I mistake them for an enemy."

She bit her tongue as soon as she said it, but it was too late. The words were already out. The pain in her jaw and the exhaustion in her bones and the fight with Eddie were bubbling away inside her, stirring up old angers.

Pine was quiet a long time. She scratched at the corner of an advertisement for a prostitute stuck to the comm unit as she waited for him to speak.

"One more thing, Miss Souza," Pine said when he finally spoke. His voice was quiet now, serious. "I want no more altercations between you and Feleti Leone or his people."

"I'll do my best, sir."

"No, your best isn't good enough. Mr Leone is a protected individual, do you understand?"

"Sir?"

"The Federation has placed significant value on Mr Leone's life. He has been a valuable source of information. He is not to be harmed in any way. The same goes for his people."

She wasn't sure she was hearing him right. "Feleti Leone is a gangster and a racketeer and a murderer."

"Feleti Leone is not your target, stalker. Penalties will be applied to your bounty if any more of his people are harmed. If Mr Leone is killed, your contract will be forfeit and further investigation will be undertaken to determine what other consequences will be handed down to you and Mr Gould. Do you understand?"

She ground her teeth. So now she had to tiptoe around a man who wanted nothing more than to see her dead. She couldn't even defend herself without incurring this paper pusher's wrath.

Pine cleared his throat. "Do you understand, Miss Souza?"

"Yes, sir. I understand. Feleti Leone will continue his fine service to this Federation for many years to come."

He ignored her sarcasm. "Keep me informed. I await your call."

She replaced the receiver and scowled at the terminal for a minute. Of all the men to leave alive on this station,

Leone was the worst. But that didn't matter. The Feds wanted him alive, and she was the Feds' dog. They told her to bark, she barked. Woof woof.

She kicked the comm terminal, stood up, and slipped back out onto the street.

25

Silence had taken root in the Green Acres apartment building, only spoiled by the scuffling of rats in the walls. Eddie crept down the hallway as quietly and as quickly as his injuries would allow. No need to spook anyone. He wanted to do this nice and calm and quiet. Take out Williams before he had a chance to fight back, before he could run. Take him out and make him talk.

And to hell with Dom. She'd insist on handing Williams over to the Feds right away. And he'd do that. But not before he had his answers. Not before he knew where Cassandra was.

He approached the door to Victoria Palmer's apartment, but his eyes touched on the apartment next door. He paused. If he was right about that hidden panel leading into the next apartment, this would be the one. He edged closer, staying against the wall so he wouldn't be seen by anyone looking out the peephole. He crouched and put his ear against the door. Silence.

He licked his lips. Calm and quiet. That was the way to do this. He examined the lock. Just a cheap pin tumbler lock, the same kind they always used in these kinds of budget apartments. He fished through his pockets and finally found a small set of lock picks in his shirt pocket. He knew he had them somewhere.

With a glance up and down the hallway to ensure he was alone, Eddie inserted a pick and a torsion wrench into the keyhole and quietly began to work. He was no master lock picker, but he'd had enough practice to be able to deal with this kind of cheap lock given enough time and patience. The time wasn't a problem, but the patience was. His heart kept up a steady rat-a-tat inside his chest as he worked. He didn't relish the idea of getting in another fistfight with Williams. The man hit like a meteor.

The last pin clicked softly into place and he felt the lock give under the pressure he put on the torsion wrench. *Here we go.* He drew his pistol, stood, and pressed gently down on the door handle. The door swung open a centimetre.

A copper stench hit him, almost enough to make him gag. Dark inside. He pushed his gun through the gap and shoved the door open with his shoulder.

A shadow sat in a chair in the centre of the room. Eddie's gun snapped towards the figure. But it wasn't Williams, it wasn't big enough. Something black pooled beneath the chair. Eddie's stomach turned at the smell. The figure wasn't moving. He wasn't breathing. He was dead.

Eddie forced the nausea down and swept through the small apartment to the bathroom. A bloody wrench sat in the shallow bathtub, trailing red down the drain. No one else here.

He swung around and returned to the main room, still moving as quietly as possible. His eyes were beginning to adjust to the darkness. He wished they hadn't.

The man in the chair was shirtless, exposing a dozen cuts across his chest. His head dangled over the back of the chair so he was staring up at the ceiling. Someone had stuffed socks into his mouth and taped them in place with duct tape. Both knees were shattered messes of bone and sinew. Eddie couldn't see exactly which wound had killed him, and he didn't want to look close enough to find out.

Roy Williams had left his handiwork behind, but he wasn't here. He had to come back eventually. Eddie went back to the apartment door, closed it, and flipped the lock.

Now he was all alone in Williams' apartment with a dead man. Great.

Keeping his pistol in his hand, Eddie started rummaging. A selection of the finest in improvised torture implements were lined up on the single bed. He supposed the fugitive must've had more important things to do than sleep.

Come to think of it, how long had it been since he'd slept? He'd lost all sense of time. He should've picked up an upper when he was at the liquor store.

Eddie pulled open the wardrobe door and found a small brown suitcase and a duffel bag. The suitcase held a handful of shirts and trousers and jackets, mostly newly acquired by the look of them. He returned the suitcase to the wardrobe and unzipped the duffel bag.

"Well, hello, big spender," Eddie whispered to himself. He reached into the bag and pulled out a bundle of ten thousand vin notes. He flicked through them. They were real, all right. And the bag was filled with them. No wonder Knox wanted to get his hands on all this. There weren't many kinds of happiness you couldn't buy with this much cash. The only thing you needed was a gun to protect it. Williams must've had the same idea, because a pistol sat on top of the pile of cash.

He tossed the bundle of cash back into the bag and zipped it up. Wouldn't be a bad idea to take the cash with him. Williams wouldn't need it where he was going.

But before he could grab the bag, he sensed movement behind him. Eddie spun, raising his gun.

The man in the chair was staring at him.

Eddie bit back a cry and took a step away from the man before he caught himself. The tortured man let out a low groan. One of his eyes was glazed, the other…the other wasn't there. How the hell could this guy still be alive? His lips moved, only air escaping. *Help me.*

"Jesus," Eddie said.

The man *was* dead, he just hadn't realised it yet. His face was grey, blood still leaked from his chest.

A scuffling sound came from the wall. Eddie tore his eyes from the bound man and looked towards the wall. His gaze fell on the seam that revealed the panel connecting this apartment to Victoria Palmer's.

"Roy?" Her voice was muffled through the wall. "Are you back?"

Eddie stood for a moment, gaze swinging between the bound man and the hidden panel. The tortured man let out another rattling groan.

The panel began to creak. She was sliding it open.

He moved quickly and quietly, pressing himself against the wall alongside the widening hole. Light spilled through from Victoria's apartment, casting the grizzly scene into stark detail.

"Roy?" Victoria said again. Her head poked through the gap between the apartments.

Eddie pressed his gun against her temple. She froze, her voice catching.

"Looks like Roy's out at the moment," Eddie said cheerily. "But you and me are going to sit nice and tight and have a little chat while we wait for him to return. Doesn't that sound like fun?"

26

Dom pushed open the door to St Reynold's Church. The scent of death still lingered. Christ the Luminary extended his hand to her as she entered the gloom. He'd taken a bullet through the chest during the gunfight, but he didn't seem concerned about it. She ignored him and made her way down the centre aisle.

No one had come to clear away the bodies. Benjamin Bollard lay at the front of the church, still wearing the preacher's outfit he hadn't earned. She wondered how he'd come across it. Had he just found it when the fugitives took over this chapel, perhaps abandoned when the original Reverend fled the city? Or was the Reverend's blood staining that black cloak? Was his body lying in a dumpster a couple of blocks away? Or hidden above the ceiling tiles?

She stopped alongside a pool of drying blood on the floor. Bones was gone. A smeared blood trail led down the aisle towards the pulpit. She rested her hand on her revolver and followed the blood.

At the end of the aisle, the trail turned aside and went around the pulpit to a curtain to the left of the room. She pulled the curtain aside and found an open door leading up a set of narrow stairs. This was where she'd heard Knox come down after the fight. The trail of blood continued up the stairs. She stood silently for a moment, listening to the sounds of the building. No creaks, no footsteps, no click of a gun's slide being pulled back. She continued up the stairs.

The staircase bent back on itself and came out on a hallway lined with three doors. These would've been offices back when the building was a pachinko joint. At the end of the hallway was a fourth door, one that looked thicker than the rest. A heavy electronic lock had been half-ripped from the wall alongside, several wires cut. The door was open a crack. The blood trail led inside. Dom quietly drew her revolver, thumbed back the hammer, and pushed open the door.

On the right side of the room was a low table, and next to that a bookshelf. The contents of both had been swept to the floor to make room for the small assortment of guns and ammunition piled there. A painting of a planet—old Earth?—hung above the guns, alongside a simple metal cross. On the opposite wall, another painting—this one of the Luminary leading a long line of people through the black of space, none of them wearing helmets or void-suits—was being used to hide a long crack running diagonally along the wall surface.

In the centre of the room sat a synth-wood desk holding a lamp, a copy of *The Word of the Luminary*, and a pistol. The pistol's grip was streaked with blood. And behind the desk, the fugitive Bones sat slumped, clothes soaked with blood and an unlit cigarette dangling from his lips.

Bones' eyes drifted half-open and stared at her. The web of criss-cross scars on his face tightened as he saw her.

"Ah, fucking hell. You just fuck right off. Fuck off or kill me if you're gonna."

She just stared at him, letting her revolver hang at her side. He didn't look like he had enough strength left to even pick up his pistol, let alone aim it.

He raised his trembling, bloodstained hand. A silver lighter was grasped in his remaining fingers. He tried to spark it, but he couldn't work the contraption. He snarled and limply tossed the lighter onto the desk in front of him.

She holstered her gun, crossed the room, and came around the side of the desk. He flinched as she approached.

She picked up the lighter, flicked the flame to life, and held it out. He eyed her warily for a moment, then leaned forward with the cigarette between his lips. The tip glowed orange as the flame caught it. She snapped the lighter closed.

Bones sucked in the smoke, eyes closed. For a few moments, the lines on his face seemed not so deep.

"I need guns and ammunition," Dom said.

"Yeah?" Bones took another drag of the cigarette and pointed with his eyes at the table to the right. "Those ones over there, I guess?"

"That's right."

"You took my people, you took my fingers, and now you're going to take my guns."

She leaned against the desk. "You tried to kill me. I wasn't going to hurt any of you. I had no contract on your heads. Yet you tried to kill me. What did you expect to happen?"

"I expected you to die, stalker."

"And how did that turn out?"

He made a noise, his eyes drifting closed. He puffed on the cigarette, then opened his eyes. "There's some stims in the bottom drawer. Whole bunch of shit, Daz's mostly."

"You want me to get it for you?"

"It's the least you could do."

She picked up his pistol from the desk and tossed it over by the other guns before she crouched down to open the drawer. As he'd said, there were a few foil packs of pills and a handful of liquid vials. She wasn't going to inject him, so she grabbed a foil pack and popped two pills out into her hand.

"Fuckin' hell, gimme more than a couple," he said. "I want to at least feel it."

"You've lost a lot of blood. Too many and your body won't be able to deal with it."

"Listen to this. You some kind of nurse as well, stalker? Want to wipe my arse for me? Gimme the goddamn pills."

She sighed and popped four more pills out. His eyes followed them greedily as she held them towards him. He raised his remaining hand, reaching for the pills.

She closed her hand into a fist and pulled the pills out of his reach. "First, we make a deal."

"Christ in the void! You really are a sadistic bitch, ain't you?"

Her hand came to rest on her revolver. She watched his eyes linger on her gun. "Should I put you out of your misery? You'll recall I don't have a contract on you. That means I'm not going to apprehend you. It also means I don't need you alive."

His tongue snaked out, licking his lips. "What the hell kind of deal are you talking about, anyway? You've got what you want." He waved his hands at the pile of guns and ammo. "Go on, take them. I can't stop you."

"They're not my guns. I'm not a thief, sir. When I take them away with me, I want you to feel compensated."

He stared at her, eyes narrowed like he couldn't understand what she was saying. "Look at me, stalker. I'm dead."

"I could find you a doctor."

"You think there's any doctors left on Temperance? They all pissed off long ago. The Federation always makes sure the high-value citizens get their travel passes."

"I could turn you over to the Feds. They'd treat you."

"And send me back to the Bolt. Fuck that. Do you know what that place is like, stalker? It's a place for people like me. That should give you a clue."

"If you're asking me to feel sorry for you, you're out of luck," she said. "Now, do you want these stims or not?"

He scowled. "Do you want me to beg, stalker? Is that it?"

"I want you to make a deal with me."

"Christ. All right. All right. You want to know what you can do for me? You're looking for Roy Williams, right? I'm guessing you ain't found him yet if you're here."

"I haven't caught him, that's correct. But I won't kill him for you. He's too valuable to me. And his money's already accounted for."

"I'm not asking you to kill him and I don't give a shit

about the money. Not anymore. I been thinking. I got something I want you to tell him. He's looking for this woman, right? Lilian Mayweather. I saw a picture of her once. He thinks Leone snitched to the Feds and then when he got sent away, Leone snatched the woman to spite him. But that ain't true. See, I know about this girl." He cracked a grin. "I was cell mates with a guy who had her picture, years ago. Only her name wasn't Lilian. It was Cassandra something. This woman ain't who he thinks she is."

"Is that so?"

"Yeah, that's so. My buddy, he ran a small syndicate on Fractured Jaw. They were getting pestered by this gang of youths, having their hauls stolen, all that. The syndicate was wild, but they could never get their hands on the kids. Then one day they got their hands on this girl. She was one of them, you see, their leader, so my buddy says. And the girl offers to sell her friends out for some cash and passage off the station. Just like that."

"Sounds suspicious," Dom said.

"That's what my buddy thought, but they eventually went along with it. And it turns out she was telling the truth. My buddy's people found those kids. And you know what they did then? They dressed up like the law and went in pretending to raid the place. And once all those kiddies were lined up against the wall, the syndicate boys pulled out their guns and wasted them. Every last one of them."

The story tugged at her memories. Something similar had happened…where? She couldn't remember. She shook her head.

"So what? This girl is the woman he's looking for?"

"Yeah. And that's just the thing. That wasn't the only time she did it. She got in bed with my buddy pretty quick after that while she was waiting to get a ship off-station. Only guess what she did then? She betrayed him too! That's how he ended up in the clink."

He laughed and it turned into a hacking cough. When it subsided, he continued.

"I bet that little whore's done the same thing half a dozen times in the last few years. And I bet even more that Leone wasn't acting alone when he got Williams sent away. I bet that woman was in on it too. And that's what I want you to tell him. When you catch him, I want you to break that fucker's precious little heart. I want you to bring him down into the mud with the rest of us fugitives. The son of a bitch always thought he was so much bigger than us. Make him realise what a pathetic excuse for a human being he is. You do that, and you can take as many guns as you want, stalker."

"I suspected you were many things, but never a gossipy teenage girl."

"That's the deal. Can I have my stims now?"

She narrowed her eyes, then held out her hand and deposited the pills into his palm. "Enjoy the rest of your life."

"I intend to." He waved her away. "Now take your guns and get the fuck out and leave me in peace." He tilted his head back and dropped all the pills into his mouth.

Without another word, she went over to the table and gathered up four handguns, a shotgun, and an assault rifle. She filled her pockets with empty magazines and as much ammunition as she could carry, then slung the longer weapons over her shoulder.

When she looked back at Bones, his eyes were closed and his lips were spread in a blissful smile. His cheeks twitched several times a second. He didn't look at her again as she left the room and pulled the door closed behind her.

As she descended the stairs and left the chapel, Bones' story continued to play at the edges of her consciousness. This woman had nothing to do with her, but she couldn't shake the feeling that there was something she was missing.

She checked the street for Leone's thugs—no one in sight—and crossed a couple of blocks to find a ransacked department store. She stepped through a broken window and went up and down the aisles until she found what she was looking for: a duffel bag long enough to carry the guns. She dumped the guns into the bag, zipped it up, and headed back to the street. All the while Bones' words rolled around in her brain.

Maybe she heard the story somewhere. Maybe it was in the news, or someone told her in a bar once, or she read it—

She stopped. She *had* read that story before. But not in the news. In a book. Fractured Jaw. She should've recognised the station's name right away. It was right there in the title. *Massacre at Fractured Jaw.* Eddie's first book.

She'd always known the character in Eddie's first book was himself, if a highly fictionalised version of him. She didn't know how much of the story was true and how much Eddie had embellished. But the titular massacre, the novel's turning point, matched Bones' description. That was Eddie's gang who'd been massacred.

The woman. She was the one Eddie was looking for. She had to be. The same woman Williams was trying to reclaim.

Eddie didn't know. He didn't know she'd betrayed him on Fractured Jaw. If he found her, if he talked to her, then what? Would he walk right into her arms? Would he even notice the gun barrel pressed against his stomach until she pulled the trigger and it all went dark?

Damn it, Eddie. What the hell had he gotten himself into now?

She strode faster, pulling her tab from her pocket as she went. She bleeped Eddie and pressed the device against her ear.

"Pick up," she said. "Pick up, pick up. Pick up the damn tab, Eddie!"

27

Eddie pressed the barrel of his pistol against Victoria Palmer's temple.

"Let's go back into your apartment," he said. "I don't like the smell in here."

He glanced back at the tortured man bound to the chair. His head had slumped forward. It looked like he'd passed out again. Maybe died. Eddie felt for the guy, but there was nothing he could do.

Victoria trembled, licked her lips. Eddie withdrew his gun a couple of centimetres.

"Calm down. Let's just be calm. Back into your apartment. Let's go."

He waved his pistol and she nodded, slowly backing up. He bent down to climb through the hole into her apartment.

She bolted for the door. Swearing, Eddie climbed through the hole and followed her. She slammed into the door, hands fumbling on the deadbolt.

Eddie came alongside her, took a deep breath, and put a hand over the lock, pushing her fingers away. He pressed the gun against her side.

"This is going to be a long wait if you don't play along. He glanced down at a suitcase sitting next to the door. "You planning on going somewhere?"

"Get out of my house," she said.

Eddie smiled. "I'm not in a particularly cooperative mood today, lady. Go and close that panel. Go on, now." He jerked his head towards the hole in the wall.

She walked across the room on wobbling legs and slid the panel closed. She was looking even worse than the first time he'd come here. Her eye shadow had smudged and she'd changed out of one ripped shirt into another. There was a bruise on her wrist he hadn't seen before. Roy Williams' doing, he didn't doubt.

Maybe that gave him an opening, an angle to play. He'd done worse things today than manipulate a woman into betraying her friend.

She slid the panel closed, but didn't turn back towards him. A few of the smaller ornaments had been cleared off the shelves, but most of the books still remained. He spotted his own still lying on the shelf.

"Let's have a seat." He gestured to the couch. Woodenly, she sat down. He angled the armchair to face both the front door and the hidden panel and took a seat, keeping the gun pointed in Victoria's general direction.

"Okay," he said. "I'm gonna do some straight talking now, and I hope you'll do the same. I don't want to hurt you and I've got no reason to. Don't get me wrong, if I need to kill you to save my own life I will shoot you down. But I don't see that that's going to be necessary."

Victoria's hands squirmed against each other in her

lap. She didn't take her eyes off them.

"I think you know who I am and why I'm here," he said. "I'm a stalker, and I'm looking to apprehend Roy Williams. That's not the only reason I'm here, but we'll get to that. I want to ask you some questions."

She rubbed her fingers, picked at her nails.

"I'd like you to answer me honestly," he said. "I get the feeling you're in deeper than you'd like with Williams. I think he scares you. I think it scares you what he's done to that man in the next room. I think he's hurt you, or threatened to. I think you've realised that anything he promised you was a lie. I think you don't want to have anything to do with the bastard anymore. So I'm going to ask you some questions. If you tell me the truth, if you help me out, then I can help you. I can take Roy out of your life."

She licked her lips. "And if I don't tell you the truth?"

He studied her for a second. "You want to know if you'll end up like the man in the next room?"

She said nothing.

"I'm not going to hurt you, Victoria. If I have to kill you it will be fast and as simple as a bullet to the head. But I'm not going to kill you for not cooperating with me. I'm not going to torture you either. If you don't want to answer, fine, don't answer. I'll just sit here and take my chances when Williams shows up. But I'm not your enemy. I'm your chance to get out of all this."

She was quiet a long time. The building creaked around them as he waited for her to work through it in her head. She was at war with herself, he could see it in the twitches that flickered across her face. A memory returned to him, a diplomacy class he'd been half-sleeping through back on Ophelia, back when he was a little rich kid so convinced of his own importance, his own immortality.

All you have to do is make them hesitate. Make your case not in facts and logic but with emotion. Appeal to their base desires: love, acceptance, safety. Just make them hesitate. Once they hesitate, they're yours. They just don't know it yet.

"I hate him," Victoria said quietly. She said it to herself at first. Then she looked at Eddie and her face twisted and her voice grew loud. "I hate him!"

Manipulation. It was so easy it made him sick.

"How did you get involved with him?" he asked.

"I was dancing and working bar at Lady Luck. I didn't know it was owned by Feleti Leone at the time. Or maybe I did, I don't know, everything around here is owned by him now. I took the job because a friend said it was a good place to work. Or I thought he was a friend." She stared through Eddie. "They didn't treat us well. I won't go into it. I'd been working there a month or two when Lilian started. Daisy, they called her. Two men brought her in, Leone's men, I guess. Took her into the back with the manager and talked for a long time. I never knew what they talked about. But she came out with a cigarette burn on her wrist and a broken look in her eyes."

Eddie's free hand curled into a fist on his knee. He should've killed Leone when he had the chance.

"She worked every night after that. Every single night. Two men would bring her in, she'd dance, they'd take her tips, and then the men would take her away. I tried to talk to her a few times, but the men were always there. At first I thought she must've owed some money or something, but it wasn't that. She was being punished for something."

"For what?"

"I didn't know. I still don't, really. I just knew they were trying to degrade her. And it was working. It went on like that for a year or more. The men—her handlers—they started to get complacent. I actually managed to talk to her after a few months. In the bathroom, as we passed on the way to the stage, just snatches of conversation. I found out her name was Lilian Mayweather. That the only pleasure she got came from reading. And then later, much later, I found out she'd been married. Still was. To a convict named Roy Williams, the man who used to run the White Hand syndicate."

"They were married?"

For some reason that little detail was like an electrodrill to the heart. How many guns had been aimed at her to make her walk down the aisle with a man like Roy Williams? Christ, what had she been through since Fractured Jaw? No wonder her songs were so sad.

If Victoria noticed his pain, she didn't give any indication. "That's what she said. It was the last time we talked. One day I came into work and she wasn't there. A few weeks later our manager torched the club and tried to flee Temperance. I…I thought Lilian might have been killed. It was just a gut feeling. Those men, her handlers, they were dangerous. I didn't want to ask any questions in case I got killed myself. It wasn't until later I heard than Lilian was working at the Crimson Curtain."

"And then Roy Williams found you," he said.

She licked her lips and nodded. "I'd run into money troubles again. I was in a bad place. Taking a lot of stims. Out on the street. Roy tracked me down. He knew I'd worked with Lilian. He set me up here." She gestured around the apartment.

"It was Lilian's place?"

"I don't know how he found it or why he decided to come here, of all the places in this city. He can be... sentimental."

"I think the guy in the next room would disagree."

"I didn't say he wasn't an evil man. Even evil men can have sentimentality."

"Sure," he said. "And some of the worst evil I've seen comes from that sentimentality."

He stood and poured himself a glass of water from the kitchenette, keeping an eye on Victoria as he did so. But she didn't move. She didn't even look up.

"You want a drink?" he said.

She shook her head, eyes still on her hands. He sat back down, sipping his water.

"All right," he said. "Sentimental or not, Williams didn't put you in this place out of the kindness of his heart. What did he want from you?"

"Information. He traded stims for information. What I knew about Lilian. What I knew about Leone. Who Lilian's handlers had been at Lady Luck." Her eyes drifted towards the hidden panel in the wall. "That man, Scott Hudson, he was one of them."

"A handler?"

She nodded. "One of the worst. Always insulting her, feeling her up, pushing her around." Her eyes went cold. "I guess he got his comeuppance. And then some."

"And now?" Eddie gestured to the suitcase. "What's happening now? You're leaving."

"He's…he's…." She clammed up.

"Victoria."

She pressed her hands against the side of her head. "I don't want to die here. He said he'd get me off the station. I believed him. Now…now I don't know. But what if he was telling the truth? I have family, I have friends. I don't want to die."

"Williams has a ship?"

"What am I going to do?" she said, ignoring him. "He doesn't care about me. He never would have saved me. Would he? Jesus. I can't stay with him any longer. The man's a monster. Drip-feeding me stims like he owns me. What am I going to do?"

Eddie stood up, put down his drink, took her by the shoulders. "Victoria. Look at me. Does he have a ship?"

She blinked, as if only just remembering he was there. "Yes. A small cruiser. He gave me the money and told me to buy it."

"What's it called? Where's it docked?"

"It's the *Sophia Almeida*. Airlock two-three-three." She looked up into his eyes. "Can you get me off Temperance? I've told you everything I know. Please."

His stomach twisted into a knot. It was going to be hard enough getting Cassandra off Temperance. He couldn't keep collecting strays. He didn't have to ask to know that

Victoria didn't have a travel pass.

"Please," she said again. Her eyes were damp. "He'll be back any second. I've helped you, haven't I? Now you have to help me."

He turned away. "I can get Williams away from you. But I can't save you from Temperance. I don't have that kind of authority. I'm sorry."

"But you're going to try to save her, aren't you?" Her voice went flat. "You'll take Lilian away."

"If I can."

"And you're going to leave me to die here."

"That's right. Just like I'm going to leave everyone else on this station . Most of them don't deserve to die either."

She was quiet a long time. He couldn't look at her. *Cassandra. You're doing this for Cassandra.*

"How can you do this?" she said. "How can you come to this place just to capture a man like Roy Williams? How can you save him and leave the rest of us to die?"

"Because you're all dead whether I capture Williams or not. I'm not paid to be anyone's saviour. I'm paid to deal justice."

"Is that what this is? Justice?"

"It's as near as anyone's going to get."

She opened her mouth. But she didn't get a chance to speak. A door creaked open in the next room. A moment later came the sound of a floorboard groaning softly.

Eddie put up his hand to silence Victoria and readied his pistol. Silently, he moved towards the panel in the wall. He pressed his ear against the panel. The sound of a zip, a swish of the wardrobe door closing. Williams was packing up, getting ready to go.

Eddie glanced back at Victoria, motioned for her to stay seated. She bit her lip and nodded.

This was it. *Calm and quiet.* Take him down. Get Cassandra back. And then everything would be all right. He pressed his palm against the panel and prepared to slide it aside.

His tab beeped wildly in his pocket. He froze at the sudden noise. The shuffling in the next room went silent. Then a creak as someone shifted their weight on the floorboards.

Eddie dived to the floor as half a dozen holes were torn in the panel. Gunshots ripped through the air above him. Victoria screamed.

Splinters rained down on him. Firing blindly back was too risky—if he killed Williams he lost everything. All he could do was crawl across the ground as the gunfire burst above him.

Victoria crouched, her hands over her head. He grabbed her and shoved her flat on the floor as another rain of bullets carved through the air. All the while his tab continued to beep at him.

Then, as suddenly as it had begun, the gunfire ceased. Eddie's ears rang. A door slammed and footsteps sprinted away down the corridor.

Eddie scrambled to his feet. Victoria still screamed.

"Get out of here!" he shouted over his shoulder at her. "Go and don't come back."

He threw open the front door to see Williams' shadow disappearing down the stairs.

No. He can't get away.

Eddie gave chase, all his aches complaining as he ran. His tab wouldn't shut up. He ripped it from his pocket and pressed it against his ear.

"What?" he snarled.

"Eddie," Dom said. "Where the hell are you? I've just been talking to—"

"Later. I'm chasing Williams." He skidded around the corner and sprinted down the stairs three at a time.

"What?"

"He's running for it. He has a ship at airlock two-three-three. Cut him off."

"I'm nowhere near—"

"Then get there!"

He cut the connection and burst out of the front door of Green Acres. Ahead, Williams shoved aside a trio of tourists and sprinted down the street. The bag of money was slung across his shoulder.

Williams paused at a corner and raised a machine pistol, aiming it at Eddie.

"Everyone down!" Eddie yelled to the scattered tourists as he ducked into a tattoo parlour doorway. A burst of gunfire rang out. People screamed.

Eddie peeked around the doorway. Williams was out of sight. The tourists were scattering in all directions. He started running again.

He came around the corner as another burst of gunfire sounded up ahead. He ran towards it. Two of Leone's thugs lay dead in the street, guns lying just out of reach of their outstretched hands. Eddie bent down and grabbed one of the pistols without slowing.

He was losing Williams. His injuries were slowing him down. He pushed his burning legs and aching ribs to keep going.

As he sprinted around another corner onto the end of the strip, the spaceport came into sight. He ran towards the stairs, passing knocked down civilians and another dead syndicate woman.

The airlocks of the spaceport were arranged in long rows stacked atop each other, with stairs and elevators leading up to the higher rows. Down below were docks for commercial ships and traders, linking directly into the underground train system. Eddie ran up the stairs to the spaceport, examining the numbers above each airlock. Leone would have men inside the spaceport authority, so there was no asking them for directions.

Through the transparent walls of the spaceport, he could see dozens of ships crammed together outside the station, maglocked in place to their respective gangway and airlock. A small cruiser, that's what he was looking for. The *Sophia Almeida*. One little ship among dozens.

Someone cried out ahead. A figure darted up a set of stairs, heading for an airlock. Above the airlock was written *233*.

Got you, you son of a bitch.

As Eddie started up the stairs, he spotted another group of figures running towards the spaceport from the opposite direction, all in long coats and hats. More of Leone's men. More than he could handle on his own.

He pulled out his tab, slipped his glasses on to use the earpiece, and jabbed at the tab's screen until it started calling Dom. He listened to the beep of the attempted connection until a crackle cut through.

"What?" Dom said.

"I'm nearly at his ship, but he killed a bunch of syndicate men and more are coming. I need you to get your arse over here and help me take them out."

"No!"

"What?"

"We're not killing any more syndicate men."

"What are you talking about? Do you want Williams or not?" he said, panting as he reached the top of the stairs.

"Pine says—never mind what Pine says. Just trust me, for the love of Man. I'm on my way."

Shit. "All right, all right. I won't kill them. But we need to keep Williams on the station. Tip off Port Authority and get the ship put on lockdown. It's the *Sophia Almeida.*"

"Don't you need backup?"

"Just do it. If he gets away, we're fucked. Shut him down and do it now."

He shoved his tab back in his pocket but kept the connection open. Leone's men were shouting from far away. He readied both his guns as he came to airlock 233. It was still open. He went in with both guns leading the way.

The time for stealth had passed. He made his way along the short umbilicus. He could see the interior of the small cruiser through the ship's airlock doors, the rust-coloured walls half-hidden in shadow.

"Williams!" he called out. "It's too late. You're not running from this one. You know Temperance Port Authority isn't going to let you disengage in a hurry. This is a gam-

bling town, Jack, and they know how much gamblers like
to skip out on their debts. They're going to check you closely, and by that time my partner will have given them good
reason to hold you here."

His voice echoed in the silence. He edged further along
the gangway.

"Leone's men are coming. Too many of them. It's the
end. Put your gun down and come on out. Come on out
and tell me where Lilian is."

A figure moved in the darkness of the ship interior.
Eddie stopped and raised his guns. But the figure wasn't
Williams. It was smaller, more slender. His heart started
hammering.

Cassandra Diaz stepped into the light and gave a small
sad smile.

"Hi, Eddie," she said. "Long time."

"Real long time," he said. He lowered his guns. "Come
here, quickly. I'm getting you out of here."

"I'm not going, Eddie." She tucked a lock of hair behind
her ear. "Roy's about to disengage the umbilicus. You have
to get out of here."

"Not without you. Come on." He couldn't stop staring
at her. "I can't believe you're alive."

Footsteps clanged out on the spaceport catwalks. They
were nearly here.

He put one of his guns away and stepped towards her,
stretching out his hand. "Come on. We have to go now."

She didn't move. Another figure appeared behind her.
Roy Williams.

Eddie's gun snapped back up. "Cassie, get down!"

Williams glared at Eddie and raised his machine pistol. The bag of money was still slung over his shoulder. Cassandra turned, put her palms against Williams' chest. She said something to him. Eddie thought it sounded like "Don't."

Dom's voice spoke in his ear. "I'm coming in on the train. Leone's men are swarming the port. If you're in there, get out."

Eddie bared his teeth, ignoring Dom. "Williams. Let her go. She's done with you. Put the gun down and you get out of this alive. Cassie, get away from him."

She shook her head slowly. "I'm not coming, Eddie. I'm…I'm sorry about Fractured Jaw."

"What?"

"I made sure you were out. I made sure you were safe."

"What are you talking about? Let's go."

"It was good to see you again." She turned and nodded to Williams.

The fugitive scowled at Eddie and punched the control panel next to him. The airlock hissed and began to close.

"No!" Eddie said. But before he could take a step forward, the airlock door shuddered to a halt, still open most of the way. A warning light flashed inside the ship.

"What is it?" Cassandra said.

Williams growled and punched the panel again. Nothing.

Then a voice came over a speaker above Eddie. "This is an automated message. By order of the Temperance Port Authority, the vessel at airlock two-three-three is now under lockdown until further notice. Ship control has been surrendered to Port Authority staff. For more information, please consult a Port Authority representative at the customer service booth."

"Shit," Williams said. He pointed his gun towards Eddie. "This is his fault!"

"Can you get us away?" Cassandra said.

"Not in time."

Eddie watched the exchange in confusion. He could understand why she was so desperate to get away from Leone. But trading a syndicate leader for a murderer and a fugitive was madness. Here he was, offering her a way out. Why wasn't she coming with him?

"Cassie," he said.

She glanced at him, then looked back to Williams. "The city. We have to find a place to hide."

He nodded and stepped through the partially closed airlock door, aiming his gun at Eddie. Cassandra followed close behind.

"Eddie!" Dom's voice yelled in his ear. She was panting, her footsteps clanging through the tab connection. "They're on you. Get out now!"

He spun around as two of Leone's men appeared at the umbilicus entrance. They raised their guns.

"Nobody move!" one said. "Drop the guns!"

Williams' machine pistol roared. The thugs ducked for cover as bullets ripped past them. Eddie stood in stunned silence as Williams and Cassandra dashed past him. He could smell her hair as she passed.

Instinctively, he reached out, his fingers brushing the skin of her hand. She glanced back, gave him one last sad smile. She said, "Run."

And then she was out of the umbilicus, following Williams. Gunfire roared. Footsteps clanged and people shouted.

Dom yelled through the earpiece, shocking him out his blank stare. "Where the hell are you? I've got sights on Williams, but I can't make a move. Get to the *Solitude*. It looks clear. Eddie?"

"Yeah. Yeah, I'm here." He started running. "Come out shooting or play it casual?"

"Casual," she said. "Port's full of scared civilians. Are you okay?"

"I'm fine."

He tucked his guns into his pockets and came out the umbilicus' entrance. The port was wild with movement and screaming. Tourists were running for cover or standing around watching the flood of gangsters and Port Authority uniforms streaming along catwalks and out of doors. Eddie dove into the chaos and moved with it. He couldn't see Williams or Cassandra, but it wasn't hard to figure out where they were by the flow of Leone's men. Williams had left a few more thugs wounded and bleeding on the floor.

"How'd you get the ship shut down so fast?" Eddie said to Dom as he ran.

"I had Knox do it. He told them it was Roy Williams. That seemed to get their attention."

His stomach sank. Leone had to know Cassandra was missing by now. And if he knew Williams was here, he'd know who had taken her. How was he supposed to get her off the station now?

He scanned the spaceport through the swirling crowds. A flash of brown hair caught his eye, the locks bobbing as Cassandra ran. Williams pulled her behind him. They were heading for the grav train platform, shoving aside the waiting tourists.

One of the men pursuing them yelled into his tab, but the grav trains were automated just like the supply trains. Shutting them down would take time. The grav train waited at the platform. The doors began to close.

Williams darted forward and grabbed the doors of the rear-most carriage, holding them open. He ushered Cassandra inside. The train began to move away from the platform.

The pop of gunfire echoed across the spaceport. Red blossomed in Williams' thigh. He toppled into the train and the doors slid closed, blocking him from view. Eddie ran towards the train, but it was hopeless. Within seconds the grav train built up speed and screamed away from the platform into the city. Eddie watched it go. He thought he glimpsed Cassandra's face through the window. Then it was gone, the train hidden by the rise of the buildings.

The chaos around him slowed. He stood in the centre of it for a moment, staring at the rails where he'd last seen the train. Then he slid his hands into his pockets and hurried towards the *Solitude*.

28

Dom made her way through the *Solitude*'s interior, shotgun at the ready. Leone's men had obviously been here—they'd cleaned out most of the armoury and emptied a dozen food containers onto the floor of the common room. But she couldn't hear any voices or footsteps now.

Anger boiled within her. The *Solitude* had been violated by these bastards. And she couldn't even kill them for it.

She swept onto the bridge, swinging her shotgun back and forth to cover the corners. But it was empty. Exhaling, she lowered the shotgun and dumped the rest of the guns in the armoury. If the thugs had been here recently, they must've been pulled into the pursuit of Roy Williams. They had a few minutes at least to regroup and hide out while the heat died down. She picked up a couple of cigarette butts from the floor of the bridge and tossed them in a trash receptacle in the wall.

The airlock door hissed. She raised her shotgun again, but lowered it when she saw Eddie limp into the main corridor. He looked even more tired than she felt. His eyes stared blankly around before finding hers.

Dom jerked her head towards the common room.

Without a word, they moved down the corridor. Eddie sat down at the small table. She went through the storage cupboards, found two metal cups that Leone's men hadn't destroyed, and set them up on the table. While Eddie sat staring into space, Dom went back to her quarters, lifted up her mattress, and retrieved the bottle of cheap vodka she kept there for special occasions.

Eddie hadn't moved by the time she got back to the common room. She half-filled each cup with vodka and sat down, resting her shotgun against her leg. Silently, they both picked up their cups and drank. Dom sipped hers, letting it burn, suppressing the urge to cough.

Eddie set his cup down in front of him. "Williams took a hit."

"Where?"

"Thigh. Could be bad if they got the artery."

"Shit," she said.

They sat silently a few more minutes, drinking.

"I was listening in over the tab," Dom said after a while. "I could hear you talking."

"Yeah?"

"That woman," Dom said. "The one with Williams. That's Cassandra?"

He nodded.

"Also known as Lilian Mayweather?" she said.

"That's the one."

"A woman from your past."

"Yup."

"And now she's with Roy Williams."

He spun the cup on the table in front of him. "Something

like that."

She nodded and was quiet for a minute. She was no good with any of this stuff. But she'd never seen Eddie like this before. He was always moody, distant, but this....

"I've got to tell you something," she said. "Maybe you're not going to like it, but it has to be said."

"Do what you gotta do, Freckles."

"I talked to one of the convicts who broke out with Williams. He knew about the girl. Knew her name. Both her names. He told me a story someone had told him. About a youth gang on Fractured Jaw, and a syndicate who wanted them out of the way. He told me this girl, she was the leader of the youth gang. But she sold them out to the syndicate. She told the syndicate everything they needed to find them and kill them."

Eddie's knuckles whitened around his cup of vodka.

Dom licked her lips. "The convict wanted me to taunt Williams with it. He thinks she helped Leone betray him to the Feds, got him locked away. Maybe that's true, maybe it's not. But the girl isn't who she says she is. She's dangerous. She betrayed you once. She can do it again. She's bad news, Eddie."

"You haven't got a shred of evidence for that." His voice was flat and sharp. "Some fugitive said he heard it somewhere or other? Come on. Gimme a break. He jerked you around and now you're jerking me around."

"I believe him," she said. "He knew her name. He knew what happened on Fractured Jaw. There's truth in there. You can feel it."

Eddie stood up and tossed his empty cup on the table. "Don't tell me what I feel." He kicked his chair, walked around in a small circle. He whirled back towards her. "You don't know shit, Freckles. I know her. I know what she's capable of and what she's not. She'd never betray her friends."

"Sit down, Eddie."

"Ah, to hell with you. I don't feel like sitting."

"Sit down and let's talk about this."

"What's there to talk about? Why do you even care?"

"You're really going to ask me that?" She stood slowly, stretching to her full height.

"Yeah. Yeah, I'm going to ask you that. Let's hear it. Why the fuck do you care so much about what I do?"

She growled. "The same reason I took a sniper rifle to the top of that building and saved your arse from Leone."

"And why's that, huh?"

"Because I'm your partner!" she roared. "Like it or not, we're in this together. And you can talk about leaving and taking your woman and flying off into the sunset with her but until that moment comes I will do everything in my power to protect you. And I thought you'd do the same for me."

"I would and I have. But now you're saying all this shit and I haven't got a goddamn clue why you believe this convict over me. Maybe you want her to be the villain in all this. Maybe you're afraid to go out into the void in this big lonely ship all by yourself."

"You really are full of yourself, aren't you? You want to go, then go. I'm trying to open your eyes to the truth you can't see."

"What the hell do you know about the truth? She's out there. She's out there in this city with a murderer. I have to find her."

She watched him across the table, the heat of anger in her cheeks. Why could he never see sense? She took a few breaths and spoke again in a calmer voice. "I heard your conversation over the tab. You asked her to come with you. So why didn't she?"

"Williams was right there. She couldn't get away from him."

"Is that really how it happened?"

He hesitated. "I know what I saw."

"You don't sound sure about that."

He shoved his hands in his pockets. "And now you're going to psychoanalyse me, huh? You're some kind of shrink? No, you're just like me. We're just a couple of thugs with guns who hunt down people for money. The only thing that separates us from our contracts is that we have the backing of the Feds. All we have is what we can hold and what we can take at the barrel of a gun. You do what you want, Freckles. I'm getting Cassandra back."

"You're making a mistake. She'll hurt you."

"Then so be it." He turned. "I'll get my stuff." He limped towards his quarters.

"Eddie, where the hell are you going?"

"I'm getting off your ship. Don't worry your pretty little head, Freckles. You won't need to save me anymore."

She followed him. "Sit down and have another drink."

"I've had too much to drink already."

"Then just sit down." She stood at the doorway to his

quarters and watched as he sifted through the wreckage left behind by the syndicate men.

"I don't have time," he said. "She's out there."

"And how do you plan to find her?"

He spun around to face her. "I don't know, all right, Freckles? Is that what you want to hear?"

He ran his hands across his bruised face. Her heart twisted to see him like this.

"I don't know how I'm going to find her," he said, quieter now. "All I know is that I have to. Maybe you're right. Maybe she did betray me all those years ago. Maybe she's the evil bitch you say she is. None of that matters. I can't explain why. I just need to find her. If she's innocent, I have to save her. And if she's guilty, I need to know."

"Are you sure? If she's guilty, do you really want to know?"

"You know me, Freckles. I'm here for the truth. That's all. She's alive. I need to know why. I need to talk to her. And that's all there is to it."

His shoulders slumped, like those last few words had taken all the strength he had left. She studied him.

"You can't do this alone, Eddie."

"Maybe not. But I can try." He opened a bag and shoved a handful of clothes and data disks into it.

"Stop," she said. "Stop packing, for the love of Man."

He stopped, but he didn't move, didn't meet her eyes.

She sighed. "We're partners. We're still partners. We help each other out. Right?"

He didn't say anything.

"If Williams is wounded, we might not have long.

We need him alive. So we work together. Williams and Cassandra, they'll be in the same place. We can capture him. You can find out the truth."

"And if I have to kill him?" Eddie said. "If I have to kill him to protect her?"

"It won't come to that."

"But if it does?"

She watched him for a long time. She could feel that leash around her neck. Lieutenant Pine's whiny voice whispered in her ear. She owed the Federation a debt, a debt she paid with men like Williams. If Williams died, what would happen to her? She hadn't lost a contract yet. What would happen if she did? Would the Feds decide she wasn't as effective a stalker as they thought? Would they come up with another way for her to repay her debt? Would she end up in the Bolt instead of Williams? Or would they just stand her up against the bulkhead and end it with the blasts of a firing squad?

"If it comes to that," she said, "you'll do what you think you have to."

He looked thoughtful for a few moments. Then he nodded slowly.

"All right. Partners."

"Partners," she agreed.

Her pocket chirped. As Eddie emptied his bag out onto the floor of his room, she pulled out her tab and answered it.

"Good, you're still alive," Knox said. "How long does it take you to get a few guns? I was starting to think I'd have to go looking for that money myself."

"We ran into some trouble."

"We? You and Skinny back together in holy matrimony, then?"

"Did you call just to mock me?"

"No," he said. "I called because the news is saying that the station's life support systems are going to fail earlier than expected. If we want to get out of here alive, we should probably get on with it. And while you two have been horsing around all over Temperance, I've been hard at work."

"You've got the tracking information?"

"Nearly. Give me thirty minutes and access to a public computer terminal and you'll have your man. And I'll have my money."

Yes. "We're coming back to the hotel now. Give us a while to dodge Leone's people."

"Bring some food with you. Real food, I mean. And something with caffeine. And maybe a—"

She hung up and returned the tab to her pocket. Eddie met her eyes.

"You ready?" she said.

"I'm always ready, Freckles."

She pointed towards the armoury. "I brought you some guns."

He grinned and slapped her on the shoulder as he passed. "You always know just how to treat your partner, don't you?"

29

Fire pulsed through Roy's thigh with every step. His trouser leg was damp and sticky with blood that wouldn't stop flowing. He took another step and nearly stumbled. If Lilian hadn't been there to take his weight, he would've fallen.

That galled him. He'd been wounded before, cut and scraped and bruised in prison fights and assassination attempts. But he'd always been able to move under his own power, at least until he found himself alone and could finally sit and deal with the pain.

But here he was, alive and walking by the grace of his wife, a woman half his size who still managed to take his weight without grimace or complaint. He loved her for that, loved her for her strength and quiet fortitude. But he was also ashamed for her to see him like this, so weak. She hadn't married a weak man.

And to think it had been nothing but a lucky shot from some syndicate thug that'd done this to him. Not a planned hit, not a bullet from the gun of a Fed hunting party. Just some faceless mook whose balls probably hadn't even dropped yet.

A nerve twinged in his thigh and he bit back a grunt as electric pain shot through him. His sweat made his clothes cling to him. He was repulsed by his own stench. But still Lilian urged him on, whispering soothing words in his ear as they crept through the dark alleys of Temperance's abandoned districts. Leone's people wouldn't be far behind. They had to get out of sight, lay low until they could make a move for another ship.

How long did they have? In a few days, the flow of tourists would slow. A few days after that and they'd begin to leave. No one wanted to be stuck here if the life support systems failed earlier than expected. And every ship that left without Roy and Lilian on it was one less ship they could use for their escape. Leone had to know Roy was on the station. He wouldn't rest until Roy was dead and Lilian was back with him.

Roy had been so close. So close to rescuing Lilian. Until the stalkers ruined everything. If Lilian died on this station, he would ensure those stalkers did too.

Roy was so deep in his thoughts he lost his sense of direction as Lilian led him through the narrow streets. He glanced around at the towering apartment blocks, dead houseplants still hanging from balconies.

"Where are we going?" His voice came out as a hoarse whisper. The machine pistol was gripped in his right hand, even though he didn't know if he had the strength to lift it.

"A safe place," she said. She had the bag of money slung over her other shoulder while she supported him. Even stained with his blood and damp with sweat, she was beautiful. His heart ached with how much he had missed her.

They emerged into the street. They'd come out behind a burned-out old building, the debris still cluttering the rear alley. She leaned him against the charred wall for a moment and pulled open the thin back door. The hinges creaked and protested.

He folded back around her shoulders as she returned to him. Slowly, she edged him through the doorway. Parts of the upper floor had collapsed, blocking the way forward. But Lilian turned and pushed through another door into a small office. One wall was completely destroyed, opening out into a wider room strewn with debris. The air stank of smoke, even though the building had clearly been this way for months.

As Roy rested against the office desk, Lilian pushed a fallen beam aside and pulled back the scorched carpet in the centre of the room. A trapdoor was revealed.

"How do you know about this place?" he said.

"You know me," she said. "I've got an eye for these sorts of things." She pulled open the trapdoor and tossed the money bag down into the darkness. She turned to him. "Can you make it down the stairs?"

He nodded and she took his weight once more. The stairs were narrow and steep, making the descent slow and awkward. Only the barest light from outside trickled in to show the way. Finally, the stairway ended and his foot touched solid ground. Lilian flipped a switch on the wall and a bulb lit up.

The room wasn't much. An empty safe sat open against one wall. A long table ran through the centre of the room, surrounded by mismatched chairs. Empty noodle boxes and drink bottles were scattered around. A cash counting machine was the only piece of technology in the room.

"Over here," Lilian said, lowering him into a chair. He exhaled as the weight was taken off his leg and the pain faded slightly.

"Will they find us here?" he asked. The machine pistol sat in his lap.

"I don't think so. Not for a while." She knelt in front of him and tore his trouser leg to expose the wound. "How bad is the pain?"

He shrugged.

She smiled up at him and took his hand, squeezing it. "I should know better than to ask you, shouldn't I? I don't have anything for the pain, so you're going to have to be brave a little longer. You've lost a bit of blood, but I don't think the artery was hit. I'm going to bandage it, okay?"

He nodded and she went to work, tearing his trouser leg into strips and using it to bandage the wound. It wasn't clean or hygienic, but he'd survive.

As she worked, he watched her face. Watched her curls sway with each movement of her head. Her hair was shorter than he remembered, but he liked it this way.

"I missed you," he said.

She flashed a smile at him that warmed his stomach. "I know you did."

"Did…what did Leone do to you?"

The smile faded. "Nothing I won't survive."

"Lilian…."

She tied off the makeshift bandage and gave his hand

another squeeze. "We'll talk about it. We will. On our way off this station. We'll have all the time in the world to talk about it. But you need to rest. Look at you, you can barely keep your eyes open."

He suddenly realised how tired he was. When was the last time he'd slept? Days ago? Had it been that long?

"Here." She took his gun from him, laid it on the ground, then helped lower him onto the floor. It wasn't the most comfortable place he'd ever slept, but it was far from the worst.

He reached out a hand to her. "I want to hold you."

"Soon," she said. "I need to go out and get some things. We need food and water and some proper medical supplies. And I need to find out what Leone's men are up to."

"No," he said. "It's too dangerous. You can't go alone."

"I've survived without you for years. I think I can last another hour." She knelt at his side and pressed her lips against his. All these years and he'd never forgotten how she tasted. He savoured that slow, soft kiss. Years' worth of tension flooded from his muscles. He wanted to stay here in this moment forever. But his body was betraying him. He was slipping into sleep.

His eyes closed by themselves. Her hand brushed his forehead and he felt her lips gently kiss each of his eyelids.

"Sleep," she whispered. "I'll be back soon."

"I love you," he mumbled.

"I love you too," she said.

And then he was out.

Roy woke with a start, clutching his leg. The muscles in

his thigh were cramping, twitching in agony beneath the bandage. He gritted his teeth and rode the wave of pain until it subsided.

The bulb overhead gave a barely audible hum. Water dripped from a pipe somewhere in the ruined building. He coughed a few times, the smoke in the air irritating his lungs.

How long had he been out? He had no idea. It didn't feel like it'd been more than an hour, but he had no way of knowing. His mouth was dry; he'd kill for a drink and a smoke. He pushed himself up onto his elbow and looked around. Lilian still wasn't back. Had Leone's men got to her?

No, she was more careful than that. It'd take time to navigate streets swarming with Leone's people. She'd be back when she could be. He knew that. But something else niggled at the back of his mind. Something was wrong. He could feel it.

He reached out, picked up his machine pistol. He couldn't hear anything, couldn't sense any movement. But his stomach was twisting. Something was missing.

The bag. The money.

He twisted, scanning the room. The bag of money was nowhere to be seen. Lilian had tossed it down here. He'd seen it. He'd passed it as he came in. So where was it?

There was only one possibility. Lilian had taken it.

He sat up, ignoring the pain in his leg, and tried to control his breathing and his swirling thoughts. There was a reasonable explanation. She needed supplies. She needed money for that.

But the whole bag? Over a million vin? He could understand her taking the pistol from inside, taking a few tens of thousands. But taking the whole bag was just dangerous. What if she had to run and leave it behind? She was a smart woman, and more careful than that. So why had she taken it?

As he shifted his weight, the corner of something hard pressed into his side. He reached into his pocket and pulled out a tab. The tab he'd picked up in Lilian's room at the hotel. He stared down at its screen, fingers tightening around its covering.

He opened her log of recent calls. Every one of them went to the same number. No name attached, but he recognised the number he'd gotten from his captive, Hudson. Feleti Leone's private number.

Why would she be calling Leone? Some of these calls were made as recently as yesterday. She called him nearly every day. What twisted game was he playing with her?

He navigated through the files on her tab, flicking rapidly through them. A name caught his eye. He stopped, scrolled back.

A digital book. No, not just one, dozens of them. She'd always loved reading. But as he scrolled through, he saw the same author's name coming up again and again. Eddie Gould.

He thought back to her apartment. She'd had one of Gould's books there as well. She knew him. That had been clear when she'd talked to him at the spaceport. She'd asked Roy to spare the stalker's life. Why?

The answer came as a whisper in the back of his head.

She betrayed you for him. Why do you think she took the money? She took it to him. She's going to lead the stalkers straight back to you. She loves him, not you. How could you ever think a woman like that would love a monster like you?

No. It wasn't true. He knew her past. He knew what she'd done to survive. She was strong, but so was her thirst for life. She'd betrayed men before to protect herself. He knew that. He respected it. She'd done what she had to.

She had never been weak. She was a leader. She'd helped him run the syndicate. She'd helped him secure territory, take over businesses, slaughter rivals. She could be as ruthless as him. That was part of why he loved her.

But she would never betray him. Not now. Not after everything he'd been through to get her back.

Fool, the voice in his head whispered. *You've already lost her. She's Gould's now. The stalkers know your secrets. They're coming for you. Just listen.*

He listened, holding his breath. And he heard the squeal of the back door opening.

He picked up his machine pistol and waited.

30

Eddie stood by the window in the lobby of the abandoned brothel, watching the street. His stomach was slowly tightening into knots. He could feel the end approaching, and he didn't like the way it felt in his gut.

From here he had a perfect view of Lady Luck Gentlemen's Club, the burned-out building still and silent in the twilight.

Knox was fiddling with his tab next to the brothel's office. Next to him, Dom knelt, checking her shotgun for the tenth time.

"How sure are you that this information of yours is correct?" she said.

Knox didn't take his eyes off his tab. "How many times are you going to ask me that? It's right, okay? Jesus Christ. It wasn't put together by gorillas like you in some sweat shop on New Calypso. This is Solar tech, painstakingly restored by Radiants on Uriel for the benefit of this great Federation. The tracker's pointing there, so Williams is there. Get it?"

"All right, calm down." She absentmindedly touched her wounded jaw. "I just wanted to be sure."

"He's there," Eddie said. "She took him there. She knows this place."

He could feel Dom's eyes on him, but she didn't say anything.

He tested the feel of the unfamiliar assault rifle against his shoulder. It was heavier and longer than he liked, especially for a close-quarters engagement like this was inevitably going to be. But he knew better than to go up against Williams poorly armed. The man was wild.

Dom produced two flashlights from the pockets of her duster coat, along with a roll of electrical tape. Eddie took one and taped it to the side of the rifle barrel. He tested the light. Bright enough.

"How are we doing this?" he said.

"Stick together. Sweep room by room."

"Doesn't look like there's many rooms left," Knox pointed out.

"That'll just make him easier to find," Dom said as she finished securing her flashlight to her shotgun. "Knox, you stay here and keep a tab connection open with us. I want to know if he tries to run."

"No problem," he said. "Just as long as you don't get any funny ideas about pocketing some of that cash while I've got my thumb up my arse out here."

"You'll get what you're due," she said. She looked to Eddie, concern creasing her forehead. "You sure you can do this?"

Eddie nodded. "Just be careful, all right? Cassandra's in there somewhere. Watch where you're shooting."

"With a bit of luck there won't be any shooting at all."

She put her earpiece in her ear as Knox twiddled the knobs on his tab. "Can you hear me?"

"Just as guttural as always," Knox said.

She racked her shotgun. "Let's get this over with."

They moved to the door. As they moved out of earshot of the augment, Eddie tapped his ear and glanced meaningfully at Dom. She took her earpiece out and covered it with her hand.

"What?"

"I just…if I take a hit in there—"

"Eddie, come on."

"Shut up, all right. If I take a hit in there, just make sure Cassandra gets out safe. Okay? Can you do that?"

She sighed. "I'll do what I can. But don't you dare get killed."

"Worried you'll miss me?"

"I just don't want to spend one more second alone with Knox. I'm about ready to plug the little bastard."

Eddie grinned as she slipped the earpiece back into position. They lingered in the doorway of the brothel for a moment, checking up and down the street.

"We're clear," Dom said. "Cover me."

She darted out of cover, swiftly crossing the street and pressing herself against the wall next to Lady Luck's ruined entrance. She paused, sweeping back and forth with her shotgun. Then she raised a hand and signalled.

Eddie took a deep breath and followed, the assault rifle hard against his shoulder. He pressed himself against the burned building's exterior and tested the door below the neon sign.

"Jammed," he whispered.

She glanced around. "No windows. Let's see if there's another way in."

They slipped around the side of the building. Nothing else moved. Eddie spotted a back door and nodded towards it. They formed up on either side, their footsteps crunching against the debris littering the ground. The back of the building wasn't so burned out; the whole rear wall was black, but intact.

Dom nodded at him and he reached out and pressed down on the door handle. The hinges squealed as he pushed the door inward. The stench of smoke filled his nostrils.

Dom flicked on her flashlight and aimed the shotgun through the entrance. Eddie followed suit. The darkness was quiet except for the creaks and groans of the injured building. Flakes of ash drifted from the ceiling, shining as they passed through the flashlight beam.

With a nod from Eddie, Dom slipped inside the building, swinging to the left and shining her beam around the debris blocking the main hallway. He followed a second after, moving to the right. His light revealed a doorway that opened into a small office. He moved inside, the beams overhead groaning with every step.

There was a carpet spread out in the centre of the office. But the corner of it was lifted, revealing a clean patch of floor. Someone had moved the carpet recently. Pushing aside the pain in his ribs, he crouched and dragged the carpet aside. There was a trapdoor set into the floor.

He turned back in the direction Dom had gone. He

could see her light playing across the walls.

"Freckles," he whispered. "Over here."

He switched off his flashlight and tugged on the trapdoor's handle. A faint light spilled out from downstairs. As he swung the door fully open, the hinges gave a long, low groan. He paused.

A rattle of gunshots burst out of the open trapdoor. Eddie scrambled out of the way as bullets skimmed the air in front of him and slammed into the ruined ceiling. Over the echoing sound of gunfire he could hear Dom's footsteps stomping through the building.

The burst of gunfire ended, leaving his ears ringing. Someone was swearing downstairs. Eddie raised his gun and prepared to descend.

The ceiling groaned above him. He glanced up to see dust falling from the tiles around the bullet holes. Something gave a loud crack.

He stumbled back as part of the office ceiling caved in. Black dust spewed out as beams clattered to the ground. Eddie put his hands over his head and dived under the office desk. Hell rained down on him. The dust got in his lungs. He suppressed a coughing fit.

The rumbling quietened; the sky stopped falling. Eddie gave it a few more seconds, then peeked out from under the desk. Dust filled the air. The hallway outside the office was completely blocked with debris.

"Freckles!" he called out.

He was answered with coughing. "I'm okay. You?"

"Just peachy."

"The door's blocked," she said. "I'm going to have to

find another way to get to you."

"Be careful. I don't want this whole damn place collapsing on our heads."

He moved to the trapdoor and flicked his flashlight back on, shining it down the steep stairs. The light barely did anything in the dust-filled air. He pulled his collar over his mouth and breathed through the fabric, trying to squint through the ash. The swearing had stopped. Whoever had shot at him had gone quiet. Probably reloading. If he waited for Dom, they'd be facing another hail of bullets. Besides, Cassandra could be down there with that madman.

He raised his gun and started slowly down the stairs. They creaked with every step.

The dust cleared the further he descended. His light revealed a small bare room with an overturned table and a chair in the middle. Small spots of blood stained the floor. A machine pistol lay discarded off to one side.

He paused at the bottom of the stairs, listening. He could smell Williams' sweat in the air, mixed with the faint tang of blood. He stepped forward.

A man crashed into the side of him, hands wrapping around the barrel of his assault rifle. Eddie had been ready for Williams to ambush him, but he wasn't prepared for the brutality and swiftness of his attack.

He slammed against the wall, his assault rifle pressed back against him as he struggled to pry it away from Williams. The fugitive snarled at him, spitting blood and saliva into his face.

Williams twisted and drove a fist into Eddie's side.

Eddie grunted, his finger involuntarily squeezing the trigger. The gun roared as bullets peppered the far wall. The barrel grew hot against his skin.

The sudden gunfire did nothing to distract Williams. As Eddie released the trigger and tried to bring a knee up into Williams' groin, the larger man twisted the gun away from him and tossed it across the room. It landed with a clatter.

Eddie could feel his pistol pressing against his hip, but he had his hands full trying to fend off Williams. His heart slapped in his chest as he stared into the eyes of a madman.

"Where is she?" Williams screamed in his face.

Before he could say anything, Williams' fist collided with the side of his head like a brick. He slid to the ground, eyes swimming. His ears rang.

Williams pulled him up by the collar of his shirt and slammed another punch into Eddie's cheek. His head swung limply to the side. He could taste blood.

"What did you do to her?" Williams yelled. "You turned her against me."

Eddie's fingers wrapped around his pistol. He drew it, aiming his shaking hand at the blur in front of him.

Williams meaty palm wrapped around his gun hand and crushed. Eddie heard himself screaming as pain stabbed through the bones of his hand. He dropped the gun.

"She was mine!" Williams slammed him back against the floor and fell on top of him. "She was mine and you took her away."

Summoning what was left of his strength, Eddie struck

out, landing a blow on Williams' already broken nose. It crunched, fresh blood spraying out. But Williams didn't even seem to notice. His hand flashed.

Eddie didn't even see the box cutter before the blade plunged into his shoulder. He grunted, no longer able to find the breath to scream.

But even through the pain, a sense of distant satisfaction gripped him. *She left him. She abandoned him. She knew what he was. Good for you, Cassie. Good for you.*

Thick fingers wrapped around his throat, crushing the air from him. His lungs spasmed. He stared up at Williams, feeling the drip of hot saliva on his face as the fugitive bared his teeth.

"You took everything from me," Williams snarled. "I told you all to leave me alone!"

His fingers tightened. Eddie tried to gasp, but no air would come. He reached out, clawing at Williams' eyes, raking his cheek with his nails.

Panic threatened to overtake Eddie's mind. He fought it, trying to stay calm despite the darkness descending around him. One hand moved to try to pry Williams' fingers away while the other fell to his side, grasping for something, anything.

His fingers brushed the corner of something hard. His pistol. He strained for it, reaching. *Almost. Almost.*

Williams slammed Eddie's head back against the ground. Dazed, his hand jerked closed. The pistol skittered a few centimetres further away. Out of reach.

Something was thudding, pulsing. The blood in his head. Lights flashed in his eyes. His vision had become a tunnel of black. Through the darkness, Cassandra's face shimmered in front of him. At least she'd got away from Williams. At least there was that.

Christ, he'd really ballsed this whole thing up.

A loud crack came from overhead. Was the ceiling collapsing again?

No. A shudder went through Williams' fingers. They loosened ever so slightly.

Another crack. The weight left Eddie's throat. He could breathe! Air rushed into his lungs and he coughed at the sudden cold burning his throat.

He rolled to the side and curled up, coughing. He could hear movement, but he couldn't make it out. His vision slowly cleared, and with it came the pain. He reached up to his shoulder, wrapped his fingers around the handle of the box cutter, and pulled. The blade came free with a sudden sting that seemed to reverberate through his entire body. He rolled back and saw a figure moving in the semi-darkness.

"Cassie?" he said, his voice hoarse.

"Sorry," Dom said. Her face resolved. "But it's nice to know how much you appreciate me after I keep saving your life."

He sucked in a breath, suppressing another coughing fit, and rolled his head to the side. Williams lay on his stomach next to him, blood trickling from his head. His hands were bound behind him in plastic cuffs. Dom put a boot under the fugitive and rolled him onto his back. His head rolled and he groaned, dazed.

"You've got impeccable timing, Freckles," Eddie said.

He pushed himself up onto his elbows and rubbed his neck. Everything hurt. "Jesus."

"You all right?"

"Not really." He put a hand to his head to try to stop the pounding. "But thanks. Thanks for coming for me."

"Had to bust down a wall to get into that office. You couldn't wait for me, huh?"

"Cassandra could've been down here." He looked up. "Have you seen her?"

Dom shook her head. "Haven't seen anyone except you and this bastard since we came in." She glanced around and put a hand over her earpiece so Knox couldn't hear. "Didn't he have money with him? Knox is going to go nuts if we don't find it."

Eddie didn't give a shit. He pushed himself onto his hands and knees and crawled over to Williams. He took the fugitive by the lapels and shook him.

"Hey. Hey, wake up."

He backhanded the man across the face. Williams' head snapped to the side. He groaned.

Eddie grabbed him again and pulled him up a few centimetres. "Look at me, Jack. Where is she? Where'd she go?"

Williams blinked away the dazed look on his face. His features twisted into a snarl.

"Don't you talk to me about her."

"I'm not in the mood for arguing, Jack. You tell me where she went, I'll make sure she gets off the station safe."

Williams' snarl faded, but his eyes remained hard. "You turned her against me."

"If she turned against you, it wasn't me who did it. I don't know why she was with you, but it wasn't because she loved you. Now where'd she go?"

Eddie was aware of Dom shifting uncomfortably behind him. He could hear the faint whisper of Knox talking in her ear. But he kept his eyes on Williams.

The fugitive licked the blood from his lips. "She took the money. She left."

"Where to?"

"I don't know," he said.

"Eddie," Dom interrupted before he could speak again. "Knox says Leone's got men incoming. The gunfire must've attracted them. We've got to move."

"Not until we find out where Cassandra is."

"She's not here," Dom said. "Look around."

"I'm not leaving the station without her."

Dom's mouth formed a line. "I didn't save your life to let you die here at the hand of some syndicate thug. Help me get Williams up and we'll talk about this on the *Solitude*."

He wanted to fight it, but he knew she was right. His battered body reminded him of that as he rose from the ground. He scowled at Williams as he took the man under his shoulder and dragged him to his feet with Dom's help.

As the fugitive rose, he turned and came nose-to-nose with Eddie. Their eyes met.

"She betrayed you too," he said slowly.

"What are you talking about?" Eddie said.

Williams nodded to himself. "I can see it in your eyes, stalker. You know it, you just don't want to admit it. You knew her long ago, didn't you? And she betrayed you. Just like she betrayed me."

Eddie grabbed the man by his shirt and pushed him against the wall. "What do you know? Huh? What do you know?"

"Eddie," Dom said sharply. "It's done. Let's get him out of here."

The two men glared at each other. Williams' nostrils flared. Growling, Eddie released the fugitive and turned back. Pressing his hand against his shoulder to staunch the bleeding there, he bent down and picked up his pistol, slipping it back into his holster.

Dom grabbed Williams and shoved him to the stairs, prodding him in the back with her shotgun. "Move."

The fugitive began to limp upstairs. Eddie followed the two, his breath rattling through his injured throat. His skull still throbbed in time with his pulse. He poked a loose tooth with his tongue. He hoped Williams had enjoyed that.

Each stair seemed a little higher than the last. Fatigue seeped into his bones, dragging him down. Dom and Williams reached the top of the stairs before he was even halfway up. He looked down at his feet and concentrated on moving each one. *Just a few more to go. Nearly there.*

How was he supposed to find Cassandra all beat up like this? He needed rest, he needed medical attention, but he couldn't afford to wait for either. She was out there somewhere, out in this station all alone. Williams could say what he wanted. Eddie knew the truth. She'd never betrayed him. He wouldn't believe it until he heard the words come from her own lips. Until then, he had to believe in her. He had to.

He reached the top of the stairs, panting, and found the hole Dom had punched through the wall. She'd risked getting herself buried in the ruins to get through to him. Her shadow disappeared around the corner. He followed through the hole, heading back towards the exit.

Ahead, Dom scanned the surroundings before prodding Williams out the back door. Eddie stumbled after them. Dust was still thick in the air. It was a relief to get outside. He limped around the edge of the building. Ahead of him, Dom and Williams were about to head across the street.

A shadow moved in the alley behind them.

For a moment, he thought he'd hallucinated it. But his hand moved of its own accord, slipping his pistol from his holster and raising it.

The shadow moved into the light. Her dark brown curls shimmered in the twilight. Cassandra still wore the same black gown he'd seen her in at the Crimson Curtain, only now it was torn and stained with rust-brown patches of blood. She hadn't seen him yet; her eyes were focused on Williams. She moved ahead of Eddie, towards Dom and the fugitive.

His heart thudded in his chest. She was here. He opened his mouth to call out.

The sound died in his throat as she raised a pistol, aiming it at Williams.

He saw the motion, but he couldn't register it. Why here? Why now? He knew she must hate Williams, but he'd get punishment enough back in the Bolt. Killing him would serve nothing. It was over. It was done.

She took another step forward, steadying the gun in both hands. She still hadn't seen him, hadn't heard him behind her. She paused, taking aim.

And then Eddie saw she wasn't aiming at Williams. She was aiming at Dom.

In that instant, he saw how it would end. He would call out for her to stop. To wait. But it would be too late. She would already have fired. He would watch the bullet punch through Dom, watch her slump to the ground streaming blood. He'd watch her die. There was nothing he could do. Nothing that would stop it.

No. There was one thing. And by the time he realised that, he'd already done it.

The gun barked in his hand. His finger was wrapped around the trigger, but he couldn't remember pulling it. The sound rang in his ears.

Cassandra half-turned, shuddering. Her arms slowly dropped to her side, the gun hanging limply from her fingers. She turned, her eyes finally meeting Eddie's. There was a hole in the left side of her chest, blood pulsing from her breast to coat her gown. She looked confused.

Then she dropped.

"No!" Williams roared.

He spun away from Dom and ran to Cassandra. He dropped to his knees at her side, wrists straining against the cuffs that bound his hands behind his back.

Dom had turned at the sound of the gunshot, bringing her shotgun up. She lowered it again. Eddie saw her looking at him, but he couldn't meet her eyes. He slipped his pistol back into his holster and stumbled woodenly towards the woman he'd killed.

Cassandra looked up at him as he approached. She wasn't dead, not quite. But he could tell she wouldn't last long. Dom moved alongside and kicked the pistol out of her grasp. It was pointless. Anyone could see she didn't have the strength to lift the thing.

"Eddie," Cassandra whispered. "You shot me. I never thought it'd be you."

He said nothing.

Tears streamed down Williams' face as he bent over at her side. Behind his back, his hands were curled into fists.

"Why?" Williams said. "Why did you come back?"

"I bought us new passes. Passage on a trader ship." Her hand gestured limply into the shadow of the alley. "It's in there. With the rest of the money. You can take it. You can be free." Her eyes were unfocused. Her forehead creased. "No. No, they got you, didn't they? I couldn't save you. I'm sorry."

Williams' faced twisted up. Eddie watched the scene, numbness creeping through him.

"The one time," Cassandra said, her voice so quiet he could barely here. "The one time I risked myself."

Her lips moved for a few more seconds, but no sound emerged. Her skin grew grey and pallid. Williams shook, like he was trying not to howl.

And then she was gone. Eddie swallowed the lump in his throat, let the coldness take him once more. His gun hand felt black and poisoned, like it needed to be amputated to stop the infection spreading.

He still didn't understand why she'd come back for Williams. He didn't understand anything. He never did. He'd loved her once, or maybe he just thought he did. How did anyone really know?

As Williams wept, Dom moved to Eddie's side.

"Are you okay?" she said.

He shook his head.

"I know. Stupid question." She paused, glanced down at Cassandra. "Thanks."

"For what?"

"You saved my life."

He thought about it. "We're partners."

"We have to go."

"I know."

"We have to leave her," she said.

"I know."

She nodded, hesitated, then moved into the dark of the alley where Cassandra had been hiding. She came back a moment later carrying the duffel bag that'd held Williams' money. It looked lighter now. She pulled it open, showed it to Eddie. Only three bundles of cash remained, along with a pair of synth-paper travel passes and a note of passage. Cassandra hadn't lied. This time, at least.

Dom took the cash, stuffed it in her pockets, and dumped the bag. Eddie could hear her earpiece squawking.

"Leone's men are a block away." She grabbed the weeping Williams by the back of his shirt and hauled him to his feet. He didn't resist. He was a broken man. "Let's go."

They left Cassandra there in that alley. Eddie didn't look back.

31

Eddie was silent the whole way back to the *Solitude*, but Dom had her hands full pushing the wounded Williams along and watching out for syndicate men. She could sense the thugs behind her, tracking them. She couldn't afford to sit around comforting Eddie.

Unfortunately, Knox wasn't nearly as silent. He followed at her heels, puffing slightly as he hurried to keep up.

"I can't help but notice you don't have a giant sack of cash, sweetcheeks."

"Later."

"I do hope you're not planning to cheat me out of my share."

"You'll get your share," she said. "Two thirds of Williams' money. And we'll take you off this station. If you stop annoying me, maybe I'll even wait until we're docked somewhere before I shove you out the airlock."

The chaos at the spaceport had subsided, the wounded syndicate men taken away. But the air was tense now, fewer tourists raucously emerging from ships. Looking through the transparent panels at the ships floating alongside the station, it seemed like there were fewer now.

As she ascended the stairs towards the airlock leading to the *Solitude*, shotgun aimed squarely at Williams' back, a uniformed man stared at her, his hand going to the gun at his side. The first lawman she'd seen since she'd arrived. Probably one of the last ones left on the station. She wondered how much Leone was paying him.

"We're stalkers!" she called out before the lawman got any ideas to start shooting. "I have a contract on this man's head, sir. Allow us to pass, in the name of the Federation."

The man hesitated. "Do you have papers?"

"I'm reaching for them. Don't shoot." She slowly reached into her pocket and produced her tab, displaying the contract on the screen. She handed it to the lawman without moving the shotgun barrel away from Williams.

The lawman licked his lips, handed her back her tab, and rubbed his ruddy cheeks. "I need to make a call."

He reached for his tab. Dom's fingers snaked around his wrist and held him tight. He stared up at her, shocked.

"Call Feleti Leone and I will shoot you down for obstructing a stalker's justice, sir."

The man removed his hand from his pocket and showed his empty palms. Dom released him and jerked her head at Eddie and Knox. She prodded Williams in the back to get him moving again.

The *Solitude*'s umbilicus was still unguarded. She hurried the three men as much as she could. She could sense the syndicate men snapping at her heels. She unlocked the airlock and shoved Williams forward through the umbilicus. He walked like a dead man, a shell.

"You, sit tight and stay out of the way," she said to Knox.

"Eddie, get Williams secured. We're getting out of here."

Eddie nodded silently and took Williams by his shirt and pushed him towards a narrow staircase that led to the cargo area and the converted brig.

Dom hurried to the bridge, sat down, and brought the electronics online. The helm's newer computers clicked and hummed as their monochrome screens flickered to life. "I'm sealing the airlock," she announced over the ship's intercom. "Requesting maglock release now. Stand by."

She started the engine sequence. Deep in the bowels of the ship, the solid fuel engines hummed to life. She relaxed at their familiar sound.

Then they cut out. Error messages flickered across her screens. The intercom crackled to life again.

"Attention all passengers and crew of the *Solitude*. Clearance to leave has been denied. Put down all weapons, relinquish door control, and prepare to be boarded."

"Shit," she said. She hammered the buttons of the helm, but nothing responded. She slammed her fist down. "Shit!"

She grabbed her shotgun and hurried back through the ship's central corridor. Knox scurried out of the common room towards her.

"What is it? What's happening?"

"Leone," she said. "He's shut us down. Can you break his control so I can get us out of here?"

"It'll take time."

"Then hurry the fuck up."

Knox squeezed past her and ran to the bridge. She met Eddie at the airlock. She could hear voices calling from the umbilicus outside.

"How many of them?" he said.

She touched a control next to the airlock and brought up a fuzzy, black-and-white image from the sensor above the airlock door. A dozen syndicate men and women crowded the umbilicus, more approaching.

"Too many," she said.

As she watched the vid screen, a figure pushed through the crowd, shoving his way to the front. Feleti Leone. His thin face showed no emotion as he stopped outside the airlock door.

"Can I kill him now?" Eddie said.

"No," she said. "But I've got an idea. Stall him."

"Stall him? We're not trying to hide a surprise party from him, Freckles."

But she was already moving back to the bridge. "Just do it!"

Eddie watched Dom hurry away, then turned his attention back to the view of the exterior airlock door. Leone held up one hideous, long-fingered hand and tapped on the door with his knuckle.

"Stalkers," he said, his voice crackling through the microphone. "Open up. You're only delaying the inevitable."

Eddie pressed the transmit button below the vid screen. "Isn't that all any of us ever do? Tell you what, Jack. You walk away from here and I won't put a hole in your head."

"Still as cocky as ever. I would've thought you might've mellowed out a little. Or do you enjoy killing women, Eddie?"

His hands tightened into fists.

Leone smiled up at the camera. "My men found the whore's body. Single shot, probably from a pistol. I assume it was you who did it. She always was Williams' girl, no matter what I did to her, no matter how hard I tried to break her. Oh, sure, she pretended to forget him. Maybe she even fooled me for a while. I never could think straight around pretty women. Then again, it seems like no one could think straight around her. Shame she's dead. But now I've got something even better. Roy Williams."

"Who?"

"Don't play dumb, Eddie. It doesn't suit you. I'm not a vindictive man. You stalkers killed some of my people, and we shed some of your blood. If it becomes necessary, I'll happily kill you both, and I'll take my time with it. But I've cooled off in the last few hours. You should've told me you were looking for Roy Williams. We could've helped each other."

"My mother always told me never to trust a stranger."

"Wise woman. But I hope you realise you have an opportunity now. I want Williams. I want him bad, Eddie. Bad enough that I'm even willing to let you stalkers live if you hand him over. I don't want to have to destroy your ship and everyone on it. That would be a complete waste. I'm leaving this station soon, and I don't want one of my last acts here to be something so violent. But if you give me no choice…." He shrugged.

"Well, hell, I didn't mean to be inconvenient," Eddie said. He paused. "What guarantees do I have that you won't harm me or my partner if I give you Williams?"

"Come, now. You've been doing this longer than that, haven't you? There are few guarantees in this game. But I can guarantee that if you don't hand Williams over to me, you will die. You will die as surely as Williams' whore died. Understand, stalker?"

Eddie felt his face split into a grim smile. "All right. You got us beat. I'm opening the airlock."

He punched the button on the panel. The mechanism hissed and groaned. The door slid slowly open. Leone's pallid, smiling face came into view, and behind him, a dozen syndicate men and women watched.

"You made the right choice, Eddie," Leone said.

"I sure did."

Eddie slipped the pistol from his holster and touched the barrel to Leone's forehead. The man went still. Behind him, all his people raised their weapons.

"They shoot, you die," Eddie said.

"Don't," Leone snapped at his men. His eyes narrowed as he glared at Eddie. "You can't kill me. I'm protected."

"You don't look very protected right now."

"You know you're not getting out of this, don't you, stalker?"

"Call her a whore again. Go on. You know you want to."

"It's not an insult. It's a fact. You couldn't imagine the things she did for me to ensure her own survival. Such a convincing actress. You know, I started to believe that she'd actually come to want me. Impressive. I've never seen someone more afraid of death. And I live on a dying station." Leone leaned forward, pressing his forehead against the gun barrel. "Not that it saved her in the end. Death comes to us all. You shouldn't still care. You made your choice. I may call her a whore. But you killed her."

"I'm leaving this station with Roy Williams. If you try to stop me, if you try to harm me or my partner, you will die. You're right, I made my choice. I killed a woman I once loved to protect my friend. So what the hell do you think I'll do to a son of a bitch like you?"

The intercom crackled overhead. "All right, all right, that's enough, all of you."

It took Eddie a moment to recognise Lieutenant Pine's voice. Dom must've been piping his connection in over the intercom.

"Feleti Leone," Pine said. "Stand down. Send your men away. Your transport is arranged to depart in forty-eight hours' time. You and the other nominated members of your organisation will be relocated in exchange for the information you have provided. And of course, for your generous donation to the Federation Navy. But that can only happen if we all avoid any inquiries coming from Babel. If two stalkers carrying a high priority fugitive are killed, well, I will no longer be able to guarantee you passage off Temperance."

Leone's face turned dark. He glared at Eddie.

"Mr Gould," Pine said. "Lower your weapon and allow Mr Leone to leave. As I told your partner, if any harm comes to Mr Leone, your contract fee will be revoked. Am I clear, gentlemen?"

Eddie showed Leone his teeth and slipped his pistol back into his holster.

"I'm disappointed," Leone said in a low voice. "I wouldn't expect two proud stalkers to go running to Mummy."

Eddie shrugged.

Leone turned back, glanced at his men, and scowled. "Go on, get out of here. Call Port Authority and let them go."

The syndicate people filed back out of the umbilicus, casting wary eyes at Eddie as they went. Leone followed them for a few steps, then turned back to Eddie.

"This isn't over, stalker. It's a small system. I'm sure we'll meet again."

Eddie made a gun with his fingers. "Bang bang."

Leone smiled back. And with that, he walked away. Eddie watched his back, smiling until he was out of sight. Only then did he lower his hand and let the smile slip from his face.

"All right," Dom called. "Are we all set to get off this damn station?"

Eddie punched the button and the airlock door slid closed. "I'll be in my room. Wake me when we get there."

32

As tired as he was, Eddie wasn't able to fall asleep on the short journey from Temperance to the Fed outpost. He lay on his cot, staring at the ceiling. He'd made the right choice. He knew that. Cassandra was his past, but Dom and the *Solitude*, this was his present. He'd never been one to wallow in the past. He wrote the story, got it on the page, and let it go. It kept him steady, kept him alive.

But how could he write this? How could he reduce Cassandra to a few words on a page? How could he describe the feeling he'd felt in the pit of his stomach as she fell, his bullet drilling through her chest?

The ship shuddered around him as the maglock clunked into place. He could hear Dom moving about in the corridor, but he didn't move until she banged on his door.

"We're here," she said.

He sighed, swung his legs over the edge of his bed, and stood. Every bit of him ached. He hoped their next stop was somewhere with a doctor and booze. Somewhere quiet.

He made his way through the *Solitude* and unlocked

the door to the brig. Roy Williams sat on the floor, his head against the wall, his arms still bound behind him. A fresh bandage had been applied to the wound on his thigh—it must've been Dom's doing. He didn't look up as Eddie leaned against the doorway.

"End of the line," Eddie said. "Up you get, Jack."

Williams' eyes tracked slowly towards him. He was quiet a few seconds. Then he spoke.

"Was it worth it? Was it worth her life to catch me?"

"She's dead, we caught you. It doesn't matter if it was worth it or not. It's what happened. Get up."

Williams put his back against the wall and pushed himself to his feet, grimacing as he put weight on his wounded leg. He took small steps towards Eddie. As Eddie moved out of the way of the door to let him past, Williams paused.

"I think I understand why you do this. You do it for the pain. You want to see the pain. Don't you?"

Eddie nodded slowly. "Yeah. I do it for the pain." He jerked his head. "Move."

Dom stood at the closed airlock as Eddie came up, pushing Williams ahead of him. Eddie met her eyes.

"Where's the midget?" he asked.

"I told him to lay low. The Feds must've scanned his pass on the way here, but I'd rather not wave him under their noses."

The airlock door hissed open. In the umbilicus, Lieutenant Pine stood with his hands behind his back, two marines flanking him with submachine guns at the ready.

Pine looked them over, a sneer forming on his boyish face.

"You two look like you've seen some action. I would offer to let my medic examine you, but you know the regulations."

"Yeah," Eddie said. "And I can see how much of a stickler for regulations you are. Remind me, which regulation says that Naval officers are allowed to take bribes from known gangsters to give them passage off a dead station?"

"Feleti Leone is a necessary evil." His eyes roamed over the two of them. "Much like many other less-than-savoury individuals I'm obliged to work with."

He stepped forward to examine Roy Williams.

"He's wounded," Pine said.

"Not by us," Dom said. "Not the gunshot wound, anyway."

"Hm." Pine pointed his chin at Williams. "Identify yourself."

Williams said nothing.

Pine stepped back and snapped open an extendable baton. "Identify yourself."

"Roy Williams," the fugitive said. "And if you touch me with that, I will tear your Fed tongue out."

"The threats are unnecessary, Mr Williams." He glanced at Dom and nodded as he retracted the baton. "He fits the description. I'll trust you've provided the right man, for now. We'll make additional checks once we have him in custody."

"The reward?" Dom said.

"A number of Mr Leone's people were killed during your hunt for this man. I have deducted two million vin from the final reward to compensate Mr Leone."

"You're fucking kidding me," Eddie said before Dom could stop him.

Pine's nostrils flared. "Is that a problem, Mr Gould?"

Eddie glanced at Dom. She shook her head ever so slightly. She could see him grinding his teeth.

"No. No problem at all, Jack."

"Very well." Pine took out his tab and touched the screen. "One quarter of the reward has been paid against your debt, Miss Souza. The rest has been transferred to your accounts."

"Then I relinquish custody of the fugitive to you." She pushed Williams forward. "And the contract has been fulfilled."

"A pleasure working with you," Pine said. He jerked his head at his men. "Take him away."

The marines stepped forward and grabbed Williams under his shoulders. The fugitive didn't look back as they dragged him away.

Alone with them now, Pine exhaled. "I'll be glad to see the back of this place. I always disliked Temperance. Too much sin for my taste. The view from up here should be much better when it dies. Of course, I won't be able to stay and enjoy it. I'll be transferred somewhere else. The life of a public servant."

Dom tried her best to smile. "Yes, sir. If there's nothing else?"

"Nothing. Enjoy your reward, stalkers. The Federation appreciates your service."

"Thanks, Jack," Eddie said. "Always happy to be of

help."

Pine turned his back and strode down the umbilicus. Dom pressed the button and the airlock door slid closed. She glanced at Eddie.

"I'm setting our course. Any requests for our next destination?"

"You're the pilot."

"How are you doing?" she said.

He shrugged. "We'll see."

"It might be a bit of a journey until the next stop. Might be a good chance for a sleep."

He shook his head. "Next book's not going to write itself."

"You're going to start so soon? I thought after...you know...."

"Me too. But it's what I'm here for." He turned away and raised his hand in a wave. "Try to make sure the ship doesn't fall apart on the way. I can hear it groaning already."

"She's fine." She patted the wall. "Aren't you, girl?"

"Whatever you say, Freckles. Whatever you say." He disappeared into his quarters and shut the hatch.

Dom returned to the bridge and started the engine sequence once more. Outside, the maglock disengaged. As she brought up the system map on the nav terminal, she heard shuffling footsteps behind her.

"Marshall's Folly," Knox said.

"What?"

"That's where I want you to drop me. Marshall's Folly."

"There's not much there. That's in the Outer Reach."

"That's why I want to go there." He leaned against the helm. "And I'll be taking my share of Williams' money, now, if you don't mind."

She shrugged. "Suit yourself." She reached into her pocket and deposited two small bundles of cash in his hands. "There you go. Don't spend it all at once."

He stared down at the wads for a minute, then looked up at her.

"What the hell is this?"

"It's your share. Two thirds of his money. Shame you weren't a bit quicker getting us that tracking information. We might've found it before that woman went and spent it all."

"This is bullshit," Knox said. "I want some of the reward money."

"That wasn't the deal."

"Fuck the deal."

She turned towards him. "Did I hear you correctly? Would you like to cancel our deal? Because I'd be happy to turn around and put you back on Temperance."

Knox glared at her, then looked down at the cash in his hands. "You're devious, stalker. I guess I should've expected this, given your upbringing."

"Make your decision. Marshall's Folly with that cash there, or I take it back and return you to Temperance. Time's running out."

Knox hesitated. "All right. All right, stalker, you win. But I get to help myself to anything in the kitchen I want."

"Fair enough," she said. "Now go be annoying somewhere else. I need to concentrate."

Knox stuffed the cash in his pockets and shuffled away. When he was gone, Dom exhaled and leaned back in her chair.

Through the viewing window, she watched the slow rotation of the blue gas giant. Temperance was barely a speck against its swirling surface, dark and grim from way out here. Tens of thousands of souls would die there in the coming days. Too many to comprehend. So she didn't try.

She could feel the *Solitude*'s engines rumble through the ship. With a few touches of the control panel, she locked in the coordinates for Marshall's Folly. She'd have to stop at a refuelling depot on the way, then they'd be jumping in and out of dark roads to get there in the next seventy-two hours. The autopilot would take care of the heavy lifting. She needed a nap anyway.

She leaned back, put her feet up on the helm, and thumbed the intercom button.

"Gentlemen, take your last look at Temperance. We are now departing Eleda VI space. Prepare for engine thrust in three…two…one…." She punched the throttle.

And the *Solitude* rocketed alone into the silence of the void.

ABOUT THE AUTHOR

Chris Strange discovered at an early age that he was completely unsuited to life among normal human beings. After experimenting with several different career paths, he said to hell with it and went back to writing, his first love.

Chris is the author of *Don't Be a Hero*, *Mayday* and the Miles Franco series of hard-boiled urban fantasy novels, beginning with *The Man Who Crossed Worlds*. He writes for the daydreamers, the losers, the cynics and the temporarily insane. His stories are full of restless energy and driven by a passion for the unorthodox. He loves writing characters on the fringe of society: the drifters, the knights errant, the down-and-out.

In his spare time, Chris is an unapologetic geek, spending far too long wrapped up in sci-fi books, watching old kaiju movies and playing video games. He lives in the far away land of New Zealand, and holds a Bachelor of Science and Postgraduate Diploma in Forensic Science.

He doesn't plan on growing up any time soon.

Want to be the first to hear about Chris's new releases? Sign up for the email list at: **http://bit.ly/StrangeList**

Contact Chris at: **chrisstrangeauthor@gmail.com**

www.chris-strange.com

17184059R00174

Printed in Great Britain
by Amazon